From a young age, Nyrae Dawn dreamed of growing up and writing stories. For years she put her dream on hold. Nyrae worked in a hospital emergency room, fell in love and married one of her best friends from high school. In 2004 Nyrae, her husband and their new baby girl made a move from Oregon to Southern California and that's when everything changed. As a stay-at-home mom for the first time, her passion for writing flared to life again. She hasn't stopped writing since. With two incredible daughters, an awesome husband and her days spent writing what she loves, Nyrae considers herself the luckiest girl in the world. She still resides in sunny Southern California, where she loves spending time with her family and sneaking away to the bookstore with her laptop. Nyrae Dawn also writes adult romance under the name Kelley Vitollo.

To find out more about Nyrae Dawn, visit www.nyraedawn.com. Find her on Facebook at nyraedawnwrites and follow her on Twitter @NyraeDawn.

ALSO BY NYRAE DAWN AND
PUBLISHED BY HEADLINE ETERNAL

THE GAMES TRILOGY
Charade
Façade
Masquerade

What a Boy Wants
What a Boy Needs

Rush

Nyrae Dawn

MASQUERADE

headline
ETERNAL

First published in Great Britain in 2014 by HEADLINE ETERNAL
An imprint of HEADLINE PUBLISHING GROUP

1

Cataloguing in Publication Data is available from the British Library

ISBN 978 1 4722 0985 6

Typeset in Electra by Palimpsest Book Production Limited,
Falkirk, Stirlingshire

Printed and bound in Great Britain by
CPI Group (UK) Ltd, Croydon CR0 4YY

Headline's policy is to use papers that are natural, renewable
and recyclable products and made from wood grown in sustainable
forests. The logging and manufacturing processes are expected to
conform to the environmental regulations of the country of origin.

HEADLINE PUBLISHING GROUP
An Hachette UK Company
338 Euston Road
London NW1 3BH

www.headlineeternal.com
www.headline.co.uk
www.hachette.co.uk

To my sister, Jessica, one of the most talented and caring people I know. I'm blessed to have a sibling with such a big, loving heart.

ACKNOWLEDGMENTS

As always I have to start with my family. My two beautiful little girls who amaze me daily and who get it when mommy is in the writing zone. To my husband who has taken over doing so many things around the house and doing them *well* in order to give me writing time. We got so lucky to find each other. I'm thankful for you every day. Huge thanks to my incredible agent Jane Dystel and everyone at Dystel and Goderich Literary Management. There is no one else I would rather have in my corner. You guys are truly amazing. To my editor, Latoya Smith. I am so lucky to be able to work with you. You not only make my books stronger but your enthusiasm never fails to make my day. Also, I would like to thank everyone at Grand Central Publishing. I still get smiley when I tell people I write for you. I wouldn't have been able to write this book without the help of my tattoo artist, Eliza from County Line Tattoo. Not only are you amazing at your job but you answered my million questions about tattooing without hesitation. Any mistakes are my own and I can't wait to schedule another appointment with you! Finally, I would like to thank my readers for everything. Your support and excitement means more to me than I could ever put into words. I couldn't do this without you!

CHAPTER ONE

BEE

I t's almost perfect. The only thing missing as I stand in the middle of Masquerade is the constant buzz of a tattoo gun. After the past few years, it's my form of comfort. Like a lullaby that sings me to sleep, massaging the tension out of my muscles. But at the same time, it shoots endorphins into my veins, bringing me happiness—something that's mine and will always belong to me.

Yes, I need to hurry up and open the doors to my tattoo parlor before I go crazy for that lullaby. Tomorrow is the day. I can't wait.

I play the words again in my head: *my tattoo parlor.* They're scary as hell and exhilarating at the same time. I'm not sure many twenty-one-year-olds can say they've already worked in five shops, but none of those places belonged to me. This one will stick. I'll stick. I have to, for a lot of reasons. One of them being, despite the fact that it's my name on all the paperwork for Masquerade, my parents footed the bill.

It doesn't matter that I'm paying them back, only

that they did it. After everything I've put them through—after the way that I struggled so much to love them the way they do me—they did it. Hell, I fight to even understand the word. People throw *love* around all the time, but I've seen it make people do crazy things. It's not something I'm sure I want. But still, they're always there.

Walking over, I straighten one of the frames filled with tattoos I've done. To the right of it is the one and only workstation here. It's exactly what I need, small without too many places to make a mess. Growing up, my parents—*shit* . . . I shake my head— Melody and Rex—had both been artists. They would get lost in their zone and the house would be a mess with supplies, but it didn't matter because they were happy.

Then I went back home and everything was different. They were happy like Melody and Rex, only not in the same way. They didn't get so deep in their art that they'd forget dinner and then order a pizza, which we would all laugh over later.

No, my real parents were perfect—are perfect—and even after eight years, it's still hard for me to be the person they need me to be instead of the one I am.

But I try. For them, I try.

"Christ," I mumble, not sure why I'm feeling so introspective today. I'm a single girl in a new town. What I need to do is get out and have some fun.

After locking up Masquerade, I climb into my Honda Insight and drive to my apartment. It doesn't take me long to get ready. I keep my blond hair down. It's so long it hangs past the middle of my back. I put on a black spaghetti-strap tank top with silver studs on it. It shows some of the tattoos I have, one on my right arm, the back of my neck, and the star on the front of each shoulder. Slipping on a pair of black heels, I walk to the bathroom and take out the small diamond stud in my nose and then I'm out the door.

It's not like Brenton is very big, so it doesn't take me long to find a club called Lunar that looks like it could be a good time. It's about 10:00 p.m., so a little early, but all I want to do is have a drink and relax anyway. More than that and I'd have to take a cab.

Music pulses through the speakers when I walk in, and I suddenly feel a tinge of guilt for being here. I guess my real dad got lost in the bottle for a while after I was kidnapped. I hate using that word— *kidnapped*—because it makes it sound like they were horrible to me when they weren't. Anyway, he's okay now. They're those kinds of people. They make it through everything together, but I wonder if they'd be disappointed I'm here.

No, I tell myself. There's nothing wrong with having a beer once in a while.

It takes a couple minutes to make my way through the crowd and up to the bar. It smells like alcohol and too many bodies, but I try to ignore it. A seat opens up and I take it. Men sit on either side of me, but none of them seem to be paying any attention, which is good. I'm not in the mood to be hit on tonight.

The bartender comes over a few minutes later. He's about my age, hot, but a little pretty for my type. He has blond hair and green eyes that run the length of me, telling me it's going to be him that tries to flirt.

"Hmm, let me guess. Cosmo?" he asks. I shake my head. "Lemon Drop? Mojito?" He keeps tossing drinks at me, and I continue shaking my head.

"You're going to have to give me a clue here. I'm drowning and I'm usually pretty damn good at knowing what a girl wants." He winks at me and I can't help but roll my eyes.

"The only thing you have that I want right now is a Corona with lime."

"Ah, a beer girl. I was way off."

He grabs a bottle, twists the top off, and then hands it to me.

"You're new. I would have noticed you before," he says.

I nod. Again, he's good-looking. Maybe on another night I would have been interested or if I were a different kind of girl—the good kind. But I'm not and I swear he looks like he belongs in a college frat, so I lean back and take a drink of my beer.

"I'm Trevor," the bartender says.

"Bee," I reply. It's amazing how the name automatically rolls off my tongue. It's almost like it gave me my new identity at eighteen years old. It was my third one, but this one I actually picked. It's the only one that feels like me. I don't remember what it was like to be the girl I'd been before I was taken, and once I went back home, I couldn't be the person I thought I was.

"Bee? As in buzz, buzz?" His question jerks me out of my thoughts. "Did I tell you how much I like honey?"

Yeah, because I haven't heard that one before. "No, as in the letter *B*. It's short for 'bitch.' Want me to demonstrate how accurate the name is?" I finish my tirade with the tiniest of wicked grins.

At that, Trevor smiles and holds up his hands. "I was kidding. Kind of. But seriously, that was hot. I think I'm in love with you."

Before I have the chance to reply, someone yells, "Trev! Stop flirting and get your ass down here. There's work to do."

That's my cue to leave. I toss a ten down and he grabs it before I walk away. I want a nice, empty corner to hang out in and finish my drink. Or, if I'm being honest, I'm not opposed to meeting someone; only that someone isn't him.

When I spot a small table in the back, I head right for it. I'm surprised no one's grabbed it yet. I sit down and lift the bottle to my lips and drink the whole thing.

I set the bottle down, and for some reason seeing the lime inside transports me back in time. Rex used to make all kinds of bottle art. He'd tell me sometimes the simplest things could be the most beautiful. We'd fill different colored bottles with different shades of objects until we found one that we thought was the most unique, and then he would let me keep it. I put it on the shelf above my bed with all my other favorite things. The things I couldn't take with me when they found me.

My hand squeezes around the bottle and I take a couple deep breaths. What's wrong with me? Why am I thinking about them so much tonight? I'm doing better. I have Masquerade. I need to remember things happened the way they were supposed to and go on with my life.

"Decided not to flirt with Trevor anymore?" a male voice says. I look over to see a guy leaning against the wall in the dark, his arms crossed. There are stairs that go up right next to him, and it's almost like he's hiding.

"Is there a problem if I was flirting with him?" I reply.

He has a tribal tattoo around his forearm. It's pretty nice work but I could have done it better.

"Not my business. I don't know why I even said anything." He turns his head and scans the crowd. My first thought is, *Now this is the kind of guy I'd be into*. He has a trail of dark stubble on his face, a tick in his tight jaw, and black hair. It has a few curls in it. Just enough to make you want to run your fingers through it to see how it feels.

I would put money on him riding a bike. He's gorgeous and trouble, and from the scowl on his face, he's probably angry at the world just like I'm confused by it.

Too bad he's an asshole.

"You're right. It's not your business. Since that didn't stop you from bringing it up, I'll keep it going for you. Let me guess, I'd probably be a slut or a tease if I was flirting with him? Let's for a minute forget that he not only came on to me, but also that men do that kind of thing all the time. It's okay for them to hook up with someone in a bar, but not for a girl to, right?"

I'd dealt with stuff like this all the time when I was in school and I hated it. I wasn't like all the other people who joined activities and smiled in everyone's face, pretending to be perfect but then going wild behind their parents' and teachers' backs. I was who I was then and I am who I am now. At home I didn't fit in, which bothered me, so I made sure I didn't care if I fit in anywhere else.

The guy doesn't reply to me but continues to look out into the sea of people.

What's his deal?

I pick up my bottle before remembering it's empty and setting it down again. I keep glancing at the guy, but he's not paying any attention to me. It frustrates me, and the fact that I'm letting it bother me annoys me even more.

Finally, he says, "I don't care who you fuck, or who anyone else does for that matter. Being a man or woman doesn't make a difference."

There's something in the raspy seriousness of his voice that makes me believe him. It makes me wonder what he does care about, if anything, because by looking at him, I'd say it isn't much.

That makes two of us.

I'm not really sure what makes me do it, but I push to my feet, walk over, and lean against the wall next to him. "Your piece is pretty nice. Could be cleaned up a bit." I point to his tat.

He huffs. "And you're an expert, right?" He makes it sound like it's a ridiculous thought.

I smirk because, of course, that's the first thing people think. I don't know why. It's not like it's so rare to be a female tattoo artist.

We keep standing there. People are dancing all

around, drinking and talking. He's wearing an earpiece, so it's pretty obvious to me now that he's security.

After a few minutes, he tosses a glance my way. "You've got some nice work too." It seems to physically pain him to say the words.

"Thanks."

All of my work was done by the Professor. He's the old guy who taught me how to tat. I don't really talk about the Professor because he's important to me and I like to keep important things to myself. Most people wouldn't get it anyway.

"What's your name?" he asks without looking at me.

"Bee. Yours?"

"Maddox." I recognize what he's doing. It's so much easier to talk to people when you don't have to look at them. Looking brings you closer, and sometimes it's too hard to get close. I was like that when I first came home. I'm still like that sometimes.

Standing here, I realize I kind of get this guy. I think he might get me, too, and I don't remember the last time I thought something like that. It's not that I need him or anyone else to understand me. Still, in this moment, it feels kind of good.

"Maddox!" a guy yells from a few feet away. "You're off early tonight. Go ahead and clock out."

Maddox turns to look at me. My skin sizzles under his stare. His eyes are gray and hot on me. Man, this guy is sexy, and for a second, I consider what it would be like to lose myself in him for a night.

"You here with anyone?" His voice is low.

A good girl would probably tell him she wasn't interested. The kind of girl I maybe should be. The kind my sister is or my mom is. I don't think it's such a bad thing to let myself have a little fun. If I'm smart . . . safe, what's the problem?

"No."

I push off the wall so I'm standing right in front of him when he speaks again.

"Do you want to leave with me?"

"We go to a hotel, not a house. And it's only one night."

"Isn't that supposed to be my line?" He smirks. It's the first time I've seen him do anything except scowl.

"I'm all about equal opportunity, remember?"

"Are you drunk?"

"No, just had the one beer."

Maddox gives me a simple nod, then tells me the name of a hotel and says he'll meet me there.

To be sure, I walk over to a different bouncer than the one who talked to him and confirm Maddox works here. You never know what kind of scams people will come up with and I need to confirm he's legit.

A few minutes later I'm in my car and driving to the hotel. Just one night. It's been crazy and stressful getting everything ready for Masquerade, and I really want to let go and have a little fun, with someone who's safe because I'll never have to see him again.

CHAPTER TWO

MADDOX

The roar of my motorcycle helps block out my thoughts as I cruise to the shitty hotel where I told Bee I'd meet her. It's not often I take a woman somewhere for the night. After dealing with Mom and taking care of my sister, Laney, for the past four years, I stay the hell away from woman drama.

Not that I really do shit for Mom.

But I owe Laney. She's the only person in this world I give a shit about, but she doesn't really need me anymore either. She's living in our old apartment with her boyfriend, Adrian, who I still don't know if I like. If he fucks with her, I'll fuck with him and he knows it. They've been together a while and started college together this month. He's good to her. Not that I admit that to her.

The tatted-up blonde was too hot to walk away from, though, and it's not like I have anything else to do. I haven't talked to Mom since her last suicide attempt in January, work can't last forever, and I just lost the only other thing I gave a shit about besides my sister—tattooing.

I take a right turn before pulling into the parking lot. Three lights are out in the VACANCY sign.

The bike rumbles underneath me and my body is all jacked up, knowing it'll soon be with a woman. It's probably been eight months since the last time I met someone here. It wasn't long after Laney and I moved to Brenton.

"Don't let your dick get you into trouble," Dad told me when I was thirteen before he tossed me a box of condoms. *"It's your own business, so I don't want to know if you need them yet—just make sure you use them when you do."*

I wonder why he didn't take his own advice about trouble. Was it his dick that betrayed him, making him need some chick on the side, or did the greed come first—the money and gambling that led to her? If he'd been stronger, he wouldn't be in prison right now for getting drunk and running down Adrian's son with his car. My sister wouldn't feel guilt because her dad killed her boyfriend's kid, and Mom never would have tried to kill herself.

And I wouldn't be sitting here lying to myself because it's really me who could have been stronger. I could have told my mother and sister about the affair before things went too far.

"You coming?" Bee's silky voice says over the sound of my bike. I didn't even hear her walk up.

Pulling the helmet off my head, I turn to her. "Eager?" Standing under the streetlight makes it so she can see my wink.

"I'm ready to go in or go home. Decide quickly before I do it for you." She crosses her arms and there's no doubt in my mind this girl will walk away. She's tough. One look at her tells me that and I respect it. I don't have room in my life for dealing with anyone else's shit.

I turn off the engine, slide the kickstand into place, and climb off my silver and black bike. It's old and needs some work, but it's mine.

"Come on." I nod toward the building and start walking.

"Why here?" she asks.

"You're the one who said a hotel."

"And you just happened to know the perfect place close by."

I shrug, not willing to sugarcoat anything for her. "Anonymous works for me. If that's not what you want, say so right now."

"I wouldn't have said a hotel in the first place if it wasn't what I needed."

I don't call her on the use of the word *need* instead of *want*. Not my business.

Gripping the handle, I pull open the glass door

and signal for her to go inside. She walks right up to the counter, with me behind her. Less than three minutes later, we're using a key to open the door to room 57. As soon as we're inside, I hit the lights.

"Condoms?" she asks.

"Obviously."

"You don't have to be a jerk. I just wanted to see if you had them or if I needed to grab mine." Bee tosses her purse onto the chair.

For some reason, the side of my mouth almost tilts up into a half-smile. This girl doesn't fuck around and I like that.

Pulling my wallet out, I grab a foil package from inside and toss it on the bed. Bee stands there, a little flicker of something I can't read in her eyes. My mind stumbles on it, making me pause.

"We doing this or not?" she asks.

The words are what I need to keep me on track. "Oh yeah. We're doing this." These are the nights that are only about me—well, and whoever I'm with, but I don't let any of the shit from my life bleed in.

Bee grins and there's a mixture of need and maybe a little bit of what almost looks like selfishness and then she's on me.

Her lips come down hard on mine, my hand cups her ass. I pull her against me, push down the back of her pants, and slightly lift her off the ground. The curve of her ass fits perfectly in my hand, but it's not enough. I need more.

Jerking away, I grab the bottom of her shirt and pull it over her head, giving me a better view of the tats on her shoulders.

She's breathing hard, her chest heaving. My hand moves toward her, my finger tracing the edge of her bra as I study her—the ring in her belly button, the edges of what I think are more stars going up her side, close to her back.

I've never been with a woman with so many tats. She's not covered in them, but they're enough to decorate her skin. I get the closest I ever come to any kind of pillow talk when I grit out, "Fuck, you're hot."

"You don't have to sweet-talk me. I'm already here."

"I don't sweet-talk."

"You next or what?" She quirks a brow at me and damned if I don't almost smile again. Before I get the chance, her hands are on me, shoving my shirt up. They stop on my chest and I help her by pulling off the material covering me.

I don't have as much ink as her. I can see her looking at the few pieces I have and it's like she's dissecting them.

This strange sort of fear spikes inside me because of the way her eyes are eating me up. Yeah it's only sexual, but I need to make sure it stays that way.

"We have way too many clothes on." I push the button on my pants through the hole, unzip, and kick out of them.

Bee's crawling onto the bed and I'm right behind her. "These have to go." I get rid of her pants just as quickly, getting a brief look at a sunflower on her calf as she lies beneath me in nothing but a purple pair of panties and a bra. She's sexy as hell, all that creamy skin with bursts of colorful artwork.

Her nails are painted black, I notice, as she pushes my boxer-briefs down, my erection springing free.

Her hand wraps around me and I groan, trying to focus enough to get her panties down. When I do, she slips free of them.

She's stroking as I push the cups of her bra down so her breasts spill over.

"This is going to be over before it starts if you don't stop with that," I tell her.

Bee lets go, for the first time letting out a real laugh that turns into a loud moan when I drop my mouth to one peak.

My moves are scripted, my body on autopilot as I get her ready—fingers and mouth teasing each mound. I grind against her, feel her wetness, wait for her little gasps and moans to increase before I'm rolling the condom down and pushing inside her—taking my quick, anonymous pleasure and hoping I'm giving her what she's looking for too.

It's not long before her nails are digging into my back and sounds fall from her lips quicker and louder. When she tenses under me, her body shaking in aftershocks, I give in. My release immediately follows, and then I'm rolling off her, our sweat-slicked bodies side by side.

"Wow . . ." she pants between breaths.

I take that as a compliment, not sure she gives many of them out. "No shit." For now, all the tension is gone from my body.

"I should go," she says, and I don't argue. It's exactly what I need it to be. We both got what we were looking for.

"Thanks," tumbles out of my mouth as I watch her get dressed.

"You don't have to thank me for sex. I wouldn't be here if it wasn't what I wanted too."

For only a second, a thought climbs its way into my head, making me wonder why she's okay with this. I mean, I've obviously done it before, but it was never this simple. The girl usually isn't the one leaving. Before the questions get their claws in, I slam the door on them.

"See ya later," she says before walking out.

I make a quick trip to the bathroom, get rid of the condom, and clean up. I consider getting dressed to head home. It's not like I have anyone there who will wonder where I am, so I grab my cigarettes, turn off the lights, and spend the rest of the night alternating between sleeping and smoking.

I reach into the bag on my bike and pull my sketchbook out. Before going in, I flip through it, again making sure I marked my favorite pages.

A thrill of excitement strums through me like I haven't felt since sitting in the tattoo parlor where I apprenticed for a few months. Before that, I hadn't felt it since I played football in school. Before I quit. Before I realized what a bastard my old man is. Before I stopped giving a shit.

Shaking my head, I head toward the building, hoping like hell this is going to work out. I left a message this morning, telling the owner that I'm interested in apprenticing here, left my number, and said I'd be down later. Then I sat around like a pussy, hoping he'd call back before I came down.

He didn't.

I pull open the door but don't see anyone inside. There's only one workstation, a desk with a computer, and then a small hallway leading to another room.

"Hello?" I call out.

"Yeah?" a female voice replies.

What the fuck? She could at least come out here. The urge to walk out hits me. I don't have time for this shit. It's probably a waste of time anyway. Still, I reply, "I called earlier. Lookin' for a place to apprentice."

"Sorry, just opened up. I don't need to take on any scratches right now." As soon as the last word clears her mouth, she steps around the corner.

Motherfucker.

Bee's eyes widen in shock, but she recovers quickly, making me do the same.

"Don't call me a scratch." My fist tightens on the book in my hand; disappointment takes control of me. Jesus, what are the odds of sleeping with one of the only tattoo artists in town? The only one left who hasn't already told me they're not looking? Especially when neither of us wanted to see each other again.

"I'm not trying to be a bitch when I say it, but it's what you are. When I first started, I was a scratch too. If you can't handle getting shit, you really don't belong here." She sits in the chair behind the desk.

Anger fills me, banging against my pride.

"You don't know me or what I can handle." *Shut up. Chill out, man. She's your last opportunity.*

I don't want it anymore, if it has to be with her. I don't see women again after I've had them. It's too fucking close.

She sighs. "That doesn't change the fact that this wouldn't work out. Let's focus on me not needing to take a scratch under my wing right now. I have too much going on."

I almost hand her my sketchbook. Almost mention she wouldn't be saying that if she saw my stuff, but fuck it. Putting myself out there isn't something I'm about to do for anyone, especially not her.

Without a word, I turn and walk out, the door pushing open so hard it slams into the wall as I go.

"Jesus Christ, Laney. What are you doing in my house?" I'm tense, my insides going a million miles an hour as I throw the sketchbook onto the couch beside her. "I'm telling you right now, if your boyfriend is here, I'm probably going to lose my shit."

She doesn't answer that and says, "So it didn't go well, huh?" My sister stands and walks over to where I'm leaning against the table, talking to me in the voice Mom used to use when we were kids. Before we realized she loved Dad more than us and that she could quickly turn love into anger. I hate it.

"Doesn't matter."

I'm not surprised when she moves closer to me and drops her head to my shoulder. She's always been like this. Sweet and innocent, trying to see the best there is in the world. We couldn't be more different, and even though she's the only important person in my life, I heft her head off me and walk away.

"Did they look at your drawings?"

"No."

"You shouldn't take no for an answer, Maddy. Go back and keep trying. They'll respect your dedication."

I can't help it—I laugh. "I'm not trying to get a job at a Walmart or something. It's a tattoo parlor. If they tell me no, I'm pretty sure they mean it."

"Want me to ask Adrian? Or Colt? They might know someone who—"

"Nope."

Laney sighs, making guilt ease its way through my anger. I'm a shitty brother to her and I know it.

"Maddox, you want this. You haven't wanted anything in a long time. You deserve it, but you might have to fight for it." She's quiet for a second before adding, "I want it for you."

I know exactly what she's trying to say. She wants to fix me. She doesn't think I fight for anything and that part is true.

It's about all I can handle today. Sometimes she believes in shit so much, she makes me want to do the same, but then I think about how I let them all down. How I knew Dad was gambling and knew about the money, but for selfish reasons kept my mouth shut. How Laney was alone when she found Mom the first time she tried to kill herself. I should have been with her. So she's wrong. Maybe I don't deserve something good.

"How do you know they're not saying no because I suck?"

"You forget I saw your book. Not that you even told me you draw. I had to find it by accident!" she yells.

Definitely time for me to get out of here. "I gotta go. I forgot I have something to take care of. Lock up for me when you leave, yeah?" I tell her. I never should have given her a key in the first place. I don't even know why I did.

"Maddy . . ."

"How many times do I have to tell you to stop calling me that?" And then I close the door and leave, just like I walked away from Masquerade. Like I walk away from everything that matters.

CHAPTER THREE

BEE

I've never been the type of person who sits around and dwells on life. Bad things happen all the time and overthinking them has never done shit to change anything. I remember when I went back home—or to the place I should consider home—I didn't really understand what was going on. At thirteen I should have, but people who are kidnapped are supposed to have been hurt. They're mistreated and locked away. They aren't happy and loved the way I had been, so the whole thing was hard to wrap my head around.

For about a week after they sent me home, that's all I thought about. The people who raised me and the people who lost me. How they both loved me even though I didn't know quite how to feel about any of them. Didn't know how I felt about that screwed up word *love* at all. Rex and Melody had always told me they'd loved me but now I knew they'd stolen me. My real parents said they loved me but they didn't really know me. I wasn't their little girl anymore. How can you love someone you don't know?

It hurt and I cried, my chest feeling hollow and broken, knowing I should feel so many things I didn't know how to.

Nothing changed.

I didn't hurt any less. My real family was still broken-hearted and confused, and I'd lost who I considered my mom and dad.

That's when I decided I wouldn't lose myself in the past anymore. I wouldn't stress and dwell on things I couldn't change or even things I could, because if I made that decision the first time, there was a reason. I would stick with my choices, even when someone didn't get them or I got shit for being closed off or hard. And I wouldn't worry about love or try to figure it out.

Girls aren't allowed to feel that way, I guess.

This is why I'm pissed that I haven't stopped thinking about Maddox since he walked out of Masquerade. I'm not daydreaming about the sex, though it was good. No, better than good. I keep seeing that look on his face when I told him no about apprenticing with me.

I recognized the expression because I've felt it before. It's more than disappointment. It's loss.

I've been lost since I was four years old, even though I didn't know it until I was thirteen. Being found didn't help that feeling of being misplaced, either.

It pisses me off and makes me feel soft.

With a towel, I wipe away the excess ink on the tat I'm giving before studying the daffodil. The girl has her hair over her opposite shoulder as she leans away from me while I work on her shoulder. She told me when she first came in that it was her first ink and she looked like she would dash at any second. She didn't and she's hardly made a peep besides to answer questions I ask her.

"What's it mean?" I ask as I put the gun to her skin again. You can always tell those people who come and get something that's forgettable. They pick a design off the wall or something like that. It's obvious when people get tattoos because they mean something. The one this girl brought in means something to her.

After a short silence, I add, "You don't have to answer if you don't want to. I have some that no one will ever know why I got them." When you engrave something into your skin, it's personal—important. Or at least it should be.

"No, it's cool," she replies, but then still doesn't talk for a few more seconds. "Daffodils are supposed to symbolize rebirth. I need that, I think."

I almost pause and pull back the tattoo gun, but I make myself keep going. Rebirth. I'm not sure how I feel about that concept. "Do you believe it? That people can be reborn?" Even though it doesn't really change anything, that's kind of what tattooing is to me—rebirth. Not sure why, but Maddox pops into my head again and I wonder if he needs to be reborn from something.

"I want to."

We don't share any more words as I finish her piece. When I'm done, I wipe it clean. "You wanna see it?" I ask her.

She stands with her back to the mirror and looks at the yellow and orange flower.

"It's gorgeous," she says. There's awe in her voice.

I love that feeling. Love knowing that I gave someone something that is a part of them. "Cool."

After she's done, I put some saran wrap on it and give her aftercare instructions. She lets her red hair fall over her shoulders again.

"Thanks. I appreciate it. I'm Camie."

Which I knew from looking at her ID and her consent form, but I still shake her hand. "Bee."

She hands me the money before walking out. I feel kind of jittery, though I don't know why. It was just a tattoo, but then I've been like this since Maddox came into my shop. I don't know what the hell is wrong with me.

It's not a minute after I'm done cleaning the equipment and disposing of the used needle when I hear the door open again. Turning around, I see a woman with long, dark hair and this happy-go-lucky smile on her face that I'm not sure I've ever worn. Actually that's a lie. I'm sure I have, but I was too young to really remember it.

"Hey," I tell her, walking over to the counter. "Can I help you?"

Her smile falters slightly as she makes her way to me. There's no question in my mind that she's not here for a tattoo. I'm not sure what else she could want.

"I'm sorry to bother you while you're at work, but I wasn't sure how else to get a hold of you," the girl tells me.

The hairs on the back of my neck stand on end, my heart going a little crazy. I don't like it when people come looking for me. Reporters wouldn't leave us alone after Rex and Melody got arrested and I was sent to live with my birth family. I couldn't go outside and they harassed everyone we knew. It's been years since I've had to deal with it, but the cramping in my stomach reminds me of how fresh it all still is.

"If it's not something you should bother me at work with, then you shouldn't be here."

I turn my back on her before walking toward my supply cabinet. Nothing will make me give this girl the time of day.

It's not five seconds later that she speaks again. "I'm here about Maddox."

I stumble, the ache in my stomach now replaced

with anger. That piece-of-shit son of a bitch. This is exactly the kind of drama I don't need.

Crossing my arms, I lean against the cabinet and face her. "I didn't know he had a girlfriend. I don't play games like that, but no offense, it shouldn't be me you're talking to right now. It should be him."

Her eyes stretch wide, shock highlighting her features. She grabs hold of the counter, making me wonder what the hell is going on here.

"You and my brother?"

"He's your brother?" I feel a little relieved because I'm not the kind of girl to sleep with a guy with a girlfriend, but family drama is almost worse than girlfriend issues. I definitely don't want to be involved here, though I don't know why she cares who her brother sleeps with.

There's no way I'm answering her question. "Why are you here?"

"I'm Laney." She holds out her hand, obviously over the surprise. She has that grin on her face again that shows how happy she is. For a minute I wonder what that would feel like but then shove it aside. What do I have to be so upset about? I have two sets of parents who "love" me—that one word that's so important to people. I was treated well. I'm standing in the middle of my dream. There's no reason I shouldn't be smiling like her, but it feels too fake. There's something inside of me that holds it back.

Still, I find myself moving toward her and taking her hand. "Bee."

"I wanted to talk to you about Maddy apprenticing for you. I know you told him no, but—"

"Maddy?"

Laney rolls her eyes. "Why does everyone have to comment on the name? It's really not that big a deal."

I shrug because she's right. Considering I named myself after an insect, I guess I don't really have room to talk.

"I know this probably isn't how things are done and my brother will freak out if he finds out I came down here, but I want to ask you to reconsider letting him learn from you. He's really good and—"

"No."

A little fire sparks in her eyes, making me see there is more to her than the smiles I saw. "No?"

"No."

"You didn't even give him a chance! He's really good. It's an apprenticeship. It's not like you have to pay him or anything."

Sighing, I shake my head, trying to figure out how to not sound like a bitch here. "Listen, I think it's really cool you're sticking up for your brother and all, but I'm not going to change my mind. I don't play real well with others and I'm pretty sure you caught from the beginning of the conversation that Maddox and I working together could be a little awkward."

"Do you care about him?" she whispers.

Oh shit. "No. I don't *know* him. It was a spur-of-the-moment thing, if you catch my drift. It didn't mean anything and it's not something either of us plan to do again."

She frowns, making me see that even though she knows what I mean, she doesn't get it. She's the kind of girl my parents deserve.

"Then what's the problem with him working here? You're both adults. Maddox is good at keeping walls between himself and other people. It shouldn't be hard for you guys to keep it professional."

It's on the tip of my tongue to ask her *why* he keeps those walls, but that would require me to knock down one of my own, and I don't plan to do that. "Again, I think it's cool you came over here for him, but it's not happening. If you'll excuse me, I need to close my shop for lunch."

Stepping around the counter, I head toward the door. My hand is on the handle and I'm pushing it open when she softly says, "Please. *Please.* He would kill me for saying this, but he needs it. He needs something to help him find his way through our past."

Her words hit me right in the chest. They're honest and raw and painful. She's really worried about him, and even though my brain is screaming at me that it isn't my business, I stop pushing the door open. Still, I don't move.

Laney speaks again. "I'm not sure this will help, but I don't know what else to do. I want my brother back. He hasn't really wanted anything for himself in so long and he wants this so badly. He's spent years dealing with painful things and taking care of me. Maddy needs this for *him*."

Don't do this. Walk away. It's not your business. Instead of doing that, I close the door again. What would I have done if the Professor hadn't given me a chance? I wouldn't have Masquerade and I wouldn't be Bee. I would be even more lost than I am now, and as much as I don't want to admit it, I *saw* that in Maddox. Saw that he's drifting alone in the world. It's probably what made me go to the hotel with him in the first place, rather than dealing with someone easy like the pretty-boy bartender. But no, I knew he would get me, and here his sister is opening herself up in a way I could never do.

Because she loves him?

"I can't help him if he's not any good."

Her face instantly brightens. "He's good. I didn't even know he could draw until recently, but he has books full. I took one from his apartment for you to see."

That makes me chuckle. She obviously takes things into her own hands. I can respect that.

Laney reaches into her purse and pulls out a black book. After grabbing it from her, I sit in one of the chairs by the door and open it.

My eyes scan page after page, soaking in each and every line and curve of Maddox's work. He's got talent, that's for sure, and he's different. His drawings have a rough, raw edge to them that doesn't look unpracticed but . . . rough in the way that you want them to look. Like somehow his pictures have seen and been through a lot but came out of it in the end. Even if it is with frayed edges and hard lines, they made it through.

I know that's a crazy way to explain drawings, but it's all I can think of.

And they're beautiful. If he could transport this onto someone's skin, it would be a waste not to share it with the world.

My hands are actually shaking when I hand her the book back.

"I have his number on my machine," I tell Laney. "I'll call him."

Her eyes pool. "Thank you. That means so much to me. I hate to ask you another favor, but could you not tell him that I came down here?"

I open my mouth, almost telling her I didn't do it for her but for him. For his talent is more like it, but I realize that would be rude. "I won't say a word."

My whole body freezes when she hugs me. I've never been a real touchy-feely kind of girl, especially when it's with someone I don't know. That thought reminds me that I'm going to be working with

Maddox—with a guy I slept with. I don't do things like that, especially when I can look into his eyes and see shades of myself. Suddenly, I feel a little nauseous.

Laney pulls away. "Thanks again. You won't regret it."

When she's gone, I whisper, "I hope not."

I don't know what makes me do it, but instead of calling Maddox, later that night, I get dressed to go to Lunar. I don't know if he's even working tonight, but this is something I want to do in person. Maybe it's because I can play things off better, which I know doesn't really make sense. I'm good at schooling my facial features—good at looking like a bitch and I need to show him that part of me. I need to keep those walls up so we can both make sure we're on the same page. This will be about tattooing and nothing else.

Lunar is even louder than it was last time I was here and even more packed with people. First, I head straight to the bar where Trevor and a few other bartenders are mixing drinks. He hands a girl with dark hair a glass before winking at her. I hate that kind of bullshit, but she seems to be eating it up.

He turns a little and his eyes catch mine and I see amusement there. "Corona with lime?"

"Yep. And then I'll be out of your way." I don't want this girl thinking I'm interested in him in any way.

"You guys know each other?" she yells, loud enough so I can hear her over the music.

"Nope," I say at the same time Trevor says, "I think she's here for someone else."

Shit. That means he knows I left with Maddox.

"Jealous?"

"Now why would I be jealous when I have Adrianna right here?" He winks at the girl again. Ugh. Definitely time for me to get out of here.

"Can I get my beer?"

"You sure can, darlin'."

I almost throw up.

As soon as he hands me my Corona, I walk away without paying. Over the music I hear him laughing before he shouts, "He's working a private party in the Back Room! You need me to get you in."

Yeah. That's what he thinks. I don't need anyone for anything.

CHAPTER FOUR

MADDOX

I feel like such a fucking cliché as I lean against the wall of "the Back Room" with my arms crossed, watching people dance and drink around me. When I first started working security at Lunar, I didn't even know the Back Room existed. Once I got hired, they told me, but new bouncers aren't allowed to work it. People pay good money for the privacy you get back here—the way you're allowed to touch instead of just looking as strippers ride your lap.

Tonight it's a bachelor party for some senator's son, or something like that, hence the strippers who aren't usually in Lunar. I don't even know why he'd be in a place like Brenton anyway, but here he is. Probably because no one would look for him here.

I push my hand to my earpiece when Trevor's voice comes through it. "You got company. Open the door."

Visitor? Who the fuck could be here for me?

"Got it."

The small hallway that leads to the door is only a short distance from me, so I make it over in no time, opening it to see who's there. My body tenses when I see blond hair and a star peeking out from under a shirt. *Fuck*. As I'm about to ask Trevor what's up, his voice sounds in my ear again. "She's hot. No one will know and she's not the type to open her mouth. Let her in. If you don't, you're fucking stupid."

As much as I hate it, I'm curious as to why she's here. Still, that tense anger is pumping through my veins as I hear her tell me no about Masquerade. I couldn't care less that I fucked her. That's not what this is about because there were no emotions there. What gives me an ache in my chest is the fact that she has what I want. I haven't cared enough about anything to feel jealous in a long-ass time, but that's exactly what comes to mind when I look at her.

"You coming to the party?" I ask her.

"I'm here to see you."

She doesn't give me a chance to reply as she pushes her way around me and inside. What I would give to kick her out of this room just because I can, but since I don't really know if she's giving me shit or if she came for the party, I hold back. It's not like Trevor to let someone in here for no reason.

Right on her heels, I follow her until she rounds the corner and pulls to a stop once she can see inside. Not having enough time to go around her, my body lines right up against hers, Bee's nice little ass tucked right against me. On reflex I reach out, my hand grabbing her slender waist to make sure she doesn't stumble forward. Damn it if that doesn't bring up all sorts of thoughts about how it felt to strip her naked and touch her everywhere.

"You have your hands on me." There's a sexy huskiness in her voice that tells me she's turned on too. It should make me rip my hand away from her as fast as I can, but I'm so pissed at her about Masquerade that I can't stop myself from being a dick.

"If I remember correctly, you liked the feel of my hands on you. You were very enthusiastic about how much you liked it."

Briefly her body stiffens and then she's the one jerking away from me.

"I can't tell you how glad I am that you just fucked up. Next time you're pissed that you don't have anywhere to tattoo, remember this moment and know you could've had it."

Everything inside me screams to stop her, to ask her what she means and why she possibly changed her mind, but I don't. I can't make myself do it. Not when I'm this keyed up because there's a part of me that wants to beg her to say yes. To show her how much this opportunity means to me and how much I fucking want it, but then I wonder if I even know *how* to open myself up anymore.

The door slams as she walks out, but I keep hearing her words in my head. Keep hearing her tell me I could've had it. I've even thought about leaving Brenton to find somewhere else to go. As fucked up as it sounds, I still can't leave Laney. Not when there's a chance she could need me. I wasn't there for her enough already.

You could have had it. When was the last time I had anything I really wanted? When was the last time I gave a shit about anything?

The rest of my shift I'm thinking about it. About how I got teased with what I want only to have it taken away. I didn't have much time in the last tattoo parlor at all, but here she is offering it to me. Or she was until I treated her the way I do everyone else.

Watching the people in the Back Room, I see them trip over each other and grab girls' asses and see those same girls laugh while the guys are doing it. It gets old fast. I can't wait to get out of this place. Maybe to some people tattooing isn't a much better occupation, but it's the only way I know how to show who I am. If I even know who in the hell that person is.

When I get off work and climb onto my bike, I head toward Masquerade. The rumble of the engine helps block out my thoughts because if I let them free, they'll eat me alive. They'll drag me under until I'm thinking about Dad sitting in prison and Mom trying to kill herself, and me missing something as stupid as football. Those thoughts will make me turn around and head home so I can then think about how much of a fucking joke I am because I ran away again.

It's late, after 2:00 a.m., so chances are she's not even at the shop, but I'm still going there anyway. When I pull up, her little Insight's parked out front, even though it looks like all the lights are out inside. After pulling out my cell phone, I look through my recent calls and since the only person I call is my sister, her number is still there.

It takes six rings before her sleep-roughened voice comes through the phone. "This better be good."

"Were you serious?"

She curses before complaining, "Your bike is too loud. Turn it off."

I do it even though I'm not used to doing what anyone says. I'm also not used to anyone having something I care about. "Were you serious?" The words sound angry even to my own ears.

Bee sighs. "Can we talk tomorrow?"

"I'm here now." Silently I'm begging her to say she'll open the door, but those words are bitter in my head. There's never been a time I've begged for anything. It makes my jaw tighten and my fingers itch to start my bike again.

"I don't know why in the hell I'm doing this, but I'll unlock the door." As soon as she speaks the last word, the line goes dead. Again I consider driving away. Forgetting her and this stupid-ass dream of

mine, to what? Be a tattoo artist? I don't know why
it's so important to me, but it's what makes me get
off my motorcycle and walk to the door.

The locks click before Bee pulls the door open,
the light from outside enabling me to see her. My
eyes scan her, taking in the really short cotton shorts
and tank top she's wearing. The girl has a killer body
and she obviously isn't afraid to show it, which makes
her even more hot. You can tell she's not flaunting;
she just is who she is and whoever doesn't like it, she
won't hesitate to tell them to fuck off.

I walk in and Bee locks the door behind me.

"You live here?" There's a light on down the
hallway. It's dim like it's only from a lamp or something, but I assume that's where she was when I called.

"No, but it's the place I'm the most comfortable,
so I stay here a lot." She clicks on the light. I'm
surprised she admitted that, but I won't call her on
it. I know I wouldn't want her to do that to me.

"Did you bring any drawings?" Bee sits at the chair
behind a desk.

I hand her a book, but the second I do, I want to
snatch it back. It's always like that showing someone
my work, even though I know it's good. "That's just
one I had with me. I have more at home."

She doesn't answer as she starts flipping through
the pages. After a couple minutes of watching her
study each page, I start to get jittery. Feel like she's

looking inside me instead of at some pages, so to distract myself, I move around the room, taking in pictures of her work and other tattoos on the walls.

She looks at the book for what seems like an hour before speaking. "These are good. They're different. Your artwork has a unique style that I haven't seen before."

I nod.

"Why do you want to be a tattoo artist?" she asks. The question shows me how serious she is about what she does because no one has brought it up before.

The urge to tell her it's none of her business surges through me, but I want this badly enough to answer. "Because when I'm around it, I feel more like myself than I probably ever have."

A brief flash of shock shows on her face, but she covers it quickly. "Good. I won't screw around with someone who's playing a game. This isn't something you do to make a quick buck. Not if you're working with me, at least. Did you get a chance to actually give anyone ink?"

"No. The apprenticeship only lasted three months before he bailed."

Bee nods. "That's good. I would rather you didn't have any experience—that way I don't have to train bad habits out of you."

"I'm not a dog."

"No one said you were. Chill out, Scratch."

I tense at the name, but before I can really say anything, she starts asking questions again. "Do you lean toward liking only black work or are you into color too?"

Everything I have so far is only black, but as I look at her again, I see a variety of black and colorful work. "Depends. I don't want to do only one or the other. I love work with shading too. I've seen some pieces that are really incredible just because of the shading."

She nods and I wonder if that was the right answer.

"I'm not saying you don't, but this is something you have to take seriously. There are a lot of dumbasses out there who think it's all fun, but it's not. Stuff like being clean and safe is even more important than the picture you put into someone's skin."

"That's a given, isn't it?"

She grins. "You'd think, but it's not always like that."

We're both quiet after that. Bee glances down at my artwork again. "I'm surprised I even let you in here tonight. It's important that you know that. I don't take shit from people."

One look at her and that's obvious. Part of me didn't expect her to open the door for me either. "I'm surprised I came, so that makes two of us." When she looks up at me, I'm not sure how I feel about the way her eyes take me in. Don't know what I think about the fact that we have shit in common or that her look is familiar to me. I give it myself.

Bee stands, walks around to the front of the desk, and then leans on it. "If we do this, can we keep things from getting awkward?"

My answer comes automatically. "I can if you can. It was one night. We don't know each other and I'm never with someone more than once anyway." I've shared this strange sort of honesty with her tonight that makes my body overheat. I want all the words back because they're a part of me and I don't want anyone to see who I am, but this is it. Saying these things to her is the only way to get what I want.

"Now that you've asked your questions and realize this isn't a game to me, I need to know if we're doing this or not."

Silently she walks toward the door and opens it. I hold in the groan, pissed at myself for fucking this up again and even more pissed that she's in control.

Bee turns toward me, her blond hair messy from sleep, but it's another thing she doesn't care about. It doesn't take away from how sexy she is either.

"We're doing this. Don't make me regret it. Now I need to get some sleep and then we'll talk tomorrow about a schedule."

I let out the breath trapped in my lungs. *Thanks*, echoes through my mind, but all that comes out is, "Cool. We'll talk later." Then I walk out the door.

Instead of going home, I head to the high school. It's such a dumb fucking thing to do, but like I've done other nights, I jump the fence and head to the football field. Sitting in the middle of it, I let my eyes trace over the whole thing, trying to remember the time this used to be important to me. And trying not to concentrate on the fact that even though I got something I want, something I *need*, I still want to take out the fucking world because of everything I've lost.

CHAPTER FIVE

BEE

KIDNAPPED GIRL HOME AFTER NINE YEARS IN CAPTIVITY

It was just like any other week when four-year-old Leila Malone went to the park with her mom. It was their Monday tradition. They played on the swings and the slide, which her mom, Katherine, said was her favorite. But on this Monday, Leila happened to slip away from her mother.

"It wasn't a minute. Not a minute and she was gone. My baby is gone!" her tearful mother had cried that day. There were searches and news conferences to follow. Private investigators and even psychics.

"I've never seen a family like the Malones. They fought the good fight and have never given up hope of finding their little girl. They love her more than anything," Detective Harris had said when he announced the case had gone cold. That didn't stop the Malones. The pictures never went away and anyone living in Virginia, maybe even the United States, knew the name Leila Malone, but nothing worked. It seemed their little girl was lost forever.

Until now.

Nine years after little Leila went missing, she's back home with the family who never stopped looking for her . . . who never stopped loving her. It's a miracle, and the world could use more of those. The two people who were responsible for taking her away from her family are safely behind bars, where they won't be able to hurt anyone again.

Good luck, little Leila. We're so glad you're home where you belong!

Opening a folder in the locked drawer in my desk, I stuff the old newspaper article back inside. I try not to think how Melody and Rex never hurt me, like the person who wrote it said. They *did* hurt me according to everyone else, and I get how that's true. My brain *knows* it is because they kidnapped me. They took me from my parents. It's my heart that has trouble remembering it because the truth is, even though I struggle with the concept of love, I didn't always. And when I remember who taught it to me, it was them because they're the only ones who hold my early memories.

These are the things no one will ever read about. How at first it wasn't a miracle for me — I'd been taken from my family. I was scared and hurting and felt guilt for those feelings.

My eyes sting, because I still feel all of those things.

Before I let myself go through the hundreds of other articles in the drawers—the ones documenting my parents' search for me, and the trail afterward, and the pictures of Melody and Rex, I shove the drawer closed again. I'm not sure why I even started looking in the first place because all it does is make me feel when I don't want to.

It's been a couple days since I agreed to let Maddox in my shop. He comes in for a couple hours every day. I hate to admit it, because I almost hoped he'd screw up, but it hasn't been bad. He's up half the night working at Lunar, but he never shows it when he's here in the afternoons.

Even though I'm not the first person to work with him, he still studies everything I do. He watches me clean equipment and does everything exactly the way I tell him to. His dedication annoys me, even though it shouldn't. He's new, but he loves it, and it feels strange having that in common with him.

For the millionth time I look at my cell. It's almost 3:00, which means Maddox will be here any minute. It's been slow as hell today and I'm hoping we get someone in not just because I want to work, but because it also helps when the scratch is here. We're both quiet and even though I'm glad he's not talking my ear off the whole time, it's awkward as hell.

When the door opens, I don't look up, knowing it's Maddox. Instead I turn to the computer to pull up my playlist so we at least have some music to listen to.

"We have anyone scheduled today?" he asks.

Now I let my eyes find him and wish he wasn't so gorgeous. He still has that dark stubble on his jaw, which I've always found sexy, and eyes that are this unique shade of gray, with long black lashes.

Eyes aren't really something I've ever cared about drawing or tattooing, but for some reason, I think I'd like to draw his. I'd like to see if I could get the curl of his lashes right and the tone of his gray.

"Nope. Hoping for some walk-ins, though. It takes a while to build up clientele."

He nods before sitting in one of the chairs. Maddox crosses his arms, and I can't help but take in the long, toned muscles as they constrict with his movement. It's crazy looking at him sometimes, because there's always this edge of anger right below the surface. I see it almost come out, but he always finds a way to hold it back. If I thought he'd ever really let it out, he wouldn't be here. Still, it's definitely always there, making me wonder what he has to be so pissed about.

But then there's something in there that reminds me of Trevor too. Not that I know him really, but he has that pretty-boy look. He's the type of guy who was popular in school and played sports and probably slept with the cheerleaders.

It doesn't fit, but I see that in Maddox too.

"You're staring at me." His voice is calm, even, like it doesn't really matter to him one way or the other.

"So?"

My reply seems to unbalance him, but he recovers quickly. "You're looking at me like you want a replay of our first night. If you don't stop, I'll be watching you the same way and that's something neither of us wants."

A shiver runs the length of me, but I don't try to hold it back. I might not get with him again, but I'm not usually one who holds back on what I feel physically. What's the point? It's who I am regardless of whether I'm Bee, Leila, or Coral. I've fought hard to make sure I know that.

"Unfortunately, you're right." Leaning back in the chair, I cross my arms as Maddox looks at me. "What?"

"I didn't think you'd admit it."

"Why not? It's true."

"Just because something's true doesn't mean people are honest about it."

I nod. He's right about that. "There's a lot of stuff we can't change. A lot people keep in. I just . . ." I shrug. "There're certain traits about me that are the way they are. Most of them I feel shitty about, so the ones I don't . . . it seems ridiculous to hide those." *It's too much to hide all the time.*

Maddox's eyes concentrate on me hard. There's a tick in his jaw, but he doesn't look angry. More curious and I don't want him or anyone else trying to figure me out. Who knows if he'll ask me anything or not. Mostly I don't think so because it doesn't fit with the quiet guy he is, but I'm also not risking it.

"That's enough about that." I push to my feet. "I'm getting antsy."

Maddox gets up right behind me and walks out the door. *What the fuck?* Did I miss something here? It's only a few seconds later that he comes back inside and I feel my body relax. Why I was so tense over him walking out, I don't know and honestly I don't like it.

Without a word, Maddox hands me a piece of paper. When I turn it over, I see it's a flyer with the same picture on it as my sign outside the door.

"You made this?" I don't know why it shocks me. Actually I do. He doesn't seem like the kind of guy to do something like this.

"If I want to learn, we need business. It only makes sense."

Ah, so there's the why. "You did this freehand from memory?"

"It's important."

"I gave some out before I opened." I don't admit that his looks better.

"I'll give some out at Lunar. My little sister is a waitress. She can maybe sneak and put them on cars at work or something. Laney and a couple of her friends go to the college. I'm sure they can hook us up with some people too."

It's on the tip of my tongue to mention something about his little sister not really being "little." They can't be far apart in age, but then I remember I'm not supposed to know about her. And really, her age doesn't matter. I'm only trying to distract myself from the fact that he put a lot of thought into this. Yeah it helps him, too, but it still means something to me.

"That'd be cool."

"I'll grab the rest of the flyers, then. We can each take some. I also thought it would help to have some specials. Did you do anything when you opened? I have a few ideas that—"

"Whoa." He's throwing so many ideas at me I'm getting dizzy. All I can think is he's trying to take over. He doesn't think I can do it. "You're getting ahead of yourself. What's all this 'we' stuff? Masquerade is mine, Scratch. I don't need you telling me how to run it."

Maddox steps back, emotions flashing through his eyes that I don't understand. I cringe, guilt layering my annoyance.

"Keep the flyer," he grits out before heading toward the door. It would be the smartest thing in the world for me to let him leave, but the paper in my hand makes the guilt burn brighter.

A voice in my head keeps telling me to apologize, but what comes out is, "You give up too easily."

Maddox stops moving. "You treat people like shit too often."

"True, but I have a feeling I'm not the only one here who does that."

With those words he turns around and looks at me. He wants to argue with me. I can tell by the set of his jaw and the tension in his features. Hell, what am I doing here with this guy? We're too much alike. I think he sees it too. There's no way this can end well.

"I'm not trying to be a bitch. This place is important to me and I'm protective."

He nods, understanding lightening his face.

"I also don't apologize well."

"I don't need apologies. They don't mean shit anyway."

In that second I realize how different I am from so many girls, because those words are sexy. Brutal honesty is underrated and I can see that he has it, like I do. If I were a different kind of girl—the kind who believed in love—Maddox would be the guy I'd fall for. Though I guess if I really wasn't me, he probably wouldn't be what I'd want.

Maddox steps closer to me, close enough that I swear I smell a faint tint of tattoo ink mixed with the scent of man. He looks down at me, strength and anger rolling off him. Not like violent anger, but frustration at the world. Like he's given up, but not in the way that he wants people to feel sorry for him. He's real and doesn't paint the universe as a happy place like so many people try to.

I suddenly want to touch him. To see if the two of us coming together like we did that first night can give the world a little more of the realness that it lacks.

Totally not a good idea and definitely not happening. I step away. "Why don't we call it a day? I don't think we're going to get much business and you work tonight. There's a lot of trouble we can get into if you stay. Trouble neither of us wants."

"It pisses me off that I want you," he says with all the honesty in the world.

"You do pissed off well, I think. And sexy too."

As he's backing toward the door, Maddox says, "Yeah . . . I'll grab the flyers for you and then I'm gone."

I'm breathing hard when I don't want to be. A slow, tingly need building in my stomach. I almost ask him to stay. We could do that—enjoy each other with nothing attached to it, but if it becomes a habit, it could be a problem. It's important I remember that, so instead of standing here, I go into the back until I hear him leave the flyers before going out front again.

CHAPTER SIX

MADDOX

The next day I'm sitting on my porch, trying to wake up with a cigarette in my hand. It was a long night at work with stupid-ass drunk people making fools of themselves. It gets tiring after a while. I've never been into shit like that. Don't do drugs and rarely drink. My one vice is cigarettes. There's something relaxing about the deep breaths in and forced breaths out. I think it was something I did to rebel when I was younger, and I haven't stopped yet. They keep me busy, as fucked up as that sounds. Maybe I have an oral fixation or some shit like that.

The only good thing about last night was I got rid of all the flyers before Trevor or his brother Tyler could give me shit about passing them out at work. They're twins even though they don't look exactly alike — rich kids who somehow own a club at twenty-two. They basically leave me alone, which works for me.

Pushing the end of my half-smoked cigarette into the concrete, I put it out before stuffing it into the old coffee can. As I'm about to go inside, Laney and her boyfriend, Adrian, walk around the corner.

Even though I'm iffy about him, there's a respect there too. He's with my sister even though our dad killed his son. He never told her that I hunted him down after he split a few months before and took some of my anger out on him with my fists. It's not as though he didn't give it right back to me.

"Hey!" Laney smiles and gives me a quick hug.

I nod toward Adrian. "What's up?"

He lifts his chin in greeting. Grabbing the door handle, I push it open and they follow me inside.

"Not too much. We're going to see Ash, but I wanted to stop by and see how things are going with you first." Laney sits on the couch and Adrian goes down right beside her.

For a second, I look at him. Watch for some flash of anger that I know he has to feel. Ash was his son. Our dad hit him and now they're going to see him at his grave. For a brief second, Adrian closes his eyes and takes a deep breath before reaching over to grab my sister's hand. Damned if he didn't make me respect him a whole hell of a lot more. He loves her and doesn't make her suffer for something she didn't cause. That's really all I ever wanted for her—not to lose out because of our parents.

"Not much," I finally reply. "You could have called to ask that, though."

"Yeah, but then it would be harder to pump you for information. This way you can't hang up on her." Adrian smirks. Fucker. Laney wouldn't have brought it up like Adrian did.

"There's nothing to tell."

"Maddox. You're learning to tattoo at a new shop. There's a lot to tell. What's she like? Is she good at what she does?"

My mind goes back to the pictures on Bee's wall. To the artwork on her body, a lot of which she told me she drew herself. Yeah, she's incredible. Way better than the guy I used to work with. "I wouldn't be working with her if she wasn't—Wait, how do you know it's a woman?"

Laney tenses for a second, making me feel like shit that I don't tell her anything that's going on in my life, before she jokingly says, "Adrian's psychic, remember?"

He taps the side of his head and I roll my eyes. I guess it was some long-standing joke around Brenton that Adrian was psychic. I don't know how it started, but he likes to play it up when the situation fits him. "You guys are funny."

"It's going around town. You know how those things work, Maddy. Everyone's talking about her."

"Then everyone needs to take their ass to the shop and get a tattoo."

"Are things going good with you guys? I mean, do you work well with her?"

The last thing I want to do is talk to Laney about Bee. "Everything's fine. How are your classes going?"

"Good. They just started. Way to change the subject." The little flash of hurt in her eyes spreads through me. I wish I could be a better brother to her.

"What about everything else? You're dealing okay? Mom hasn't given you shit or anything?" Laney has always been a little sensitive. She's *nice* and she expects everyone else to be too. She's the kind who always looks on the bright side of things, but it means she gets hurt easily too. A little before the summer, she cut off contact with our mom. She needed to because for four years Laney tried to take care of Mom, but she just treated Laney like shit. I always worry my sister will let her back in.

"She's good." Adrian puts his arm around her. "I wouldn't let anyone hurt her. I take care of her."

"We take care of each other," she whispers back at him, and he nods in agreement. It's true too.

Suddenly I get this sort of ache in my gut and I want to be out on my bike or working in the shop. Anything but being here. She's happy and I'm fucking glad, but it makes the emptiness I usually welcome inside me threaten to pull me under.

We all could have been happy, until everything got too screwed up. Instead she had to fight for it and live through hell to be where she is. That's the one thing I want to fix more than anything else.

"You look sad, Maddy." Laney stands up, but I shake my head and she doesn't come closer. She's a toucher. She wants to hug and be affectionate, but all those things do is remind me of how I failed. They're emotional when I try not to focus on emotions. It's easier to shut down.

"You guys caught me right before I was going to get in the shower. I have to head to the shop soon."

The sad look she gives me tells me she knows it's an excuse. Yeah, I'm supposed to go to Masquerade. Even if I wasn't, I wouldn't let them stay. Adrian stands, shaking his head before taking her hand. "Come on, Little Ghost. We need to get going."

She waves good-bye before Adrian leads her out. I take a step toward the door, guilt mixing with my blood and running through my veins, but there's really no point in going after her. I still don't want to open up and pretend the world is going to become a better place because I share my feelings.

Annoyed at myself, I grab my phone the second it rings. "Yeah."

"Maddox. I'm so glad you answered!" When Mom's voice comes through the phone, I wish like hell I would've checked to see who was calling first. "Please. Don't hang up."

She sounds so nice. Like the perfect, happy mom we all used to think she was, the one she maybe used to be. But the older Laney got, the worse she treated her. What kind of parent is jealous of their own child? She blamed Laney for Dad—because he gave her attention. Somehow it was Laney's fault when he started gambling and sleeping around too.

It was also Laney's fault that she didn't walk away as Mom lay bleeding on the floor. She called 911 and held her and cried for her mother, while Mom blamed Laney for letting her live.

She wouldn't have cared if I did the same thing, and she doesn't know that *I* could have been the one to stop it all. I didn't tell her that I knew what Dad was doing and to this day I'm too big a pussy to admit it to her.

Even though she's cared more about herself than anyone since Dad went to prison and even though she treats my sister like shit, I owe her because I kept my mouth shut about what Dad was doing. If I hadn't, things might not have gotten as bad as they did.

"How are you?" The words burn my tongue. They're a betrayal to Laney even though she would never see it like that, but it's an apology to Mom for being weak too.

"How do you think I am? My husband is in jail, my son won't speak to me, and they're making me see a shrink."

Nowhere in there does she say a word about Laney. I have to fight to bite my tongue and not mention it. "You've tried to kill yourself multiple times in four and a half years. Maybe it wouldn't hurt to talk to someone."

"Do *you*?"

I sigh, wondering why I didn't see that coming. "I'm not suicidal. And I didn't hurt my family."

"Don't do that, Maddox. I'm not the one who hurt our family. Your father did. He's the one who cheated on me and ruined our family."

What about the fact that he killed a kid? Hurt Laney and I? None of that comes out of her mouth.

"We could have been a family without him." Or hell, maybe Laney was right and we don't deserve it because someone died. A little fucking kid.

I hear the tears in her voice before she starts to speak. It always happens this way. "Are you saying it's my fault? I was a victim here too. It's not that easy to turn it off."

No shit. I wish it was. "You think I don't know that? That I don't live with this shit every day? That Laney doesn't? She has to look at Adrian and know what our family took from him!"

"Blah, blah, blah, blah! It always comes back to her, doesn't it? What kind of hold does she have on the men in this family? What did she do to you, Maddox? Why do you love her more than your own mother? That's what she wants. You know that, don't—"

Her words are cut off when I end the call. I should

have fucking known it would end up like that. It always does.

My hands are shaking. My heart racing. I'm supposed to be at Masquerade in an hour, but I can't go in like this. Not when I'm raw and open, when I know in my head that I just need to get the fuck over it.

But damn do I want to be there. I think I might need it.

My shower is quick. My thoughts turned off like it's so easy for me to do. Stoic, unemotional. People like my sister don't get it, but closing myself off is how I make it through.

Still, I find myself driving to Masquerade, when my brain is telling me not to. When I know how shitty I am to be around when I'm in a mood like this. Pretty soon she's not going to take my shit and she'll call this whole thing off. It's only been a week and we've already gotten into it more than once.

Maybe she should kick me out. What the hell am I doing here anyway?

It doesn't stop me from wanting it. From getting off my bike and walking to the door. I'm surprised to see the CLOSED sign is up. Glancing at my cell, I see it's almost two, the time she said I should come in. I start to dial her number, but something makes me try the door instead.

I squint when the door easily opens. She's a smart

girl. She pays attention and doesn't let people get the drop on her. I didn't expect Bee to leave the shop unlocked with the CLOSED sign up and the lights turned off inside.

"Bee?" I call out.

Her answer is immediate, but her voice softer, sadder than I've ever heard it. "Not in the mood, Scratch. Come back tomorrow."

This is where I walk out. I want to. I'm used to it. Has there ever been a time in my life when I didn't walk away? Instead I go off instinct and flick the lock. If we're going to be in the back, I don't want anyone getting in.

My muscles are tight and my brain is telling me I'm being a fucking idiot the whole time I walk down the hall, toward her office in the back.

Bee's sitting on a black couch wearing a pair of jeans and a shirt with slits in the sleeves. For the first time, she's not wearing makeup. It doesn't make her any less gorgeous, maybe younger and a little more innocent.

The light in the room flashes off the small diamond in her nose.

I've never been back here before. Boxes are everywhere. Next to her sits her cell phone.

"I said not today. I'm in a shitty mood."

Her eyes are red and puffy like she's been crying. For some reason, I can't stop looking at them. Tears seem like such a foreign thing. They would be from me and they seem like they should be from her too. Mom always cried a lot. Laney too. I never wanted to deal with a woman's tears. Still, I don't turn around and leave. "That makes two of us. All the more reason we both need the distraction of Masquerade."

She picks up her phone, turning it over and over in her hand.

"Distractions aren't always a good thing. You have to face your life head-on and keep moving. No matter how confused you are or how much something hurts, you keep going."

I haven't known her long, but those aren't her words. "Whoever said that doesn't know shit. They haven't been through anything."

She sighs and looks up at me. "But she has. My family has been through worse things than I have, because they didn't know what happened. They deal with it better than I do."

"What happened?" I squeeze the doorknob, shocked and pissed the question came out.

"Nothing."

"I hung up on my mom not an hour ago. She was wrong, but me even more so. Not because of that. For . . . things I won't tell you. Stuff I probably never will." The words sound harsh but somehow I know she'll understand them.

For the first time, real, honest sadness shows on

her face—in her eyes. Not because of me, but for whatever she's dealing with. "And I'll never ask. You're lucky your mom is wrong sometimes. Mine never is. She's perfect and loving and understanding, even though she doesn't get me."

She bites her bottom lip, looking unsure.

"And you're not perfect. Neither am I. I'll never give you shit for that. I get it."

This time, I can't read the look she gives me, but I don't have long to try. Bee pushes to her feet, slowly walking over to me. I notice the swells of her breasts from the V-neck of her shirt and her slender hips. Her purposeful steps and sexy lips.

Fuck, do I want her.

Bee stops right in front of me, the heat of lust and need rolling off her. I don't question what she wants, just pull the neck of her shirt down and press my mouth to the star on one shoulder, then the other before tracing it with my tongue.

"I guess that means you're okay with this?" Her voice is breathless as she drops her head back.

"I shouldn't be, but I am so fucking okay with this."

CHAPTER SEVEN

BEE

Most women probably would have walked out when he said he didn't want to be okay with it, but just like Maddox said about me, I *get* it.

Those three simple words helped to calm the storm inside me. No one has ever told me they got it—that they got *me*. It was awkward when I came home. My family tried too hard to be what I needed and even though it kills me to admit it, what I needed was Melody and Rex.

I tried to be who my real family expected me to be and I *know* they tried to understand me. Tried to make sense of the connection I felt with the people who took me away. And as I got older, they tried to understand the girl who was different from most of the other girls at school but didn't care. The one who became obsessed with tattooing and didn't go to college like my sister, the one who moves around.

I'm the only Malone who didn't go to school and

they've never come out and told me I'm a disappointment to them, but the truth is, I know I have to be.
That even though they try to "get" me—and the fact
that I'm blunt and don't have a plan other than
Masquerade or the ink that's such a part of me—they
don't.

*"I know you want this but remember Masquerade
might not work out. Odds are it won't. It's important
to have something to fall back on."*

*"Your sister is doing so well. She might possibly be
making top of her class."*

I don't want another plan besides Masquerade. It's
what I love and I needed their help. So what, I'm
not doing as well and they have never met a guy I've
dated in my life. Those things are so little . . . only
to them, they make me different. The lone Malone
who isn't like the rest.

Thoughts of the phone call with Mom are replaced
by Maddox. He said he gets me and there isn't
anything inside me that doesn't believe him.

"We're still on the same page, right? Original rules
apply?" I shiver as he speaks into my neck, somehow
his lips still kissing the tender skin there simul-
taneously.

"Don't worry. I'm not the type of girl who sleeps
with someone and thinks she's destined to be with
him forever."

That seems to be all the motivation Maddox needs.

He pulls me closer, higher into his arms. My legs automatically wrap around his waist. His mouth is on mine now, kissing me more slowly than he did the first night. More like a girlfriend than a lover, and it makes me pull away. "More," I tell him as he walks me over to the couch.

"Then stop talking."

"Pushy, pushy."

"You're still doing it," Maddox grits out before his lips are on mine. He doesn't lose his groove as he lays me on the couch, fitting between my legs. His erection grinds against me as his tongue explores my mouth.

He knows what he's doing. I realized that the first night, but even more so now. One of his hands expertly unbuttons my pants, his lips and hips still moving. I tug slightly at his hair, hearing a moan from him.

Then he's kissing down my neck and taking off my shirt. His tongue swirls around my belly button. "Oh God," I say huskily as that beginning tingle already forms in the pit of my stomach.

"This is hot." Maddox nips at my belly-button ring.

"*All* piercings are hot."

Maddox slides my zipper down and I lift my hips while he slowly pulls my jeans down. "I want to get my nipple done."

My eyes widen at that. I'm not sure if he's joking or not. "I'll do it for you."

"Hell no."

A laugh tumbles out of my mouth. When it hits my ears, I snap my mouth closed. I don't think I've ever laughed during sex. Not in a good way at least.

Suddenly Maddox feels too close. My body is hungry for him, *enjoying* him and begging for more, but all sorts of thoughts are rolling through me. *He gets me . . . I'm laughing with him . . . It feels too close.*

As soon as my jeans are gone, my panties follow and then he's pushing a finger inside and I don't have to remind myself not to laugh. My emotions are safely tucked away and I allow myself to feel.

Feel his finger pump in and out and feel his mouth as he teases my breasts through my bra.

With his teeth he somehow lowers one cup and then, *"Oh God,"* I gasp as his mouth covers my sensitive peak.

The heat in my belly is building higher and hotter, but I'm not ready to finish yet. Neither of us will let ourselves do this again and he's so good at what he does that I don't want to go over that ledge without him. I want to take the plunge with Maddox, which is strange in itself, but I don't know how to really say that.

"I don't need the foreplay."

"You sound like you're enjoying it." His hand moves faster.

Struggling, I find his button and pull it open before taking his zipper down. When I begin working his pants, he has to pull back, his hand and his mouth suddenly gone, making me wonder what I was thinking. My body craves his touch again.

Unfortunately, Maddox does what I made him think I want, and stands up. He pushes his pants down, his shirt right after, making me change that to *fortunately*.

He is so, so sexy—all tanned skin and defined muscles. Suddenly I really wonder what he would look like with that piercing we were talking about.

Before my imagination can run too wildly, he's grabbing a condom from his wallet and sliding it down his length. It's not nearly enough time to admire, but then he's leaning over me, pushing inside, and my nails are digging into his back and the feeling is *so* much better than admiring.

"Oh God," I say again, wondering why that seems to be my phrase of choice when I'm with him.

"You don't have to keep calling me that."

His joke springs out of nowhere and I can't stop myself from laughing. "This is no time for jokes." I fight to take control and then we're both quiet as we move together.

The heat is back, blazing into an inferno and I know I'm going to take that leap over the edge at any second.

Maddox's movements come quicker and his breathing more hurried and when I can't hold it back any longer, I'm spiraling into oblivion with Maddox right behind me.

His body collapses on top of mine. I can tell he's not resting his full weight on me. Still his weight and this slick, hard body feels . . . almost comforting? I don't know, but it freaks me out and makes me try to wiggle out from under him.

"Don't worry," Maddox mumbles. "I'm not trying to cuddle. I just can't move yet."

Well, that's putting things into perspective.

Then he shifts, taking care of the condom before tossing it into the can by the couch. "I'll take the trash out in a minute."

He relaxes on me again. I almost put my hand on his head, but stop at the last second. It feels too strange, though now I'm not sure what to do with it, so I have one arm on the back of the couch and the other hanging over the edge.

We lie there for a few minutes, no sound in the room except for the mixing of our breaths. Most of the time I feel suffocated when people are too close like this, but as I lie here waiting for that sensation, it doesn't come. He's just here and I'm just here, nothing threatening to take me over and freak me out. He gets what I feel, so he doesn't want to change me and for a few seconds, I want to live in that.

Without warning, Maddox pushes off the couch and stands up. He doesn't hide his body, not that he would have a reason to, but it's almost as if it's normal to walk around naked in front of me. Or not me, I guess, but any woman? A heaviness settles into my gut.

Bending over, he grabs my shirt and tosses it to me before picking up his boxer-briefs. "I'm going to the bathroom to clean up."

"What happened to ladies first?"

"Really? I would have thought you'd give me shit if I tried to pull that one."

Eh, I guess he's right. I can't have it both ways and want him to act like a gentleman only when it fits me. "You're right." Then, on instinct, I reach out and flick his nipple. "So you going to let me do it?" I ask.

"Nope. Not changing my mind either." Maddox picks up the rest of my clothes and hands them to me. "You got your clothes first. Guess that means you get the bathroom first too."

He hardly looks at me as he speaks. It isn't like the tone of his voice changed or he got all flirty when he said the words either, but my heart does this sort of stutter. It's a little piece of niceness that I didn't expect from him. Something small and simple. Those are the best kinds of nice things, aren't they?

Rex and Melody used to say the small things matter

more than the big. I didn't get it when I was younger. I definitely do now.

And it makes me take a step backward. Then another one.

"Hey," he says right before I step into the restroom. "Is Bee your real name?"

That question somehow reminds me of who I am. Of more of my earlier call.

"Your sister's boyfriend proposed. I wasn't surprised when she told me. He's such a sweet boy. They'll finish school first, of course. They both know it's the most important thing."

What she didn't say is that's what Malones do. They're responsible and proper. They don't change their names and then fuck some guy because they're upset about not being who they were born to be. Not that Mom would have ever said that. She's too kind and loving for that. "No."

"What is it?"

"If I wanted people to know, I wouldn't go by Bee."

He gets this strange look on his face that I can only explain as disconnected. That he's unplugging or hitting the power button, a look I only recognize because I do it as well. Now I also feel like a bitch. I'm taking my internal shit out on him, which almost feels like opening up. Like being honest. "I'll tell you when you let me pierce your nipple," slips out of my mouth, without my planning on it, but it's perfect.

Maddox doesn't smile or step closer to me, though now that I think about it, he doesn't smile often at all. But he suddenly doesn't seem so far away either.

"You play dirty, Bee."

"You better believe it, Scratch."

It's Maddox's turn in the bathroom when I hear knocking coming from the front of Masquerade. The second I hear it, I remember I had an appointment set up for today. Holy shit. I totally would have forgotten. Not a real cool way to start my business, but when I let myself get upset, that's what happens. I sort of shut down, like I did after my phone call with Mom.

Jogging down the hall, I turn into the main area of Masquerade before twisting the lock and opening the door. "Sorry. Something came up," I tell the guy standing outside the door. I met him the other day when he came in to look at my portfolio. He's about my age, reddish hair, and already has a little ink on him.

"No problem," he tells me. About then Maddox comes down the hall, his hair all messed up and looking like he just did exactly what we were doing.

"What's up?" Maddox nods at him.

"What was your name again?" I ask.

"Dustin."

"Maddox, Dustin. Dustin this is Maddox. He's working with me, so he'll be sitting in."

Dustin nods as I head to my desk. "I'll show you what I drew up for you."

He wants a tree. All black, but he wants it to look old and sort of creepy. It's going on his bicep.

Both Maddox and Dustin follow me over. I open one of the drawers and pull out the sketch.

"Nice," Dustin says as he looks at the detailed drawing. The branches have an aged look that I can't really explain, each of them bent and twisted into different directions. When I look at it, I think it has a story to tell and I'm suddenly upset that the piece is for someone else. It's experienced and worldly, which probably doesn't make sense to most people.

"Thanks," I reply as Maddox says, "Who is it?"

His words make me snap my head toward him, my heart beating faster all of a sudden.

"What do you mean, who is it?"

"There's a face in the trunk." He points.

"Oh shit. That's bad-ass. I didn't even notice that." This from Dustin.

Maddox is right. There is, but I say, "It's not anyone specific. It's a tree. He wanted it to look scary, and unique. This is how it came out." And honestly, I didn't think anyone would notice it.

He gazes down at me as though he doesn't

believe me. I turn away, unable to continue looking at him.

"You did awesome. It's perfect," Dustin says, excitement bouncing around in his voice.

"It's not right . . ." I shake my head, looking down at it. "It's missing something."

Maddox leans over me and points to the paper. "Look at the branches right here. You've got part of something right there and you don't know it. Are you seeing what I am?"

For a minute, I study it, trying to see what Maddox does. I squint, trying to make it out.

And that's when I see it. All the branches together, with all the little parts sticking off, lying a certain way and somehow resembling feathers. "It's almost a bird."

"A crow. The black would blend right in. See this part?" Maddox points again. "Curve it a little. Make the head come around this way. Not everyone will see it, but that makes it more incredible." He shrugs and steps back. "Only a thought. Not sure if it fits what you're looking for but—"

"It's perfect." I'm seeing it in my head, on the paper, and wondering how I could have missed it before.

"What do you think?" I lean back while Dustin looks it over.

"It's fucking awesome. I'm down."

"Cool. Let me fix the sketch real quick." I tell Dustin to have a seat. Maddox washes his hands before he starts getting the equipment ready for me while I lean over the paper to add Maddox's bird, wondering how he saw it. Wishing I had. And thinking this tat would have been shit without it.

CHAPTER EIGHT

MADDOX

I talked to Laney once and she mentioned how Adrian is always paying attention. Not that she wants to hide anything from him, but that it's almost impossible to because he notices things. It wasn't like I really wanted to sit and have a heart-to-heart with her about her boyfriend, but I'd listened to her, partly because he makes me curious.

I know who I am. It might not be pretty, but I'm honest about it. I'm shut down now, and honestly, I can't imagine how he does it. I gave him shit and called him a pussy for walking out on Laney and I do believe that, but I also know he's a better man than I am. I couldn't be with someone if her family took from me what ours took from him.

Laney said he grew up with an abusive dad. That he kind of lived inside himself, making him see the world and other people differently. I don't fully get it, but I guess it kind of explains how he notices more than other people do. Why he looks a little deeper.

That's never been me, except when I had sex with Bee today I suddenly saw a part of her that is buried a little deeper.

I watched her eyes as she began to close off when we were having sex. How there was this sort of veil that separates her from other people. I've been with women I knew a whole lot less than I know her, yet there was still some kind of emotion, feelings. Something there that Bee doesn't have. Or that she keeps locked away.

She lost it afterward when she gave me shit about my piercing, but then when I asked her about her name, it was right back. Not that I'm not pissed at myself for bringing it up anyway.

"You see how I'm doing the shading right here?" Her question wakes me up from wherever I was. "Shading is an art in itself. Not everyone can do it well, but if you can, it's going to make your piece stand out."

I watch her hand guide the gun along his skin. The brushed blackness of her shading showing me the branches blowing in the wind. His skin is red, little beads of blood pushing to the surface and mixing with the ink and Vaseline. Bee wipes it away.

Fuck she's good.

"Is the pressure the same when you have the shader on?" I ask her.

Her eyes don't leave her work as she speaks. "Less

pressure for shading and the amp is almost always turned down."

I nod and keep watching her work, the look of concentration on her face. When I was at the old shop, it wasn't like this. He basically admitted that it was a way to make money for him. It's not like that with Bee. You can see how important it is to her, making me feel like a piece of shit because even though I want this, I don't know if anything other than my sister has ever mattered to me as much as tattooing obviously matters to her.

It takes about three hours for her to finish Dustin's tat. The whole time I study everything she does and ask questions even though it's not like me. It's almost like needing someone and I won't let myself need anyone, but then, I think maybe someday I could look at tattooing the way she does.

After she's done, I wash my hands before cleaning his tat, wrapping it and giving him a sheet with the aftercare instructions. Dustin thanks her and then he's gone, leaving just the two of us again.

She has her back to me, her nice, little ass perfectly shaped in the tight jeans she's wearing. I wish like hell I could touch her again, because she's gorgeous and I want to study every bit of ink on her body.

Without turning to look at me, she says, "Good call on the bird."

I shrug, turning away from her, too, because seeing

that bird was nothing. "It wasn't a big deal." *Was it?*

"Yeah it was." I can tell by the sound of her voice that she's facing me, so I follow her lead. If she can brave looking at me, I need to man up and do the same.

"All I did was say what I saw."

"Which makes it even more incredible. Not a lot of people would have seen it. *I* drew the fucking thing and I didn't see it until you mentioned it. You have instinct and you're not afraid to look for things that might not always be there. A good eye is a good quality to have. I don't give compliments often, so when I do, you know it's real."

For a second, I just stand there. My throat feeling all fucking tight for some reason. I don't know what to say. I don't need her to tell me she doesn't give compliments often to know it's true, but hearing what she said? It's almost like this sort of respect in her voice that I've never heard from her before.

Even as I want to tell her thank you, my skin feels itchy too. Her words scratch across my skin like that needle on the gun, like they want to push below the surface the same way the ink does when she's creating magic on someone's body.

"It's hard to take credit for something that I didn't really have to work for." There's a good chance she'll take that the wrong way and maybe some people would, but she nods.

"Fair enough."

We clean the equipment and put everything away. I'm suddenly craving a cigarette even though they aren't usually something I crave—they're just something I compulsively do.

"I'm going outside for a smoke."

I'm surprised when she follows me out. I lean against the building on one side of the door while she sits on the ground, the side of the building holding her up.

"It's a good thing I slept with you before I knew you smoked—otherwise we both would have missed out on a good time."

"Twice," I tease her before taking a drag. Though I have to admit, it's a relief she can joke about it.

"Don't remind me."

I don't even consider getting offended because I feel the same way she does.

Surprise takes over me when I open my mouth and say, "Is it fucked up that we can sit around and joke about having sex with each other like this? I've never spent a lot of time with anyone I've been with."

"Slut," she teases. "Who knows if it's fucked up or not? I don't care. You don't care. That's why it works. We both want the same thing, so it's not like we're going to get all attached or get our feelings hurt because the other doesn't call the next day, ya know? We both know what it is."

"What is *was*." The need to stress that comes out of nowhere. Even talking like this feels foreign to me. I don't do shit like this.

"Exactly." She moves slightly and something makes me walk over and hold my hand out. I feel like an idiot for a second, but then Bee grabs it and lets me help her up. "Thanks."

"No problem." After putting out my cigarette, we go inside.

"I feel like getting out tonight."

The way she says it makes me think there's more to it than that. Maybe not that she feels like it, but she needs to. *What the hell is my problem? Why do I think I suddenly know this girl?* It's not like I've ever tried to figure anyone out before. I'm not sure why it keeps happening with Bee.

Because she's like me . . .

"I'm down to go to Lunar." It's not like I'd be doing anything except sitting in my apartment anyway.

"Yeah?" She stalls for a second. "We could do that. Have a beer or something."

"Typical thing for people to do after work."

"And like we said before, we both know there's nothing more than that going on."

I leave it at that. It doesn't matter if we end up going or not. I don't want to get into some big fucking conversation on if, why, or when we'll go have a drink. Instead, I do a quick sweep of Masquerade. When I don't find anything I missed while cleaning up, I tell Bee, "I'm going to go. I have some shit to take care of. Let me know if you wanna go and I'll meet you there."

She nods. I make it to the door and pull it open before she speaks. "Maddox?"

"Yeah?" I don't turn around to face her.

"Thanks."

There's more than one thing she could be thanking me for: the bird in the tattoo, cleaning up the shop, talking to her, or even some of the shit that went down in her office. But I wonder if it's maybe a combination of all of them.

With a simple nod, I walk out, knowing both of us will do better without verbally acknowledging her gratitude.

Bee doesn't call until 9:00 p.m. I change my shirt before heading toward Lunar. I'd already showered.

It doesn't take me long to get there. I'm surprised to find Bee waiting outside for me. I figured she would have gone in.

She's wearing this short black skirt and her shirt is another tank top, this one camo.

When I reach her, the stupidest fucking thing comes out of my mouth. "I don't do anything more than T-shirts." Anger then starts sizzling through me. Why the hell did I say that? It doesn't matter what I wear and even if she did care, I don't.

"Let me give you a hint, Maddox. When you look as good as you do, women don't need you to wear anything more than a T-shirt. They're hoping to get you out of it anyway."

Her words throw water on the flames of my anger, but all they do is burn to life again, but this time blending with lust. I don't say shit like "I don't do anything more than T-shirts," and knowing I did puts me on edge. Yet hearing her say she thinks I'm sexy too? It makes me want her again. "Let's go inside."

Since it's not a weekend, there isn't a line. Not that we would have to stand in one anyway. It doesn't mean it's not busy inside. The music is still loud, drunk people are still everywhere, dancing, drinking, and looking for someone to take home.

It's already getting old spending my nights here.

Trevor is behind the bar like always. He never takes a night off. It's different than it is with his brother, who keeps to himself and only wants to get shit done. Trevor likes to be here because he never shuts up, and when he's at Lunar, there's always someone for him to talk to. Like when he let Bee in the Back Room. He's the type who thinks shit like that is funny, seeing how people react.

The bar's crowded when we walk up. Trevor and some other bartender I don't really know are handing out drinks. Bee's right by my side as we wait. It takes a few minutes before it clears out a little and we step up. Trevor makes his way right over to us.

"Corona with a lime?" He winks at Bee.

"Shot of tequila." She winks right back.

"You're breakin' my heart, darlin'."

"Pfft." I cross my arms. What a fucking idiot.

They both ignore me, and she has to yell over the music. "What I drink depends on my mood and what my plans are." I can't help but wonder what her response means.

Trevor looks over at me. "Coors?"

I nod. When I drink, it's only ever a beer or two.

Trevor pours her shot first and then hands me my bottle. We both watch as Bee shakes a little salt on her hand, licks it, downs the shot, and then sucks on a lime.

"Do that often?" I raise an eyebrow at her.

"Nope." Leaning back on my barstool, I take a gulp of my beer. Trevor's standing in front of us and it's annoying the fuck out of me. "We'll let you know if we need anything else."

He laughs and holds up his hand. "I got you, man. My bad." And then he walks down the bar.

"Idiot," I mumble.

"He's got you, huh?" Bee grins.

Even though I heard her, I lean close anyway. "What?" My mouth's close to her ear, which puts her close to mine too.

I repeat what he said. "Just giving you shit, but somehow I think you know that."

"No idea what you're talking about," I say, even closer to her than I was before, and then I back away.

Bee rolls her eyes, but I can see the smirk on her face. We sit there quietly for a few minutes, me drinking my beer while she sways her body to the music. Fucking A, this woman is trying to get to me, but I refuse to sleep with her again. It's not going to happen. I've got a good thing going as her apprentice and I don't want to ruin it. She already shakes me up too much as it is.

The other bartender heads our way and Bee orders another shot. I watch her take that one, too, watch her swallow, her lips as they close over the lime, wishing like hell I could feel that mouth on other parts of my body.

"Dance with me, Scratch." Bee grabs my hand, but I shake my head.

"I don't dance. Even if I did, I don't think that's a good idea." My eyes are on her hard, showing her what I mean by that.

"You're right. First guy I've ever met who thinks with the right head."

"I don't want to. Believe me, I really don't fucking want to."

"That's my cue to go. I'll be out there." She nods

toward the dance floor and starts to walk away. I down the rest of my beer as I watch her go.

"You're a fucking idiot, Cross." Trevor grabs my bottle, but I don't reply.

Bee rolls her hips, her arms in the air as her body keeps perfect beat with the music. She's all confidence out there, open and obviously enjoying herself in a way I've never seen her. Those walls aren't up. She's not hiding behind her veil or sarcasm—just losing herself in the song.

She's out there forever, coming up for another shot before heading right back to the dance floor.

As she's moving, some guy with a Mohawk slips behind her. My hands fist and my teeth grind together. Bee turns toward him and says something. He laughs, making my anger kick up another notch; then he holds up his hands, like he's surrendering before taking a couple steps away.

She goes right back into dancing but Mohawk is still close behind her. Easing forward, I sit up straighter, my feet planted on the ground as I fight the urge to stand up and go over there. It's not my business. She's not mine and I don't want her to be.

But what if he won't leave her alone?

I don't want to protect someone else.

It's so much fucking pressure to be what other people need you to be. Especially when you fail at it over and over like I did. I tried so fucking hard for

Laney, but she's my sister. I don't give a shit about anyone else.

When Mohawk turns back to her, trying to dance and grind against her ass, I push to my feet. Trevor grabs my arm.

"A woman like her doesn't need to be protected. She's only going to get pissed at you for trying."

Jerking my arm away, I head toward Bee. Fuck what Trevor said or if he's right. Fuck if Bee gets pissed at me or not, and fuck that stupid voice in my head telling me to back off. That I've dealt with too much of other people's shit in my life. That there's a hundred other guys in here who can step in so I don't have to get involved. I'm not going to let any guy give her or anyone shit while I'm here.

I'm about halfway to her when Bee turns around and shoves him. Mohawk stumbles backward, but she doesn't stop, she keeps going at him, screaming something as she does.

"Settle the fuck down, you crazy bitch. I was only dancing," Mohawk yells.

"Don't touch me. Don't fucking touch me unless I say you can." When she tries to leap at him again, I grab her around the waist. She's twisting and fighting the whole time but I stay between her and him.

One of the bouncers on shift grabs Mohawk.

"She told you once. Stay the fuck away from her," I grit out at him as I stand between them. Bee's trying to get around me. Everyone's yelling. When I turn to look at her, she's shut down again, nothing but fire in her eyes.

"Don't want the bitch anyway." The asshole laughs.

I don't hold back this time; letting my fist fly forward, I hit him in the face. He drops to the ground as Bee tries to go for him again, but I grab her waist. She doesn't stop trying to get free.

When she almost slips out of my arms, I squeeze tighter, hefting her over my shoulder like a goddamned caveman or something, her fists coming down on my back the whole way out of the club.

CHAPTER NINE

BEE

I'm not the type of girl to make a scene. I don't freak out for no reason, and I definitely don't get thrown over a guy's shoulder because I went postal on someone in a club.

Yeah, I'm on edge because of the call from Mom and maybe a little bit because of Maddox, too, but that's not what this is about. The second he put his arms around me from behind, I had this strange flashback. A weird almost déjà vu of being grabbed. It was familiar, too, and a part of me wants to dip back into that flash from my mind and explore what it was.

The other part is pissed it was there in the first place.

"Let me go!" I shove at Maddox, trying to get out of his arms. A chilly blast of night air hits me as he steps outside.

Maddox doesn't listen but walks around the corner until we're a good distance from Lunar. When he sets me down, I realize we're next to his bike.

"What the hell was that?" My voice cracks as I scream at him.

His voice is more measured but equally as angry as mine. "That was me saving your ass. By the way, I'm not the hero type. I've dealt with enough shit in my life."

His words make my thoughts stumble slightly. He did save my ass, even if it was from me making too big a fool of myself. This strange urge rumbles through me, to ask him what he's dealt with, why he's so adamant not to be a savior; then I realize it's not like I need that from him anyway.

"And I don't need a guy on a white horse to save me. I'm drunk. He grabbed me—"

"He deserved what he got for putting his hands on you. Just don't give me hell for pulling you out of a bad situation."

I don't call him on the fact that he pretty much admitted that, regardless, he would have tried to be the hero tonight. I can see that in him. I didn't realize it until right now, but Maddox is that guy who can't stop himself from doing the right thing, even when it goes against who he thinks he needs to be.

Why?

"Thanks. I . . ." I let my words trail off there. Even if I was the type to tell him everything on my mind, I'm not sure what I would say. That it made me wonder if I was ever grabbed like that before. Or that it made little flashes of something pass through my mind that I don't understand. Not going to happen.

"I know you've already done your hero duty for tonight, but I need a ride home. I don't think I can drive. Do you mind?"

A slow grin slides across Maddox's face before disappearing. "Don't have another helmet. It's a bummer because that could have been fun."

"Stop being a sexy flirt. You're too angry for that," I tease him. This time he doesn't laugh or smile but kind of squints his eyes as though he's working something out in his head. I don't want it to be me.

"I can call a cab. People won't mess with my car here, will they?"

"You're drunk. You're not taking a cab home by yourself. Give me your keys and I'll drive you."

I shake my head. "I can handle a cab, and that leaves your bike here."

My breath hitches when Maddox steps so close to me I smell his masculine, spicy scent. He reaches for me as I say, "And I'm not that drunk." Though I kind of am.

When his fingers push into the pocket of my jean skirt, I try to step back. It gives him enough time to grab my keys and pull them out. "I'm not asking what you think I am either. Although I'm sure you wish I was."

"Shut up, Scratch." I'm trying to be pissy at him, but the smile on my face is ruining it.

And he's ruining me because I'm supposed to be annoyed by him right now. *It's the tequila,* I tell myself. He doesn't give me much time to think about it, because Maddox is already walking toward my car. And I'm following him.

In the car, I'm thinking about the fact that he grabbed my keys, and I let him.

"Where do you live?" he asks, his voice rough.

"Why are you doing this?" I ask, instead of replying. He's a struggle to figure out, and I'm not sure if I want to or not. I'm already feeling comfortable with him, and that's not what I'm looking for.

"Okay, I'll bring you back to Masquerade, then."

A foreign feeling of respect for him hits me. I don't mean that I didn't respect him before. It's just not something I let myself think about often. But here I am, thinking about it, about Maddox. There's no doubt in my mind that he will take me back to Masquerade, and even though I do stay there some-times, I'm not thinking it's a good idea tonight. Not with the scent and memories of Maddox and I still so fresh.

"Go left on Canopy. It's a few streets up."

I cross my arms, not sure if I'm suddenly annoyed at Maddox, myself, or both of us.

My house is only about a ten-minute drive from

Lunar, so it doesn't take us long to get there. It's on the tip of my tongue to ask Maddox again why he's doing this, but he didn't answer the first time and I don't beg.

If he wants to play the quiet martyr while denying he's doing it, that's his business.

Still I can't stop myself from wondering about him. Wondering what he hides. He doesn't pretend, even though it's obvious there's more to him than he lets come to the surface. Maddox is a contradiction. He's so closed off in some ways, yet in others he is who he is and he doesn't disguise himself as anyone else . . . *Like me?* Or how I want to be?

"Shit. You passed it. I'm a few streets back."

"I don't know where you live. I didn't pass it. You did." That's all he says before turning around and heading back the other way.

I point to my house and Maddox pulls into my driveway. He kills the engine and sets my keys in my lap.

"You can stay," I tell him without thinking about it. "You can have my spare room and I'll take you back to your bike in the morning."

"What's your address?"

"It's rude to ignore people or not acknowledge when they offer you something." The words make my chest tight. They're true, but they don't sound like me. They sound like my mom. It's a scary thought.

Not because there's anything wrong with her. Someone would be lucky to be like her. I'm just not.

Maddox sighs. "I'm not staying here and you know why. You don't want me to and I know I shouldn't."

The back of the seat catches my head when I drop it back. He's right. We both know what will happen if he stays, and we've both already broken our rule with each other once. The second time we slept together never should have happened, so boundaries are a must right now.

"You're right. I'm drunk and not thinking." I almost tell him it's his fault for being so hot, but I have a feeling that would break the floodgates we're trying to hold in place.

"Let me pay for your cab." It's the least I can do.

"You're not paying," he snaps.

"Why? First I couldn't leave by myself and now I can't return your favor? I'm a big girl, Scratch. I can take care of myself." *But thank you . . .*

He pulls out his phone and I can't help but wish I could see the expression on his face in the darkness.

"Tell me your address."

He's more like the Maddox from the first night, even more locked tight with short, angry answers. Maybe that's a good thing.

He dials information and asks for the number for a cab. When he gets them on the line, I give him my address.

"They'll be here in twenty." He drops his cell to his lap.

We're both quiet for a few minutes. The whole time I know I should go in the house, but my legs are a little weak, the alcohol taking the energy out of me, so I don't move. *Really? Is that really why?*

"You coming in tomorrow?" I ask, needing to fill the silence. It's a stupid question because he's at Masquerade every day.

"Yeah. We got anything?"

"A couple appointments. I have a piercing. You can watch me in action and see how good I am."

At that he chuckles. "Still ain't happening."

"Who said I still want to pierce you? I don't do people who are scared."

He laughs a little harder at that. "I'm so scared I could cry."

"Wuss," I toss back at him in this easy banter that I refuse to let myself question right now.

It's more silence after that. The quiet makes me a little jittery, though I'm not sure why. "Did I frighten you away?" My voice sounds light, but there's a part of me really begging for the answer. Sometimes I'm too much for people and usually it works fine for me. I should get out of the car right now and tell him he can't come back because of the way I'm waiting for his answer.

"Nah. You just made me go over my word quota for the day." His voice is honest.

Lights shine through the window, burning my eyes. "Cab." *Yeah, like he didn't notice that.*

We both get out of the car and Maddox says, "Go inside."

I open my mouth to tell him to fuck off. I can handle standing outside my own house in the middle of the night if I want to. But he's been cool tonight. He drove me here when he didn't have to, and I think there's a white knight inside him who really couldn't let himself leave if I stayed out here.

And then he would hate himself for staying too.

"FYI, I'm going in because I'm tired. Not because you told me to. See ya tomorrow, Scratch."

When I get inside, I don't turn on the light. There's a window right by the door and I peek out, watching as the cab takes Maddox away.

CHAPTER TEN

MADDOX

My sister wants to talk about everything. If she's upset, happy, sad, whatever, she has words for it. Mom's like that too. Not in the same way Laney is. Mom goes off—yells, screams, cries, and tries to make people feel bad. Laney likes to be close to people. She has this big fucking heart. I don't know where she got it from because no one else in our family is like that.

I grew up around this woman who wanted to tell me about every fucking thing, and sometimes it was hard because all I wanted to do was fix it, but I've never been able to.

It's been two weeks since I went to Lunar with Bee and she hasn't mentioned it. Not the sex or the fight or sitting in her car. It's a relief. I was tense as hell the next couple times I saw her, but she just went on with her life the way I like to pretend to go on with mine.

I respect that about her.

So, when she mentioned she planned to come in

on Monday when Masquerade was closed to organize some of the shit inside, I told her I would help.

She didn't react, which means I didn't have to be a prick, and here I am, parking my bike in front of the shop, knowing it'll only be the two of us all day.

I don't usually do one-on-one real well, but I also want to be a part of everything when it comes to Masquerade.

The door's locked when I get there. Bee's not in the front, so I have to knock for her to let me in.

"You need a key," she says as she closes and locks the door behind me.

My pulse spikes in a way I actually enjoy. She'd give me a key? Bee doesn't trust and that's a huge fucking bit of it right there. "Would make things easier." I shrug.

"Of course, I'd have to kill you if you screwed with anything in my shop."

"You think you're so fucking tough, don't you?" Playfully, I ruffle her hair before realizing what the hell I'm doing and jerking my hand back.

She laughs. "No, but I know a guy who knows a guy."

That makes me laugh too. "Your guys ain't shit."

She rolls her eyes and it's something so normal, it takes me back for a second. Bee is so different from any girl I know, that even something as simple as rolling her eyes is too ordinary for her.

"So what are we doing?" I need to get my mind off her and stop having fun and get to work. That's what I'm here for.

"I started a little already. I have tons more supplies I've been organizing in the supply closet and I have a box full of pictures. I'm thinking about changing out some of the samples in my portfolios. I don't like to put it all out, but if I switch it up from time to time, it gives my clients fresh material." She winks. "Makes it look like I'm doing a lot more work than I really am right now."

Crossing my arms, I also shake my head. "That's dirty."

"You don't like dirty?" she tosses back, making me smile.

"I didn't say that." My gut clenches when I think about this back-and-forth we have going. It's easy when nothing's been easy in so fucking long.

"Yeah, I had a feeling you'd say that."

Without replying, I go toward the back. There's not much more to say without dragging on this moment that I'm still unsure how I feel about. We rearrange the boxes, pulling out what she needs and packing away what she doesn't. I take what she needs to the supply closet while Bee unpacks and puts everything where she needs it.

She's had enough out for Masquerade to run, but something makes me wonder why she hasn't unpacked everything before now. It's almost like she wasn't sure she'd stay, but I know this place is hers, so that doesn't make sense.

Why does it matter? It's not my business either way.

A couple hours later we're done with all that, so I pull out the small box with her pictures of her tattoos. We go into the front of the shop, Bee sitting at the table at her desk and me in another chair in front of it.

I open the box and stick my hand in before something makes me meet Bee's eyes. She nods as if to say, *Go for it*, so I pull out a stack and start looking through them.

I only make it through a couple photos before I think, *Jesus, she's good. Really fucking good.*

"How'd you get into tattooing?" I ask.

"Same as you, I guess. I asked someone if I could apprentice and they said yes."

My first reaction is to be pissed at her half-answer, but I bury it with all the other thoughts and feelings I want to keep as far from the surface as I can. I don't really need to know every detail about her, do I?

"We should make an art portfolio for you that you wouldn't mind sharing. We could put it up in the shop, or if you wanted to wait until you start tatting, we could put it out then."

"Nah. Not yet." What's the point when they're only drawings?

"You should. Think about it, Scratch. Eventually

you're going to want to leave your mark in someone's skin. They're trusting you to create art on their body. You don't have tattoo experience to show them, but you have some really incredible raw talent that's going to get their attention. You'd be smart to do it."

This urge fights to make it to the surface—one that wants to ask her if she really thinks I'm talented. She's said so before, but words are just fucking words sometimes. They don't always mean something. She doesn't strike me as a person who says something she doesn't mean, though.

And as much as I don't like them to, her compliment feels good. "Hey—"

Knock, knock, knock.

Turning, I look at the door to see who's there. Everything inside me seems to shut off in an instant when I see Laney on the other side of the glass.

In what feels like a second, I'm standing, unlocking the door, and pushing it open. "What happened?" Adrian stands behind her. His friend Colt is behind him and Colt's girlfriend, Cheyenne, is next to Colt.

Then I'm disconnected for a different reason. Nothing's wrong, but they're all here, pushing their way into the only part of my life that actually feels like it's mine. It's a clash of my worlds. Laney doesn't feel like she belongs here.

Laney says, "I didn't know the shop was closed today. I want a tattoo."

"Me too!" Cheyenne pipes in from behind them.

"We're closed." Which they obviously know. My hand tightens on the door handle, selfishly not wanting to share this with them.

"Who's this?" Bee walks up behind me and grabs the door. It takes everything inside me to let her open it.

I'm going to kill my sister. She won't look at me because she knows I'm pissed. Before she came down here, she knew I would be. "My sister." I fight to keep my voice steady.

"Laney," she says, looking at Bee. "This is my boyfriend, Adrian, and this is Colt and Cheyenne."

"Hey." Bee nods at them. "You want ink?"

"We're closed," I remind her.

Bee doesn't hesitate to lock her eyes with mine. "And I own the shop, so I can change that whenever I want." She pulls the door open wide and all four of them file inside.

My hands sink into my pockets so no one will see how tense they are.

"Yeah, I wanted to get something. Cheyenne too. Like I said, I didn't know you'd be closed, though. We can come back," Laney tells her.

"Nah, it's cool. We can do this."

"What are you talking about, Laney? You've never said you wanted a tattoo." I step between her and Bee. I'm not completely sure why it bothers me so much—maybe because it doesn't feel like something my sister would do? Because it's easier for me to keep my worlds separate? It feels wrong.

"So. I do now. What's wrong with that?"

I know why she's doing this. It's because of me. She's trying to do what she always does and fit herself into a situation so she can try and fix things or check on me. How many times can I tell her I don't need her to fix me?

"Where do you want me to start? Don't be stupid."

"Hey." Adrian grabs my arm. "Back up. You talk to her like that and we're going rounds again."

I jerk my arm away. Who the fuck does he think he is? I'm her family. I'm the one who's supposed to take care of her. *I'm the one who failed her. Failed them all.*

"And I'll kick your ass again."

He steps up and Laney grabs him. I try to step forward, too, but then . . . Bee grabs me.

"Hey . . . Scratch."

My body's tight, so fucking tense, my jaw locked. It would feel good to hit Adrian again. To hit something, but then, as if on autopilot, I'm turning to face Bee instead. "What?" I grit out.

"What? She's too good for ink? I'm not and you're not and all the people you plan to tattoo in the future aren't, but it's a big fucking deal if it's your sister?"

My jaw starts to slacken. "That's not what I meant."

Is it? "She's being impulsive and that's not usually like her."

Bee's green eyes penetrate the fog around me. Work through this anger that I don't get about my sister getting ink. The urge to pull away tugs at me, wants me to escape so she can stop trying to read me.

She lowers her voice, looking at me pointedly. "She's a big girl. Don't worry about it, Scratch. I'll take care of her."

The honesty in her words rolls through me. It's a stupid thing to get pissed about, I get it, but she's my sister and I don't want anything for her that's not perfect. She deserves it. *Don't worry about it, Scratch. I'll take care of her.* I kind of hate that I believe her.

Bee's hand briefly squeezes mine. Fuck, I hadn't even realized she was holding it. I yank away.

"Whatever." Eyes on the desk, I walk over and lean on it. Bee starts talking to Laney, getting ideas about what she wants. My sister keeps glancing at me before looking at Bee again. Adrian has his hands on her hips, not letting go of her, while Colt and Cheyenne walk around, looking at the pictures on the walls.

I see the questions in Laney's eyes, but I fight to ignore them, even in my own head. She's trying to see something in the fact that I quit arguing. *It's a tattoo. It's what I want to do with my life. Not a big deal.*

Then why was it at first?

Bee walks over as Adrian and Laney head to the chair.

"Look at you, being such a papa bear over your sister. *Tsk, tsk.* It's only a little ink." She fingers the tattoo on my arm, and I jerk away again.

"You're pouting. She wants two Chinese symbols. It's not a big deal."

"Of what?" I grunt because at least if she's going to get work, it should be something cool.

"Love, I'm assuming for him." She nods toward Adrian. "And family for her brother."

Her words hit me harder than the satisfied look on Bee's face. It does exactly what it's supposed to, guilt spreading through me like wildfire.

I look at the four of them on the other side of the room and whisper, "It's not a big deal. I really don't care if she gets inked. We've been through a lot. I don't like to see her hurt. I don't want her to have any regrets."

There's movement in the corner of my eye, so I glance back at Bee. Her head's cocked a little, her eyes trying to work me out. As if she realizes it, she straightens up and offers me a small smile. "I said I'd take care of her. Come watch. That's what you're here for, right?"

I nod because she's right. "I'll set up," I tell her before walking away. Bee sits down at the desk and prints out the images for Laney's piece.

As I walk to the sink, my sister steps up to me. "Still freaking out over nothing?"

"Nope."

She pauses. I hate that fucking stall because I know it means she's going to say something I don't want to hear. She's always trying to look for emotional shit that's not there. She wants to analyze me when I don't need it. "You . . . you listened to her."

My jaw ticks, but I don't turn to look at her. "I don't listen to her. It's not a big deal."

Without another word, I wash my hands before getting everything set up. Only a few minutes later, Bee's placing the thermographic transfer paper to the back of Laney's neck, leaving the two symbols behind.

"Look good?" she asks my sister after handing her a mirror. Laney uses the reflection from the one behind her to check it out.

"Perfect," she answers before looking at Adrian.

"So sexy, Little Ghost," he replies before nuzzling her neck.

My body tenses up when Laney leans over the chair. Adrian sits in front of her, smiles, and grabs her hands. I watch as he raises one to his mouth and kisses it. I feel like a pervert for watching them, but I don't fucking get it. I don't understand that need to touch and hold someone, or how it helps when things are shitty. But it does help her, because I see the nerves leak from my sister's body, which makes the same thing happen to Adrian.

It's like they're one fucking person and even though I hate it, I can't help studying it too.

Bee washes her hands and snaps on her gloves. That steady *buzz* of the tattoo gun fires up. I flinch when it comes down on Laney's skin. She doesn't. Not when Adrian is sitting in front of her, holding her.

How? I don't get how they can trust someone like that.

As Bee works, I can't help moving forward until I'm standing next to her and watching as she puts a permanent mark on Laney's neck.

The top symbol—love—is red and the other is black. It takes Bee longer than I thought it would since it's not that in-depth. When she's done, leaving behind the tattoo and red, puffy skin, she looks up at me and I know—I fucking know she took her time, made it perfect to keep her word. To take care of my sister.

Thank you.

CHAPTER ELEVEN

BEE

Cheyenne's boyfriend, Colt, holds her almost the same way Laney's did as I give her a tattoo. Hers goes even quicker than Maddox's sister's because she's only getting a quote. A cool quote about making your own fate.

My mind isn't much on that, though. It's stupid. I see couples in here all the time and don't really pay it any attention, but I can't help but study the way Maddox's four friends are. Though maybe *friends* isn't the right word. He obviously doesn't get along well with Adrian and he's only said a couple words to Colt.

There's something about them that catches my attention. It's the way each couple is with each other, like they've fought the world to be where they are, and I kind of envy that. It's not as though I'm looking for a partner or I haven't been through stuff, because I have, but for the first time, I wish I dealt with it differently. Not because of my family, but for me.

"All done," I tell Cheyenne. Colt still holds her hand as she goes to the mirror to look at it.

Maddox steps up next to me. "I like the font."

"Yeah, it's one of my favorites." It's sort of old-fashioned-looking, almost medieval, yet thin, feminine. "It fits your art style, actually," I tell him. "It's almost like there's knowledge to it."

Maddox glances over at me, those gray eyes that have the same knowledgeable quality. "Yeah?" he asks, with a hit of vulnerability I'm not used to from him.

"Yep." And then I turn away, because he suddenly feels too close. "You like it?" I ask Cheyenne. It looks good on her shoulder.

"Absolutely. It's gorgeous." She's still looking in the mirror while Colt traces a tattoo on his wrist that says *Mom*. Yeah, these people have definitely been through more than most.

"You do great work." Laney steps up next to her brother.

"Thanks. I'm glad you guys like them."

"How much do we owe you?"

Without thinking, I shake my head. "Don't worry about it. You're with Scratch, so—"

"No," Maddox interrupts.

I almost argue with him that I don't usually do things like that and not to look a gift horse in the mouth when I realize what his answer's about. He thinks he'll owe me if we do that. I'm not sure I want him to owe me either. Luckily, Adrian jumps in and speaks. "He's right. This is your business. It's not a big deal." Nodding, I head over to the desk to check the time. After I tell them how much they owe, and they pay, Laney says, "You should hang out with us sometime."

Maddox tenses and a small smile curves Adrian's lips. The two guys obviously feel differently about what she asked, which tells me it has a deeper meaning than saying hi to the new girl in town.

Not a good idea, but it's not like I can be rude to her either. "Cool. Thanks. I don't have much extra time right now since I'm trying to get Masquerade off the ground, but maybe we can figure something out sometime."

The little downturn of her lips says she realizes the answer is no. It's not smart to entangle my life any more with Maddox's. I've already slept with him twice and he's here with me practically every day.

"Okay. Sure. You can get a hold of me through Maddy if you're interested."

"Maddy, huh?" I lift my eyebrows at Maddox, but he shakes his head.

Laney gives him a hug. He quickly pats her on the back and pulls away. Then the four of them walk out, leaving Maddox and I alone again. He leans against the front of my desk and I move over to stand next to him. I'm not sure why I do.

"You're protective," I say.

"She's all I have." The words have to squeeze past his lips his mouth is so tight.

I've never been one to pry in other people's business because I've never let myself really care enough to do it, but everything inside of me is begging to ask him why. Why is it only two of them? What are their secrets? Why does Maddox think it's his job to take care of her?

Even though I want to, I don't. Wondering about him shouldn't be something I'm trying to keep myself from doing. It usually happens automatically.

So instead of asking, something equally as crazy falls out of my mouth. "You do a good job."

A blast of heat seems to shoot off Maddox and slam right into me. Anger? Pain? I'm not sure.

"Not really. You don't know anything about us."

Moving over, I stand in front of him and cross my arms. "I do have eyes. She's happy, you care about her, and she cares about you. Feels like about as close to success as a person can get."

And she does love him. Even if she hadn't come in here begging me to give him a chance, I would have been able to see that today.

"Looks can be deceiving."

A little jolt hits me in the chest. He's right. People assume my life was horrible because I was kidnapped. They think it was automatically perfect when I went home. Feelings and situations behind the scenes often make things look like something other than what they are. "You need to stop saying things like that to me." My voice is low. When Maddox raises his eyes to me, I know he sees what I mean. Words like that make me feel close to him.

Instead of taking them back, he continues to stare at me, this smoldering look in his eyes that threatens to burn me alive. I welcome the forbidden flames.

His finger hooks through the belt loop on my jeans. His tug is gentle, but I come easily, the whole time yelling at myself, *Back up! It's too much. You can't do this with him again.*

"Stop making me want you." The same heat from his eyes is now in his words.

"Stop letting me have you," I reply, and it seems to inflame him more.

He pulls me closer again, right between his legs, as the other hand moves up to cup my cheek. His stare alone is burning me alive. Neither of us are smiling, both torn by this wild desire and the need to push the other away.

"Pretty soon we're going to hate each other if we keep doing this." The knowledge makes me a little sad, but I fight to bury it beneath my craving for him.

"I know." And yet, he still leans forward and I do too. Our lips are close, so so close, that I smell him and feel him and almost taste him when—"Oh my

God! Told you they're open! I knew I saw someone inside."

My body jerks away from Maddox as two girls laugh while they're stepping inside. Neither of them are looking at us, so I don't think we were caught.

"Hey! You're open, right? The sign says closed, but we saw you in here and the door is unlocked," the perky blonde says.

The girl standing next to her is dark-skinned with hundreds of long, black braids in her hair.

"Are we interrupting?" she asks.

"Nope." I head toward them. "Yeah, we're open. I forgot to change the sign." Total lie, but it'll keep Maddox and I away from each other, something we need.

"What are you looking for?" I ask the girl with the braids.

"Not me. Her." She points to her friend.

The blonde shows me a little sun design she brought in and I give her a quote. When she agrees, I tell her, "Cool. I'm Bee. This is Maddox. He's learning the biz."

Braids eyes him. "Hi. I'm Christine and this is Aimee."

"Hey." Maddox nods at them and then turns to me. "I'll get the equipment set up."

We go through our usual routine and it's not long before I'm sitting down and tattooing a sun on the swell of Aimee's breast. Maddox sits close like he always does, studying what I'm doing and asking questions. I can still feel the heat rolling off him.

"So you're looking to get into tattooing?" Christine asks him.

Obviously.

"Yeah."

"That's cool. You've had some nice work done."

"Thanks," he tells her. And on and on and on. She wants him. That much I can tell and she has every right to want him. I'm not one of those girls who's going to hate her because she has eyes in her head and knows a good-looking guy when she sees one. Plus, Maddox isn't mine.

Even though he's giving short answers, he's not being a dick to her. He's into watching Aimee get tattooed. That's what he's here for. Every once in a while, I glance his way and honestly, I can't even tell if he realizes this woman wants him. I don't mean that I think he's oblivious to things, it's . . . I don't think Maddox works that way. He doesn't run off emotions unless it's for his family. He keeps his distance, which means he's not paying attention.

Whoa. Why do I suddenly think I know him so well?

I pull the tattoo gun away from the client's skin to wipe away some of the excess ink.

"It looks good," Maddox tells me. "The white

around the sun makes it stick out more. I was iffy about it at first."

"You don't trust me?" I try to tease him, hoping it will get my thoughts away from things that are real.

But when he replies, "More than I trust others," my heart stumbles. I put my needle back to work on Aimee's tattoo as his reply rolls over and over in my mind. In the same vein, I almost feel like I trust him more than I do others too. The way he still stays here watching me tattoo and the easy set of his body tells me he didn't mean anything by his comment. It wasn't some big declaration, but still, it feels like *something*. I've had too many of those moments with him.

When I'm finished with the tattoo, Christine says to Maddox, "I'll have to come back when you're tattooing. You can give me my first one."

Hello, flirty.

Again, she's not doing anything wrong. More power to her for going after what she wants but I still find myself feeling pissy when I grit out, "He won't be here when he's on his own. Masquerade is mine."

Maddox's face flashes a different kind of fire than the look he gave me by the desk. This one is hard and I know it's my fault. I have no idea what's gotten into me; I only know I don't like it. I'd turned the atmosphere in the room to awkward as hell.

Without a reply to me, or Christine, Maddox heads over and starts taking care of the equipment. My brain keeps telling me to take the words back, to apologize to the customer, and to Scratch, but I can't make my mouth listen.

As soon as they leave, Maddox is grabbing his stuff. He didn't even have to stay here this long, I remind myself. He helped me this morning and we did three tattoos on a day we weren't supposed to do any.

"Hey," I start to say to him as he's heading toward the door.

"I gotta run. I didn't plan on being here this long."

"Maddox . . ." *I'm sorry. I'm freaking out and I don't know why.* "I'm—"

"Don't," he cuts me off.

"Don't what?"

"You're honest—that's what you are. You told her the truth. It's important that we both remember that. I'll see ya later." After that, Maddox walks out of my shop.

Guilt trickles through me before becoming a massive waterfall. I jump when my cell phone vibrates on the desk. "Relax," I mumble as I walk over to look at it.

MOM lights up on the screen.

I wait, telling myself I'm going to pick it up on the next ring. I don't. And then I don't again. Finally it stops. It's not the first time her call has gone unanswered since we spoke about my sister.

It's another reason to feel like crap.

And then I remember the vision, memory, whatever I should call it about being grabbed and wonder if it's real. I shiver. A flash of sitting in the corner, scared, floods my vision. I never had any of those memories, dreams, before. And if they are real, I know it had to be from when I was taken from the person whose phone calls I ignore.

What's wrong with me?

CHAPTER TWELVE

MADDOX

"I love Chinese food." Laney takes a forkful of her fried rice and then smiles at me.

I shake my head. "You have food on your lip." She wipes it off before grinning again. Crossing my arms, I rest them on the picnic table where we're eating lunch. Fall's setting in and the weather's cooling down slightly, but today's a pretty decent day. She puts another bite into her mouth happily as though everything is right and perfect in the world.

Sometimes I wonder how we can be siblings. She's always been like that in a way. Laney's been through a lot like me and she's grown up fast because of it, but she's also always had this sunshine and happiness outlook that I've never come close to having. She's emotional and takes things to heart yet still can see the beauty in things that I couldn't give a shit about.

It's part of the reason I've always wanted to shelter her from the bad. Why try and taint that good? There's enough negative in the world already. Plus, she always got the shit end of the stick when she didn't deserve it. Everything that I got I had coming to me because I kept my mouth shut about Dad.

I'm still keeping my mouth shut to protect myself.

"How's your tattoo?" I ask her.

"It's awesome. I love it. You freaked for no reason, Maddy. I don't get you sometimes."

Yep, she's right there. I know it was for no reason, but I don't say it.

"And school?"

"It's great. I love my classes. Lots of prereqs right now. I can't wait to get into more of the nursing stuff."

When we were kids, I thought I would be in the NFL and she always wanted to be a nurse and take care of little kids. It fits her and she'll make it happen. I'm glad she'll get her dream, though mine is such a distant memory. I don't feel like that same person anymore.

In reply to her, I nod.

"What about you? How's the tattooing going?"

This time it's my turn to take a bite of my food. I knew she'd ask, like I'm sure she knows I don't want to answer. The why of it I don't get myself. Even while I'm shutting her out, I always feel like shit about it.

"Good. You're doin' it all okay? With work and school?"

Laney sighs and pushes her dark hair out of her

face, looking at me with the same gray eyes I see in the mirror every day. "Yes."

"What about money? You're working part-time—"

"Yes, *Dad*."

My body turns to stone at that. He's the last motherfucker I want someone to call me, though maybe it's not really far from the truth.

"You know I didn't mean it like that, Maddy." She read my mind. "But it's ridiculous. You worry about me, not yourself. You want to know everything about me but don't want to tell me anything about you. We need . . . we need to try to move past it, ya know?"

There's the logical part of me that knows that. Fuck, Adrian's son is dead. He'd do anything for my sister though. "We're not all built the same way." I shrug. It's the only answer I have. My instincts are to keep myself closed up. I don't do the comforting thing, and it's not something I can decide to change and do it. Hell, I don't even know if I want to. "Just because I'm different than you doesn't mean I'm not over it."

Her eyes close at that and I know she's sad. Guilt tugs at me, telling me to try and fix it, but I don't know how to be the person I used to be. I went from a kid who only wanted to play football to going gambling with my dad who told me it was the only way to pay for college. I wanted college and football, right? I became good at keeping my mouth shut for my own fucking good and now I don't know how to open it again.

"Remember when we were younger? It was before everything went down. God, Maddy. You couldn't have been any older than ten. You used to collect cans and do yard work and then you'd take your money down and buy us Chinese food."

An ache forms in my chest. I ignore it. Ignore the need to walk away too.

"One time we ate Chinese at a park like this and then you tried to teach me to play football."

"You sucked." I'm surprised the words came out.

"I did, and you spent hours out there teaching me to throw. To me, it didn't really matter that I sucked. Well, that's a lie. It kind of did because you liked football. I looked up to you. All I wanted was to be like my big brother and even way back then, you tried to take care of me."

I drum my thumbs on the picnic table and then reach into my pocket, pull out a cigarette, and light it. "You don't wanna be like me, Laney."

She knows that now. I don't even have to tell her I'm no one to look up to.

"You were my best friend. You still are. You've always been more than my brother."

I take a drag of my cigarette, hoping this conversation is going to end soon.

"Mom called me . . ."

My eyes snap to Laney. "What did she say to you? Did she give you shit?" Laney was the one to hold Mom while she lay bleeding. She was also the one Mom blamed for saving her.

My sister closes her box of Chinese. "She started to. She tried to make me feel guilty because you don't talk to her. She thinks it's my fault. I hung up. I told her if she was going to harass me, I wouldn't talk to her."

The urge to smile hits me at that. She's stronger now. Sticking up for herself. That makes me feel good. "Don't answer anymore. If she calls you again, tell me and I'll take care of it."

Laney shakes her head and I know she's upset. "I don't *need* you to take care of it. That's not why I told you. I can take care of myself. It's time for you to take care of yourself too. I'm good, Maddy. And I have Adrian. I want . . . I want you to have someone too."

At that, I push to my feet. *"Just one more time, Maddox. Be a man. Sometimes men have to do things that aren't right to take care of their family. I do this for you guys and if you tell your mom, it will kill her."*

I should have opened my mouth. I should have known it was more than the gambling he was trying to hide. If I hadn't listened to him, he wouldn't have left that weekend. Maybe Adrian's son Ash would still be alive. Why would I want someone else in my life to depend on me when I obviously make shitty decisions? The men in my family only let people down.

"I gotta go."

She pushes to her feet right behind me. "You always have to go. Anytime we talk about something important, you have to go. Maddox, I want you to be happy."

"Who said I'm not? I'm doing the tattoo thing. I have a job—"

"You keep yourself so closed off from any and everything important. You don't date. What about you and Bee? I saw something there."

Bee is definitely not someone I'm going to talk to my sister about. "I thought your boyfriend was supposed to be the psychic one, not you."

"Whatever, Maddox." There's an edge to her voice I'm not used to hearing from my sister, like she's getting fed up, and then for the first time, it's her who walks away from me.

I'm in a shitty mood. I text Bee that I'm not coming to Masquerade before work today. She's probably going to be pissed. I'm the one who pushed her into this and now I'm not showing up. Right now, I can't find it in me to care.

I head home and get ready to go to Lunar. The last thing I feel like is being around a bunch of drunk people. I'm pissed about my fight with Laney and feeling like shit because of the way I treat her. And her boyfriend too. Fuck, I can hardly talk to the guy. It hurts too much to think of what my family did to him. Real stand-up fucking guy I am.

I don't know what makes me do it, but I head to the bar first. I'm early and I try to avoid Trevor as much as I can. He's too hyper for me.

It's only about 8:00, and a weekday, so Lunar's not too packed. Both Trevor and Tyler are behind the counter. I try to take a quick turn to head to the back before they see me, but Tyler calls out, "Hey, Cross. Come here, man."

Shit. I'm not really in the mood to get involved with whatever the owners of Lunar need.

"What's up? I gotta clock on in a minute," I tell them when I reach the bar.

"We have a problem." Tyler leans against the counter, arms crossed. He's wearing a silk button-up shirt and slacks. What a joke. He owns a club where meth-heads get caught getting high in the alley, they have private stripper parties, and his brother fucks everything that walks, yet he's always dressed like he's sitting in a fiftieth-floor office somewhere.

"And it has something to do with me, how?" I ask.

I see Trevor try and cover a laugh, but Tyler just hardens that stern-ass businessman look.

"Because you're security and we're having a security issue. Unless you don't like your job here and then I'm sure something can be arranged."

No. No, I don't like my shitty job here, but I need it. "What do you need?" I grit my teeth. Tyler nods and so I walk around to their side of the bar.

"Turbo's out of here. He got caught dealing. You ready to step up?"

Wow. Didn't expect that. Turbo was the head of security.

"Why me?"

"I'm wondering that, too, but Trev says you're right for it." Tyler's stare is hard. I look at his brother, surprised he went to bat for me.

"What other responsibilities will I have?"

"First and foremost, don't sell drugs in my club," Tyler says.

I shake my head. "I don't fuck around with that shit."

"Yeah, that's what Trev said."

I'm wondering how in the hell Trevor knows or thinks he knows so much about me.

"You do the schedule. Your hours shouldn't change unless we need help. Someone's sick or needs time off, you man up and step in. You take responsibility too. One of the guys fucks up, it's on you. We have private parties. They're all yours or you make sure the right guy gets it. Extra money's on the table too. You down?"

Fuck no. Then again, what else do I have? Yeah, I'm tattooing with Bee, but what if that doesn't last? Not only that, but she said so herself, once I'm done training, I'm out. It's not like I have the money to open my own shop and if I can't get anyone to let me apprentice under them, I'll probably have trouble getting a job too. This? It's guaranteed money, even though I hate this place.

"I'm in."

Tyler nods. "I'll be in touch." And then he walks away. When I look at Trevor, he has a big-ass smile on his face.

"What?" I ask.

"You're welcome."

"I didn't know you were the one who earned the job. I thought it was me."

"You're such a prick, Cross. That's why I like you, though. How's your girl?"

I fight the urge to tell him Bee's none of his business. "She's not my girl."

"No?" His eyebrows go up.

The urge to hit him suddenly makes my fists tighten. "Nope."

"That's good to hear. She's fucking hot. Bring her in with you again, yeah? If you don't want her, I'd definitely like to get to know her better."

Before I know what's happening, I have the front of his shirt in my grip and I've shoved Trevor up against the wall. As soon as he starts laughing, I know what he did and know I stepped right into his plan. I still don't let go of him.

"I'm kidding, man. You know I don't play like that. Plenty of fish in the sea . . . though maybe not as feisty as her."

Don't fucking hit him. Don't fucking hit him. I can't afford to lose this job.

"Judging by your reaction, I'm taking it she's more your girl than you're willing to admit."

"Fuck off, Masterson." I shove a little before letting go of him.

"Relax, man. I'm giving you shit. Trying to lighten you up a bit. Life's too fucking fun to walk around as pissed at the world as you are."

"That's easy for you to say. You were born with a silver spoon stuck up your ass. Twenty-two years old and you own a club with your brother. Life must be real fucking hard."

As I walk away from him, my chest feels tight and my jaw hurts it's so tense. When my phone rings, I pull it out to see Laney's name. Instead of answering, I turn my phone off. I've heard enough shit for one day. I'm not in the mood to deal with any more.

CHAPTER THIRTEEN

BEE

Maddox is pissing me off. His text today about not coming in pushes me over the edge, which in turn makes my anger shift from Scratch to myself. Why the hell do I care if he comes in or not? That he's been acting strange ever since we almost kissed after his sister's tattoo?

We've slept together twice, and yet it's always been as if nothing happened right afterward. Not this time.

There's nothing more intimate than a kiss . . .

I shake my head at that, not willing to let myself think of it or what it would mean for Maddox and I.

I've spent way too much time thinking about him—I mean *it*—already.

A client left a few minutes ago and there's not much going on here. I play around online, looking up some of my favorite font sites, always looking for something new and different that I can use.

When the shop phone rings, I revert from stressing about Maddox to being a horrible daughter and checking the number to make sure it's not my mom before I pick it up. It's a number I don't recognize, so I grab the phone. "Masquerade."

"Bee? This is Laney. Maddox's sister." Her words are dragged out, her speech a little slow. My heart rate makes up for it, though, suddenly speeding.

"Yeah. What's up? Is Maddox okay?"

She giggles at that, relieving some of the stress and making me think she's really drunk or something. "Worried about Maddox are you?" She giggles again before adding, "I'm sorry. I don't handle pain meds very well."

There goes my rapid beating heart again, though I'm not sure why.

"It's cool. Is everything okay?" I ask her.

"Yeah, I think so. They said I could go home, so I'm assuming."

"Who said you could go home?"

"The hospital, silly."

Oh yeah. This girl is on something good. "Are you looking for your brother, Laney?"

She sighs. "Yeah. We got into a fight today and he's going to feel guilty now. Not that he wouldn't have felt guilty before, but 'specially since I got into a car accident. I'm fine, though. Just a little neck pain and a hurt wrist."

Worry takes me over, though for some reason it's not about Laney. She said she's fine and I believe her, but I hear what she's saying too. I've seen how

Maddox is with her and if they got in a fight and then she got into an accident, he's going to be pissed at himself.

"Maddox isn't here," I tell her.

"Shit . . . Adrian's phone is broken. We haven't gotten him a new one yet. He's going to feel guilty too. What's with these boys we love feeling like everything's their fault? The world isn't their responsibility."

I don't call her on the fact that I don't love Maddox. I'm not even sure how much I like him, but what I do know is what we have doesn't belong in the same sentence with her and Adrian. I've seen them together once and I know that.

"I was hoping Maddox was at the shop. He's going to freak if I don't tell him. I tried his phone, but I think he turned it off."

"He texted earlier that he wasn't coming in today. I know he works this evening, though I'm not sure if he's in already or not." He almost lost it when she got a tattoo; this is going to make him go through the roof. *Why?* I can't help but wonder. I mean, I get it—she's his sister and he loves her—but why is he *so* protective of her?

"Well, thanks anyway. I need to try and get a hold of Cheyenne or maybe Colt. Even if my car was running, not like I can drive right now." She giggles again.

"I could . . . I could come and get you if you want?" I feel strangely nervous as I ask, but the girl doesn't deserve to sit around in the hospital trying to get a hold of her friends. Not when I'm sitting right here doing nothing. Something also tells me it will be easier on Maddox to see her at home rather than at the hospital. Ugh. This should have nothing to do with him.

"Really? You don't mind? I hate hospitals. Maddy and I, we've spent a lot of time in them with our mom."

Why? What's wrong with her? "Yeah, sure. No problem. I'll be there in a few minutes, okay?"

"Thanks, Bee. I appreciate it." She pauses. "He looks at you different, you know? The fact that he looks at you at all says something."

Everything inside me begins shutting down. *Don't do that. Don't tell me that.* Instead I laugh it off. "You tell them to lay off those pain meds, okay? You're not making any sense." After hanging up the phone, I shut everything down in Masquerade, lock the door, and head straight to the hospital.

The whole way there, I consider stopping by Lunar to tell Maddox what happened. Unsure if it's the right thing to do or not, I steer clear. I don't think busting into his work to tell him the only person in the world he cares about is in the hospital is smart. It would be different if she wasn't okay, but they're sending her home, so she has to be.

When I get to the emergency room, I realize something very important. I don't know her last name. Which means I don't know Maddox's last name either. That's strange, right? I've slept with this guy twice and I work with him almost every day, but I don't even know his last name?

"I'm looking for Laney," I tell the ER registration clerk.

"Laney . . .?"

"Actually it's Delaney. She goes by Laney."

She waits for more.

"Dark hair, gray eyes, and she got into a car accident. Does her last name really matter? She called me to pick her up. How would I know she's here if she didn't call?"

Her lips purse and I can tell she doesn't like my attitude. Not that I blame her.

"What's your name?"

"Bee." Ha. I don't have a last name either. At least not one I'm giving her.

"I'll be right back."

She leaves, I'm assuming to go ask Laney if the tatted up bitch outside is really here for her. A minute later, the sliding doors open and she leads me to one of the curtained rooms.

When I slip inside, Laney's sitting in a wheelchair

with a neck brace on, a wrap around her wrist, and a big bruise on the side of her head. My heart does this tumble-and-drop thing before trying to work its way back up from my feet. Oh yeah, Maddox is going to flip.

"It's fine. They want me to wear this for whiplash. I'm seriously okay."

"Your brother's not going to think so."

"Neither is my boyfriend. I'm surrounded by brokenly noble men. You get used to it after a while."

I let out a little laugh. "I'm not really the kind of girl who gets used to something like that."

There's a small smirk on her face that says she doesn't believe me.

The nurse comes in then and goes over Laney's discharge instructions with her. Pain meds, appointment with her doc the next day, and rest. The nurse looks at me. "So she's okay? Just wear that stuff and check in with her doctor? There's nothing else we need to know?"

She shakes her head. "If the pain increases, come back, but she's fine. Just a little banged up. I doubt she'll even have to keep wearing the neck brace. Her X-rays looked good."

I nod and the nurse leads us out. She helps Laney get into my car and then we're on our way. Laney begins giving me directions to her apartment; then she gets quiet.

"He's a good guy, ya know," she says after a few minutes. There's no question about who she's talking about.

"I know."

"He cares too much sometimes, but he doesn't know how to show it. He keeps it locked in."

I can see that too . . . "Why are you telling me this?"

She's stiff in the passenger seat and I can't tell if it's because of my question or her injuries.

"I'm not sure. I thought you should know, I guess. He's not the easiest person to get to know. He's my brother and he's been my best friend my whole life and he still won't really let me know him."

The sadness in her voice, her words, works its way inside me, making me feel heavy. And maybe slightly alone. "He's lucky to have someone like you who cares about him so much."

The same way I have people who love me? People I lock out the same way Maddox does with his sister? Then again, love doesn't always make sense. Look at Rex and Melody. It made them steal me.

"I'd do anything for him and I think it's pretty obvious he would do anything for me too."

"You don't need him in the same way you used to." I'm not sure where the words came from but as soon as they leave my mouth, I know they're true.

"I leaned on him more than I should have. I asked

a lot of him where our mom is concerned and that was hard on him. But . . . meeting Adrian? I grew up a bit after that. I know how to be strong on my own and if I need help, I have Adrian there. He supports me instead of taking over the way Maddox does. We're stronger together than either of us ever were alone. I want that for Maddy one day." She pauses for a second. "He's my brother. I'll always need him. Still, things aren't the same now."

I nod but don't reply. This isn't a conversation I am going to get into with her. When she opens her mouth to say something, her cell phone rings. "I'm okay, Maddy," she says instead of hello. She pauses while he says something. "I only have a few bumps and bruises. I'm already on my way home. Bee is taking me."

I can't help but wonder what he has to say about that.

"You don't have to come . . . chill out, okay? I'm not in the mood."

He says something else and then she replies with, "See you in a few minutes." Laney groans. "That went well."

I can't help but laugh and think she's pretty cool.

"You had to have an upstairs apartment?" I tease as I help Laney up the stairs.

"I'm sorry. I don't know why my body feels so stiff.

I'm going to kick Adrian's ass for his phone. I feel bad you have to help."

"Nah, no worries. I'm only giving you a hard time."

As we turn the corner, I hear muffled voices ahead of us. Down the hall, Adrian stands next to an open door, laughing with Colt. As if he senses her, he turns around, his eyes landing right on Laney. Even from thirty feet away, I see the fear flash in his face and then he's here, wrapping his arms around her.

"Christ, Laney. What the fuck happened, baby? Are you okay?"

"Shhh. I'm fine. I accidentally rear-ended someone, but everything's good."

He doesn't seem convinced. His dark eyes are wide, lost. He runs a hand through her hair, down her back, her arms, as though he's trying to make sure she's really there.

"It's okay, Adrian. I'm good. I promise." Still, there are tears in her eyes. Not from pain, I can tell.

Adrian wipes them with his thumbs. "Come here, Little Ghost," he whispers in her ear, and then lifts her into his arms. Colt and Cheyenne have come out of their apartment or maybe Adrian and Laney's. I'm not sure, but my question is answered when Adrian doesn't go to the same door. He's carrying her away, Colt and Cheyenne right next to him, all of them asking her what happened.

I turn, realizing my job is done. I'm not going to

interfere with the four friends. The only thing I needed to do was get her home, which I did.

"Bee. Don't go. Come with us." Laney's looking over Adrian's shoulder and then he turns.

"Shit. I'm sorry. Yeah, come on."

The need to walk away tugs at my feet; then Laney adds, "Please?"

"Yeah, come on. Someone has to help us calm these knuckleheads down. They'll be freaking out over her all night," Cheyenne laughs.

A ball of awkward energy forms in my stomach as I step toward them. I follow the foursome to Adrian and Laney's apartment. As soon as we get in, Adrian carries her right back to her room.

"I'm thinking he's going to want to strip her bare and make sure she's okay all over." Colt grins and Cheyenne smacks his arm. "What? It's what I'd do to you, Tiny Dancer."

And there goes that feeling to run again.

He gets closer to her and lowers his voice, but I still hear him when he says, "In fact, I think I'll do it anyway. You know, just to be fucking safe and all."

"Oh my God—"

"Where is she?" Maddox cuts Cheyenne off as he pushes into the apartment.

"She's in her room with Adrian. She's okay, Scratch."

He ignores me and heads for the hallway. The

bedroom door is open so I know they're not really doing what Colt said. Automatically, I follow him. Colt and Cheyenne must be just as worried because they're coming too.

"I'm *fine*," Laney stresses as Maddox turns into the room. She's sitting up on the bed, Adrian kneeling in front of her with a hand on her hip.

"What happened?"

"I accidentally hit someone."

"Shit," Adrian mumbles at the same time Maddox asks, "Is it your brakes? Christ, Laney. I told you to get those checked."

At that, Adrian pushes to his feet. "You need to back the fuck off right now. She's not a kid. The last thing she needs is you making her feel like shit about it."

Colt steps closer as I do the same, my breathing fast.

"Fuck you," Maddox tells him before moving closer to his sister. "Are you okay? What did the hospital say?"

Adrian doesn't stop there. He grabs Maddox's arm. "You're in my house, man, with my girl. I know she's your sister, but I'm tired of dealing with this shit. You need to have a little bit of respect."

"The same respect you have for her by not making sure she's driving around in a car with brakes that work?"

Adrian's face goes cold and hard at that. "I've dealt

with a lot of shit from you, but don't *ever* make it sound like I wouldn't do any-fucking-thing to take care of her."

Colt gets closer, taking Adrian's arm. "Both of you need to calm the fuck down."

Laney pushes to her feet and wobbles slightly. "I am so tired of dealing with this from both of you guys. I got into a fender bender! It's not the end of the world." She turns to Maddox. "I love you, Maddy, but Adrian's right. You need to have more respect for him. I love him too. He'll always be a part of my life. And he loves me. It's not his job to take care of me . . . We take care of each other."

I'm surprised when Adrian looks Maddox in the face, his anger gone. "I get it. You know I fucking get what you've been through together. If anyone knows how much I love her, it's you. She brought me back. She makes me become someone Ash would be proud of. I would take on the whole fucking world for her and you need to open your eyes and see that."

It's as though all the air has been sucked out of the room. Everyone is deadly quiet. Even though I'm obviously the only person in the room who doesn't know the history of that, even my own pulse pounds in my ears. What have they been through together? Who is Ash?

I'm surprised when Maddox steps back and gives Adrian a small nod.

"You're okay?" he asks his sister.

"Yeah, I'm fine. There's nothing to worry about and Bee was great too. She came down, picked me up, and helped me get home."

Maddox turns and acknowledges me with the briefest glance before he gives her another nod.

"Thanks for that. I owe you one," Adrian tells me. I shake my head, all my attention on Maddox.

"I'm gonna go. I'm supposed to go back to work. I'm glad you're okay." And then he looks at Adrian. In typical male fashion, they don't speak, only nod at each other again.

Instinct makes me follow Maddox out. He doesn't say a word to me as he takes the stairs quickly. It's not until we get to the parking lot that I speak. "Hey. Good to see you too."

"I gotta go," is all he says. Then he gets onto his motorcycle and he's gone, leaving me alone.

No. He's not leaving *me*; he has no responsibility to stay. I don't want him to either. I need to start remembering that.

I get into my car and head back to Masquerade. It's more a home than my house is. It's where I always go when I need to be reminded of who I am. Of Bee.

I don't turn on the OPEN sign and I lock the door behind me. There are new blinds I just put on the glass door, so I close those too.

Hours later, I'm still sitting in Masquerade, thinking

about what went down at Laney's house today and wondering all sorts of things that I usually don't let myself get close enough to anyone to think about. I jump when a clap of thunder sounds. It's dark outside, nothing but the sound of the sudden rain slapping against Masquerade and the ground and me.

That's when I hear it. That familiar rumble. And then I see the lights. Without looking through the blinds, I unlock and open the door. My breath catches in my throat when I see Maddox standing on the other side. His midnight hair flat against his head and rainwater pouring down him.

In this moment, he's sexier than he's ever been. He's beautiful.

CHAPTER FOURTEEN

MADDOX

I rode around for hours, trying not to let myself think about much of anything, except thinking ended up to be all I did.

Christ, Adrian is right. Who the fuck do I think I am? She's my little sister and she has her shit together more than I do. She doesn't need me. And him? If the fact that he's with her at all doesn't prove how much he loves her, nothing else will.

I swore when it started raining that I was going home, yet here I am, standing in front of Masquerade — in front of Bee, the girl who took care of my sister.

"Are you going to let me in?"

Without a word, she steps aside and I walk in. I hear the door close and the lock click into place behind me. I'm soaking wet, a pool of water beneath me on the floor.

"I think I have some towels in the back," she tells me. When she walks by, I reach out and grab her wrist. It surprises me when she stops so easily.

"You took care of my sister twice. The first time it

was your job. The second time, you didn't have to but you did. You closed your shop and you picked her up when I was being an asshole and ignoring her calls."

I wait for her to pull her hand away. She doesn't. Instead, she stands there and looks straight at me.

"All I did was give her a ride. It's not a big deal."

"I wasn't there. I told her I would always be, and I wasn't. You were. That . . ." I close my eyes. *Means something to me.* When I open them again, I grab the bottom of my shirt and pull it over my head. Tossing it into the sink, I open the cabinet and pull out the piercing supplies and set them down. Then I walk over to the display of barbells and pull one out. Behind me, Bee hasn't moved or spoken yet.

There's a voice in my head that tells me how fucking ridiculous I am. How hard is it to say *thank you?* Words have never been easy for me. Actions speak louder and this is the only thing I can think of. I told her I wouldn't let her pierce me because I didn't trust her, but she was there for my sister. That's the best kind of trust I can think of.

"A simple thank-you would work." Her voice cracks slightly. I've never heard it from her. She's always calm and in control. Not now.

"What the fuck are words? People put too much stock in them when they don't mean shit. Anyone can use them. People lie every day. I may not be good with words, but this I can do."

"Okay." She walks toward me. "I'm grabbing the towels. I'll be right back."

It means a lot to me that she doesn't ask if I'm sure or doesn't try to talk me out of it. Most people would. If I wasn't sure, I wouldn't be doing it, and I wonder if she knows that about me.

"Take off your pants," she says when she walks back in the room. "You're getting water everywhere."

She tosses me a towel and then begins to lay the other one on the chair before reclining it. My jeans stick to my legs as I pull them off. They go into the sink with my shirt.

I can't believe my hand actually fucking shakes as I dry myself off. I run the towel over my hair, too, but it doesn't do much and I toss it and sit in the chair.

"I guess the rain helped one thing—they're already hard." She rasps her finger, with black-painted nails, over my nipples. I hiss, suddenly wanting her to touch me somewhere other than my chest.

If I were in the mood to laugh right now, I would. I'm sitting in a tattoo chair, wet, in nothing but a pair of boxer-briefs. When her eyes skate down my body with almost as much heat as a touch, I groan.

"We doing this?" It's the same thing I asked the first night I met her.

Bee walks to the sink and washes her hands. Then she opens a new needle and the barbell package before grabbing a disinfecting wipe. I close my eyes when she cleans my left nipple.

"One or both?"

"One."

Bee leans over me with a marker in her hand. She is so fucking sexy, all blond hair and tattoos, that small piercing in her nose, and I suddenly want my teeth tugging gently on the one in her belly button.

She puts a small dot on each side of my nipple, measuring it with her eyes to make sure it's straight.

"What do you think?" she asks, still looking down. I don't take my eyes off her.

"You're the professional." *I trust you. At least in this I trust you.*

"Maddox?"

"Don't. Don't ruin it with words. Please."

"It's going to hurt like a bitch," she says.

"Most things do," I reply. We both know I'm not talking about physically.

She nods before picking up the needle. Her hands are steady. Somehow it doesn't surprise me. Not with her. The barbell fits on the end of the needle, and then she grabs the piercing forceps and clamps them down on my nipple. Bee lines the point up with the spot from the marker.

"Don't move. It'll be quick. You need to stay still. I'll be careful."

I nod, start to close my eyes, but then think, *Fuck*

that, and watch her instead. I don't take my eyes off her when a sharp, stinging pain shoots through me. Christ it fucking hurts. My whole body tenses up as the little needle stabs me. *"Fuck!"* I grit out, but then the barbell is in and she's twisting the balls on each end.

"It takes a long time to heal. Like six months. You have to be really careful. You don't want it to get infected. Shit, I can't believe I did this without talking to you about it—Maddox."

I grab her and pull her onto my lap so she's straddling me. "What the hell are you doing?"

"I don't know," I say, and then I pull her mouth to mine. My chest throbs like a bitch. It has nothing on the desire I feel for her right now.

She doesn't pull back as I take her lips. She shudders and there's a little bit of pride in me that likes that. She's rock-steady while working, but I made her shake.

Her legs straddle me in the tattoo chair. My tongue slides in and out of her mouth, taking the kiss as deep as I can. She matches me stroke for stroke, the whole time keeping clear of my piercing.

"We shouldn't be doing this." She drops her head back so I can kiss her neck.

"Say the word and I'll stop, but fuck, I want you right now." I think I might need her.

Her hand slides between us before she pushes it

under my boxer-briefs. This time it's me who shudders when she wraps her hand around me. The same hand that pierced me.

She stills and I'm actually *scared* she's going to pull away but then she says, "I can't sleep with you in this tattoo chair. There's something wrong about that."

It only takes me a second to push to my feet. "Take your shirt off," I tell her as I start to work the buttons on her jeans. She does it. Then her bra while I'm stripping her bottom half. The urge to kiss every tattoo hits me again, but I don't. Instead, I stand. "Please tell me you have condoms."

"They're in my purse." She grabs one, her tight little ass on display, while I kick out of my underwear. When she hands it to me, I rip it open and sheathe myself.

As I lift her, she wraps her legs around my waist. I take her mouth before holding her up between a wall and myself. *Take her to the couch. At least take her somewhere to lay her down.* I feel like an animal, the way I come at her, but she's rotating her hips against me and digging her nails in my shoulders.

"Maddox . . . please."

It's all I need. I take her nipple between my teeth before pushing inside her. We both cry out as I pull back and push forward again. It's fast and furious, like every time we've been together.

And yet, it feels like more too—as though there's

something here that wasn't there before. I quicken my thrusts, needing this to be about what she makes me feel physically. Telling myself that's what it is.

I rasp my tongue over her nipple before pulling back slightly and wondering how it would feel if she could do the same to my pierced one.

My thumb brushes over the stars on her side as I push in, harder . . . faster.

I feel her stiffen before she cries out in completion and I'm right behind her. Her body squeezing everything out of me.

"Oh my God. I don't know if I can stand," she says, so I carry her to the back room and lay her on the couch. I take a quick trip to the bathroom to get rid of the condom, clean up, and grab a washcloth for her.

"Ummm . . . here." I hand it to her awkwardly.

"I am so going to sleep well tonight." A lazy smile tilts her mouth and I have the strange urge to kiss it. I never kiss someone after sex.

"Are you staying here?"

"Mmm-hmm."

"Okay . . . yeah . . ."

Then as if she realizes what we did and who we are, she opens her eyes and says, "You can stay. Though I don't know if you want to and honestly I don't know if we should."

I love her honesty.

Yes. "We shouldn't."

"Yeah." She nods. "I guess you're right."

I go to the closet she has back here and pull out the blanket and pillow I know she keeps. I hand her the pillow and then lay the blanket over her.

"I'll lock up." *Thank you. Not just for grounding me tonight, but also for caring for my family.*

The honesty in those thoughts scares the hell out of me. It's exactly what I feel. Grounded.

"Thanks. Read the aftercare instructions for your piercing, okay? You need to clean it a few times a day, and I want to see it tomorrow, okay? I really fucked up tonight, Maddox. I didn't even have you sign a consent."

"I'll sign one. And it wasn't your fault. I sprung it on you. I needed it. It was all me."

"Still. I don't lose my head like that. It's . . . I don't like that I did."

My mouth wants to close up. The words try to bury themselves so they won't come out, but I owe her something too. Tit for tat. "It wasn't just you. I lost my head too."

She nods.

"It's . . . it's too much. I'm going. You're okay here? You sure?"

"I stay here all the time, Maddox. I don't need to be taken care of, remember? I'm not that girl."

"I know." I turn for the door, really wishing I didn't

have to go out there and put on wet clothes again. I make it halfway down the hall before I turn and go back. Quickly, before I change my mind, I kiss her forehead. "Thanks."

Before she can reply, I walk out, fight my wet clothes back on, sign the consent and leave it on the desk for her, and grab the aftercare instructions. It's not until I'm on my bike driving away that her words play back. *I don't need to be taken care of, remember? I'm not that girl.*

For years I've avoided that. I've never wanted to take care of a woman. I've had my hands full with Mom and Laney, but for once I find myself wishing someone needed me, maybe even just a little bit.

CHAPTER FIFTEEN

BEE

I'm determined to act completely normal around Maddox today.

No, I tell myself. What's that? There's no reason to act normal because what happened between us last night is what I've done with him before and what he's done with other women before as well. We enjoyed each other. End of story. Today we go back to him watching me tattoo.

I have one little tattoo and a piercing before he comes in. Right on time I hear his motorcycle pull up in front of Masquerade. The shop's empty when he comes in a minute later in a pair of jeans and a black shirt. It's a little windy out today, even though it's supposed to be like sixty-five degrees. Something makes me wonder if he's cold, though.

Melody and Rex used to tease me about how easily I get cold.

"What's up?" he asks. His eyes are puffy like he didn't get much sleep last night and I wonder if it has anything to do with what we did. *Or it could be that his sister got in a car accident.* I don't know what made me automatically tie it to myself.

"Take off your shirt." My voice comes out as light as I fight to make it.

"Want more of me already?" He quirks a half-grin, which shocks me, as does the joke.

"Ha-ha. Take off your shirt and let me look at your piercing."

Maddox stops at the end of my desk and I stand up. He doesn't take his shirt all the way off, but lifts it so I can see his chest. "Does it hurt?" I ask, letting my finger trace the slightly reddened skin around it.

"Hell yeah it does. I have tats, and I broke my ankle playing football when I was younger and none of them touch this."

"You played football?" sort of tumbles out of my mouth.

He shrugs. "It was another lifetime ago."

We both had another life, floats through my head, but I try to wash it away, with his piercing. "I'm going to put some cream on it." I run to grab what I'm looking for before going back out to Maddox. After squeezing a little on the tip of my finger, I gently rub it on his nipple.

It's crazy stupid, but I can't help myself from watching my finger as it moves against him in a really sexy place.

"It's not too swollen."

"Then that's about the only thing on me that isn't."

I think for the first time in my life someone makes me gasp. Looking down, I see a very obvious erection beneath the fly of his jeans.

"I don't see anything," I tease, and then Maddox does something I never expected. He lets out the first real laugh I've ever heard from him—all throaty and sexy and *scary* because I enjoy the sound.

Then I laugh, too, because he's right and the bulge is huge and he made a joke, which he doesn't do very often. Suddenly we're both laughing together and it's strange and cool at the same time. It's then I realize my finger is still on his nipple and then he lets out this sexy moan and I do, too, before we both separate.

Distance. We definitely need distance.

"It looks good. Make sure you keep taking care of it, okay? They're not the easiest piercings to have. I'd hate it if it got infected or you regretted it . . . What?" I ask. He's cocking his head at me, studying me in this way I don't understand.

"You." He turns his back to me, walks to the supply cabinet, and looks inside, moving stuff around.

"Me, what?"

He doesn't answer right away and I can't help but wonder if he's trying to figure out what to say. He's mentioned he's not a fan of words, and I can see that. He doesn't talk a lot, but the words he does say usually really mean something. They're not emotional or in depth, yet when he says them, you know they're important.

"The caretaker bit. It shocked me." He still has his back to me. His voice is tight, though not like anger . . . confusion maybe.

"I don't try to take care of people. I'm doing my job."

"Are you?" he asks, and I suddenly want to tell him to shut up. He's always so quiet—words never coming easy for him. It's strange that suddenly he wants to use them.

"What about you? You're cracking jokes. Like that's not different for you?"

"I know." There's the anger. It's found its way to his voice, only it doesn't feel like it's directed at me.

Turn around. At least look at me if we're doing this.

I wait for him to say more. He doesn't. Nothing comes out of my mouth either, so I sit back at my desk and look at some of the tattoo blogs I visit. I get two more people who come in for piercings, which Maddox watches. It's obvious he's not nearly as into those as he is tattooing.

We're still not talking. Honestly I'm not sure what's going on or why it's on my mind. Unfortunately it is. We had this easy conversation this morning, and now it's as though we took ten steps backward. The space between us isn't anger, but there's definitely space.

I like space. He likes space. What's the big deal?

The longer it goes on, the more it upsets me. The more I upset me. "If you're going to pout all day, you might as well go home."

Maddox crosses his arms and stares at me. "I didn't know I was pouting. I'm taking care of shit, Bee."

The way my name rolls off his tongue unexpectedly makes me shiver.

"You're pouting."

"Why do you care?"

I shake my head, knowing I'm being a bitch. He's not innocent either, though. Maybe that's what makes things different between us than they are with other people. Neither of us gets close or uses words to show who we are, but we use actions. We both use strength as our defense. I've never known someone who was like me before. Who *got* me.

"I'll be right back." I'm the one pouting now as I head to the back office. I hear Maddox sigh and then the creak of the chair at my computer desk. I can't help but glance over my shoulder. He's leaned back enough that I can see him down the hall. Quickly I turn away.

The sound of the glass door opening drifts through the shop.

"Can I help you?" Maddox asks. The chair moves and I watch him as he pushes to his feet.

"Hello."

Everything inside me freezes at the voice. *Yep, that's right. I'm a bitch.*

"I'm looking for L—Bee. I'm looking for Bee."

I close my eyes, feeling myself shrink until I'm about two inches high. Before I open them, I know Maddox is looking down the hall at me. I give a small shake of my head, open my eyes, and plead with them.

"Um . . . no. She's not in today. I'm Maddox. I help her out."

"Oh," my mother says. "It's very nice to meet you. I didn't know Bee had anyone working with her. I have to admit, I'm glad to hear it."

Smaller. I'm getting smaller and smaller as I stand hidden.

"I've always worried about her being alone all day and night in the shop. It's a scary world out there." There's nothing but sincerity in her voice.

"She's strong. I think people know not to mess with her. I'm here a lot, though. I mean, not that I think it's my job to protect her or anything," Maddox backpedals.

"Yes. She is strong, isn't she?" I can practically see my mom through the walls. Her perfectly styled blond hair. She's probably wearing some sort of diamond earrings that most likely came from my father. Flowers, I bet, and a dress. The opposite of me.

Instead of replying to her question, Maddox asks, "Can I tell her who came by?"

He knows. With one look it's obvious.

"I'm her mom, Katherine. It's nice to . . . what did you say your name is again?"

"Maddox."

I watch him lean forward and know they're shaking hands.

"I'm passing through on business. I wanted to stop by and see her. I've been trying to call, but I can't get a hold of her. I know it sounds silly to worry . . ."

Don't tell him why. Don't say anything that will make him question my past.

"I know her phone has been acting up. I think she's planning on getting a new one." Silently I thank him for the lie while I continue to get smaller and smaller. I'm a coward for hiding back here. Worse than that because she's here out of concern for me— she's always cared about me—but I'm still trying to figure out how to love anyone. Or if I want to.

And like when I was taken, she's still not giving up on me.

Mom laughs. "See? Perfectly logical explanation. It's like a mother to worry. I'm sure yours is the same way."

There's no reply from Maddox at that.

"Okay. I guess I better head out, then. Can you tell her I stopped by?" she asks.

Go out there. Go out there and say hi.

"Yeah, I'll tell her."

Footsteps. Then the door opens. I exhale, thinking I'm in the clear, when she speaks again. "She's okay? She's happy?"

I can see Maddox tense from down the hall. The thoughts that must be going through his head right now scare me.

"She's good. She's real good at what she does. I'm honored to learn from her."

I imagine Mom's smile—part proud, part confusion.

"Thank you. I hope to see you again sometime, Maddox. Tell her I love her."

And then she's gone.

Maddox doesn't come back to me, and I don't go to him right away either. I give it time—time for Mom to be gone. As I wait, I feel itchy, my feet wanting to run, my brain already checked out. The only thing left is the guilt eating me alive.

Another little flash of a memory flitters through my head. I'm young; I'm crying. Why am I crying?

"She's gone," Maddox calls out.

I grab my sweatshirt off the couch and turn off my thoughts.

"Can you take me for a ride on your bike?"

He doesn't ask where, which is a good thing since I don't know. Instead he grabs his keys off the desk. "Let's go."

CHAPTER SIXTEEN

MADDOX

When I bought my bike, the first thing I did was get an extra helmet for my sister. If shit went down and I had to pick her up, I wanted to make sure she had something to wear. She's never ridden the fucking thing once, but if she has to, I want to be prepared. It's probably one of my shitty ways of trying to make up for the past, for not being there. I don't usually keep it with me all the time, but for whatever reason, after I drove Bee home the other night in her car, I started keeping the helmet with me.

I've never had a woman on my bike with me. That's not something I do. It's mine and I like to keep the things that are mine away from other people.

Still, when we step outside, I automatically hand Bee my extra helmet. She slips it on her head, and I ease her hands out of the way to latch it.

Neither of us speak, which is a goddamned blessing because words would ruin it. If we just go through the motions, we can both pretend this isn't a big deal.

As soon as I'm straddling the bike, Bee gets on right behind me. I have no idea if she's ridden before. Her arms wrap around my waist, and her legs squeeze, and suddenly I want to lay her on it, strip her, and lose myself in her. Maybe it would help her fight off whatever monsters she's battling right now too.

The engine growls, sending a vibration through me, and then I rip out of the parking lot. Masquerade is toward the end of town, so it doesn't take long before there aren't lights or stores or anything else around us except space.

Even though she doesn't say it, I know she wants to go fast. Sometimes I think if I go fast enough, I can leave everything behind. That's what I want to do for her. I don't let myself wonder why or even acknowledge the fact that we're riding together. I just try to help her fly.

Bee's grip on me tightens as we speed down the highway.

Without planning it, I drive to a town a couple miles over and end up by the high school football field. The lights are on, evening setting in.

And then . . . I stop. I'm not sure why. There's no reason to pull over next to a high school football game. Or none that she would know or care of at least.

The stands are full. The scoreboard is lit up, saying it's the third quarter. At first Bee doesn't speak.

Questions have to be going through her mind, but I think she's good at that—not pushing. She doesn't want anyone pushing her, but fuck, I almost wish she would. I almost want to tell her something—something I would never give to another person.

With her arms still holding me, she says, "I've never been. To a game, I mean. It wasn't really my thing in school."

"It was my life." My body tenses with the words, but I don't try to take them back. "Things have changed. I'm not that person and know I never could be. Still, sometimes I like to watch. I watch and pretend that it's still me and that I'm still the kind of guy who would thrive out there, ya know?" Honesty pours out of me. The same shit that's usually so locked inside I didn't even know it was there. I couldn't be that person again. There are some people who can get it back, who can change. I'm not one of them. That person could never be me. Still, that doesn't mean I don't wonder how that life would have been different.

"Let's watch the game." Bee nudges me with her arm. Without replying, I pull away, skip the front entrance, and drive to the far end of the parking lot. There's a field on the other side with a chain-link fence separating it from the game.

Bike parked, Bee climbs off and I'm right behind her.

Why are we here?

What are we doing?

It's so fucking strange, being with someone like this. It isn't me, but the crazy part is, I don't want to be anywhere else.

We walk through the open field, stopping about midway in and pretty far from the fence. For a second I wonder why she didn't go closer; then I realize she's like me — it's easier to participate from a safe distance.

Bee sits in the grass and I look down at her. Her hair is in a messy ponytail and Christ her eyes are so green. I never really noticed before.

"I don't have a blanket or anything for you to sit on." My brain and my mouth don't feel connected. I don't remember planning those words, but they're what came out.

She shrugs. "I don't need one."

Beside her, I sit with my feet flat on the ground, knees up. A tall weed sticks up between my feet, so I grab it and twist it around my finger, not sure what else to do.

"You don't seem like the football type."

"I'm not. The old Maddox was." This is where anyone else would ask questions. What happened to change you? You're still the same person, ya know? And maybe it's like that for some people, but not everyone.

"What position did you play?"

"Quarterback. Are there others?"

She grins. "You're asking the wrong person, Scratch. I know jack shit about football."

Testing the words on my tongue, I ask, "Want me to tell you?"

Bee looks over at me, probably more seriously than I've ever seen her. "Sure."

And now I really have to fucking do it. I'm the one who asked. Long conversations aren't really my thing, but once I start, the words kind of flow. We talk positions, offense and defense. She nods and looks interested, though she probably really isn't. Even though this isn't the game I love anymore, it still feels good to talk about it.

Glancing over, I study Bee as she looks at the football game. She's different. So fucking different than any other woman I've known. All my instincts are telling me to walk away. I've never wanted to be close enough to someone to have to deal with shit in their lives, yet I've done it with her. How easy would it have been to walk away this afternoon? Call her out of the office? But I didn't.

The lines are blurring for the first time in my life and I don't know how the hell I feel about it. Don't know why I'm not walking away. It's not as if I want to end up like my folks. My brain knows I still fuck up and I've let people down and that, really, I don't have shit to give away. I'm pissed half the time and

I don't deal with shit well, but . . . those instincts to run are ghosting away. I want to understand why.

"I've never done this before." An ache lands in my gut at the vulnerability in my own fucking voice. I've never heard that. And why? Because we rode on my bike and I'm watching a game with her? Or because her mom came to see her and for the first time I saw real vulnerability in *her*?

"Me either."

We're quiet and, I have to admit, I revel in it. Ever since she walked out of the office and asked to go for a ride, things have felt too deep. But then, no matter how comforting it is, my stupid fucking mouth is the one that opens first. "Your mom seems nice."

Bee reaches over and for a second, everything inside me turns to stone because I think she's going for my hand. Instead, she pulls that long weed from my fingers that I forgot I even had and starts playing with it herself.

"She is nice. Remember? I told you she's perfect." Another pause. "What about yours?"

"She tries to kill herself. The first time she did it so Laney would find her. She likes to hurt my sister." The coldness in my voice hits me. Words might not be something I do well, but those I can say. I won't hide from that or let Mom do it.

"Wow . . . that's rough. How is she with you?"

The door I didn't even realize was inside me slams

shut. I didn't tell. I knew what Dad was doing. If anything, I'm as guilty as he is.

"How she treats me doesn't matter. I don't matter when it comes to them."

Restless, I tap a foot, knowing if she asks why, this time I *will* leave.

She doesn't.

Instead, she leans her head over and rests on my shoulder, making me tense. Sucking a deep breath into my lungs, I . . . relax. The tension eases out with my exhale and I wait, wondering if she'll give me a piece of her or if we'll start the same old masquerade again.

CHAPTER SEVENTEEN

BEE

I *don't matter when it comes to them.*
No matter what I've gone through in my life, I've always known I mattered. When Rex and Melody looked at me with concern or bandaged my scrapes, I knew I mattered.

When I came home and found out how hard Mom and Dad looked for me and saw that my old room never changed and found all the old newspaper interviews online, I discovered I was important to them too.

Does he feel the same?

What's wrong with me that I can't return the love I get? That I can't understand it when so many people long to receive a little of it?

My throat tightens, almost like a fist squeezing me. His mother tries to kill herself yet mine fought for me, still fights for me, and I ignore her.

Maddox is as closed off as I am, yet he's given some of himself to me. He's given me way more than I've shared with him. He covered for me today when he didn't have to. And I feel . . . normal when I'm with him. It doesn't matter that I'm the tattooed, pierced chick with the bad mouth. I'm just Bee.

That means something to me.

The urge to give him a part of me in return takes over.

"His name was the Professor." Even though I should, I don't lift my head from his shoulder. Despite the fact that I haven't said who the Professor is, Maddox doesn't ask. He's letting me go at my pace. *He knows me* . . . Somehow through all of this, he knows me. I swallow the lump in my throat.

"I never really fit in when I was in high school and honestly, I didn't give a shit."

Tell him why. I can tell him why. That I was taken when I was young. Then when I went back home, I felt like I didn't fit with my family. It hurt too. I wouldn't let myself care if I fit anywhere else.

"I always drew, so that's what I focused on—drawing and doing my own thing. When I turned eighteen, I decided to get my first tattoo and that's where I met the Professor. He was old as hell, but good at what he did."

I startle a little when Maddox's arm lifts and wraps around my waist. Crazily, I can't find the urge to pull away.

"So yeah, I went in to see the Professor and I had my own drawing of what I wanted." I bite my lip, hating to admit this next part. "I don't know why, but I couldn't do it. It's like my hands wouldn't work and I couldn't grab the drawing out of my pocket to give it to him. I was freaked out, so I left."

"I don't believe that." There's a hitch to his voice that makes him sound different than he usually does. I'm pretty sure it's because he's trying to make me feel better.

"Nice try."

"Was worth a shot."

"I appreciate it." That's Maddox, I'm realizing. I can see him doing something like that for his sister—can see him trying to make her feel better.

"For the next week I was pissed at myself. I *wanted* that ink and I wasn't the type of person to get scared of something. So I went back and then kind of freaked out again. Every week for a month, Maddox. I went back four separate times. By then the Professor started calling me 'the B-Back.' It's what they call—"

"People who chicken out getting a tat," he interrupts.

Not sure why I didn't think he'd know that. "Yep. I was the girl who always said she'd 'be back.' Crazy, isn't it?"

He moves a little as though he's getting more comfortable. *You can move your arm*, plays on my tongue, but I don't let the words free. I should want him to move away. I don't.

"I've heard crazier."

At that I pull away enough so I can look at him, wondering how in the hell we got here. How I got here with anyone. "Careful, I might start thinking you're nice."

He tilts his head down and the urge to reach up and kiss him teases me.

"I could start thinking the same about you."

Then he says nothing—back to his quiet and waiting for me to finish the story.

I look away again. "I was pretty pissed at myself. It was a tattoo. I'd been through way too much in my lifetime to freak out over that, so I went back, the drawing in my hand. Without a word, I handed it to him and he said he knew I'd do it.

"So I did. I let the Professor give me my first tattoo. He's given me all of them, actually. I've never trusted anyone else to do it."

"Which one?" Maddox asks.

"The Gemini sign on my lower back. It's—"

"The twins. Two complete opposites living in one body. The yin and yang."

Trying to play it off like my stomach isn't quivering because he knew exactly what it means, I laugh. "You're usually so damn quiet and now I can't shut you up. That's the second time you interrupted me."

"And I never thought you would be the type to keep avoiding what you're trying to say. You always say whatever the hell you want, and if you didn't want to tell me this story, you wouldn't have started, so do it. What's up with the Gemini?"

The hairs on the back of my neck rise but I ignore them. After sitting up, I pull away from Maddox to see the challenge in his eyes. "I've always felt like there are two of me. Getting it tatted made it real. Then I realized not getting it done didn't make it false either." *Wanna play hardball, we'll play hardball.* "Why don't you matter when it comes to your mom and sister?"

"Because I kept my mouth shut when I should have spoken up, and they got hurt."

I cross my arms, running his response over in my mind. For some reason, I didn't expect him to answer.

My eyes continue to study Maddox as he does the same to me, as though we're picking each other apart and categorizing the other. "You take responsibility for everything that's gone wrong in your family's lives, the same way you try to take care of your sister, don't you?"

I wait for it. Wait for the anger that I know Maddox is capable of. Not violence, because that's not him, but the anger he feels at the world—the same emotion I see every time I look in the mirror.

"I don't do this, Bee." He shakes his head, looks out at the football game again.

My eyes travel the same line of sight as his, watching

the game but not taking it in. "Me either . . ." After taking a couple deep breaths, I continue. "The Professor asked me who did the drawing and I told him I did. He asked if I was lost and I told him I was. I felt like that for years . . . lost, like I didn't really know who I was. Then he asked, 'Wanna come back tomorrow, B? Maybe work with me?' I know it sounds crazy but everything kind of clicked into place then. I could come back to his tattoo parlor and I could become Bee. Not because I was a B-Back, but because it's who I wanted to become. Bee—the girl who chose who she was and didn't let anyone pick it for her."

It's almost like this weight lifted off my shoulders to say this to him. My back straightens, pride teasing me and asking for permission in. *I* decided who I am.

Maddox turns his head in my direction. There's a relaxed air about him that he doesn't usually have. With my eyes, I take in the stubble on his jaw and his dark, messy hair. It would really help things if he wasn't so damn sexy. *Keep lyin' to yourself, Bee. If it was just his looks, you wouldn't be here right now.*

"That takes guts. Not everyone can do that." He's staring at me and I'm still staring at him. I can't keep from thinking about the ring in his nipple and want to run my tongue over it.

Then he reaches toward me. Automatically I flinch

and then feel like an idiot. He pauses for a second, touches my hair, and the movement is almost . . . tender. I've slept with Maddox three times. He's not the only guy I've ever been with but that touch—the way he lets my hair almost float and fall from his fingertips—feels like the most intimate moment of my life.

"Who told you who you should be?" Then his hand falls, as does my stomach.

No one, but that doesn't make it easier. I know who they want me to be and I should love them enough to do it.

"Next question."

Maddox laughs this rich, throaty sound that makes my insides flip. "No shit. I'm going to use that one from now on."

"Deal."

A whistle blows, signaling the football game is over. Time flew by because I didn't even realize we'd been out here this long. I watch as Maddox stands and then holds out his hand. I surprise myself by letting him help me up. "I'm driving." I look over my shoulder at him as I walk toward the motorcycle.

He gives another laugh. "Where'd you hide the alcohol because you must be drunk."

"Asshole." I shake my head and roll my eyes.

When we get to the bike, I reach for the helmet but Maddox's hand on my arm stops me. His eyes have transformed from the lightness they held at his last comment.

"What's your real name, Bee?"

And that's what does it—the fact that he used Bee when asking. It's almost like he's telling me it's okay to be who I want. That to him I'm Bee, the pierced tattoo girl, and he's okay with that.

Or maybe I'm going crazy and seeing things I want to see. Still, I open my mouth and let the words tumble out. "Leila . . . or Coral. I guess it depends on how you look at it."

Questions swim through his eyes, but he doesn't ask any of them.

"Grab the helmet, Bee. Let's go." Without another word, Maddox climbs onto the bike and waits. Words bubble in my throat. I can't sort through them enough to let them free. I'm not sure what I want to say, so I settle on nothing.

After pushing the helmet onto my head, I climb onto the bike behind him. My arms go around his waist and he revs the engine before pulling away. We speed through the field and onto the road and I swear it feels like freedom. The wind is cold, but I revel in it. Love the feel of it as it rushes past me.

It's then I realize I'm not really freaking out about having told him about the Professor. He knows my name and it's kind of okay. It's different than how it is with people like my family where I know on some level I'm hurting them but can't seem to change it. He only knows Bee and he doesn't expect Leila or Coral when he looks at me. I press my cheek to his back and relax.

Maddox leans to the side as we take a corner. My body goes along with his, hugging him as he controls the bike.

It's not long until we're pulling back into town. I'm buzzing, getting that same tingle under my skin like I'm getting a new tattoo.

When Maddox stops at a red light, more words start fumbling out of my mouth. "I don't want to be alone tonight, Scratch." Immediately I feel on display. Maddox tenses and I want the words back, but then the light changes, the motorcycle accelerates, and Maddox speeds off again.

What the hell is wrong with me? If he could hear me, I'd tell him to let me off the bike right now. We shouldn't be out here together in the first place. We shouldn't have done any of it.

The wind no longer feels right as it washes around me and my stomach is nauseous.

I pushed. I'm always the one who keeps the walls up but I pushed him.

But then . . . then he turns away from my house — away from Masquerade. My fist tightens in his shirt as we take another turn, then another one.

Maddox pulls into the driveway of a brown house.

It's a little run-down, some of the paint peeling. *It's his . . .*

It's a shock to my system when the bike suddenly shuts off under me. Maddox climbs off, then I do. He pulls off his helmet, then I do.

"It's not much." Maddox tucks the helmet under his arm.

"It's yours, that's what's important." We're standing in his driveway, only a foot away from each other.

"I don't do this."

"I don't either."

He sighs. It's like a breath being pulled from me too. Confusion mixes around inside me.

"What do you want, Bee?"

"Nothing." And it's true. "Just to hang out. I'm not here to sleep with you. I . . ." *Feel like I can be myself with you.*

"I've never really done the friends thing, Scratch, but . . ." I shrug and he nods toward the house before starting to walk away.

I don't hesitate before following him.

CHAPTER EIGHTEEN

MADDOX

I've never taken a girl home with me. I've never gone home with a girl. I've never fucked a girl in a bed that I considered mine. She said she wasn't sleeping with me again and my brain knows that's smart. We're somehow all tied up in each other when I've never been connected to anyone before.

But then, we've also both always been on the same page. We don't do attachments, so my head is all fucked up about why we're going into my house together if it's not for something physical.

Or maybe I think I should feel screwed up about it. Crazy, but I actually *feel* and that's what has the fist squeezing my insides.

Shake it off, man. "Watch your step." With my hand flat on the door, I push it open while stepping back so Bee can walk in.

Slowly, she goes inside. Bee stops when she gets far enough away from the door that I can close it behind us. Even though it's dark outside by now, I can see inside because of the small lamp I left on this morning.

Automatically, my eyes scan the room, trying to see it the way she does. My couch is against the back wall. Fifty-buck special from a yard sale. Next to it, the little oak side table with the black lamp. A matching coffee table in front, pieces of paper scattered all over it: some flat, others balled up. Some blank, others filled with different drawings.

There's a small TV, but I only have a few channels. Another yard sale special is in the kitchen, a small round table with two chairs.

"This is strange . . ." Her back is to me as she looks around the room. Yet, I know, somehow I know, she doesn't mean my house. She's talking about being in it.

"Yeah . . . You thirsty or anything?" Scratching the back of my head, I walk into the kitchen. My first instinct is to watch her, to see if she explores. It's not that I really give a shit about anything I have, but it's mine and bringing her here is showing her who I am.

"Sure, I'll have some water."

It's a good thing because that's all I have.

After pulling two water bottles from the fridge, I toss one to Bee. She catches it easily and then we both stand there drinking, not knowing what to do.

It's not even a minute later she puts the lid on and turns. "I shouldn't have asked to come here."

Before she gets more than three feet away from me and toward the door, "You didn't," sort of tumbles out of my mouth. "You said you didn't want to be alone. I brought you here. It was my choice."

Slowly she looks my way and gives a small nod. My brain starts searching for words. I find none. I don't know why I want to. She makes me itch under my skin. It's not annoying but it's always there, and I don't know what it means. It's like I feel her, even when we're not touching.

"How's the piercing?"

"Don't know. You're the expert. Why don't you check it for me."

She rolls her eyes and grins, not at all taken aback by my words. Not that she would be. Not Bee.

She sets the water bottle down and steps toward me. My breath gets caught up in my lungs. Holy shit. I'm actually holding my breath as she pushes my jacket off my shoulder.

Neither of us reaches for it as it falls to the floor.

Bee looks at me and winks. Her voice is low and feisty when she says, "Sure thing. Just remember, you're the one who asked. The torture we both feel for the rest of the night will be all your fault."

Without planning it, my hand reaches for hers,

my fingers wrapping around her wrist. "You don't play fair."

"Like I said, you asked for it." And then she pulls her hand out of my grasp. Puts both hands flat on my stomach and starts to push my shirt up—slowly. So fucking slowly I feel like I could lose it.

"We agreed . . ." she says. "No more sex, remember?"

"Shit," I hiss. "Why did we say that?" Slower . . . higher, her hands warm and smooth against my skin.

"You know why."

I can't believe it when I close my eyes. It sounds fucked up but it makes me feel more vulnerable. Like she can do anything she wants to me and I wouldn't know before she strikes. Still, I don't open them, just keep letting her push my shirt up until my chest shows.

My hands are begging me to rip it off, to strip her and take her right in my kitchen but I fight it.

"Looks good." Bee's breath ghosts across my pierced nipple.

"You did that on purpose." I make myself open my eyes.

She shrugs. "I'm bad like that," she says before she steps toward the sink and washes her hands. It means she's planning to touch me.

She is so bad. I like that about her—like that she's different from any woman I've ever known.

The fact that she's standing here right now proves that.

"It's a little pink, but not too bad. We need to keep an eye on it, okay? Does it hurt?"

Her first finger traces around my nipple and my mouth waters to do the same thing to her. "Tender. Nothing too bad, though."

"Make sure you clean it tonight. You've been using the antibacterial soap, right?"

The sexiness in her voice is gone and even though I shouldn't, I want it back.

"Yep." Stepping away from her, I lower my shirt, pick up my jacket, and set it on the counter. "Let's go sit down."

Bee grabs her water again and follows me to the living room. Before she makes it to the couch, I'm already starting to pick up the drawings, trying to put them away so she can't see them. My whole body tenses when she grabs my arm.

"You don't have to hide that from me. I do it, too, remember?"

The papers fall from my hand. "So show me something."

There's blank paper and pencils and erasers all over the table. Bee pulls off her sweatshirt and sets it on the couch before sitting on the floor. I go down next to her, both our backs against the couch as we sit around the small table.

"This is going to be quick, so no laughing." Bee bends over, her arm and body trying to hide the paper from me as she starts drawing.

"What the hell is that? I thought you were showing me something?"

She looks over her shoulder at me and smiles. Really fucking smiles and I think it's the first real, bone-deep smile I've seen from her. If I wasn't already sitting down, she'd knock me on my ass.

"When I'm done, Scratch. Have some patience."

It's crazy how that name doesn't bother me anymore. Trying to block out her smile, I shake my head. "Hell, maybe I shouldn't be workin' under you, if you don't even trust your drawing skills."

My teasing comment doesn't even faze her. Bee looks at the paper, me, and then the paper again. The only sound in the room is her pencil scratching out whatever she's drawing.

Quiet I can do, so I watch her while she works. Wondering what she's doing and how in the hell we got here. That urge to pull away, to question what she's doing here is still pulsing beneath my skin, but not strong enough for me to do something about it. Right now I'm watching the way she puts her blond hair behind her ear with her black-painted fingernails.

It hasn't been more than a couple minutes, but I realize I'm *watching* this woman the whole time, studying her, and it's like a jolt, pushing me to my feet. This is so fucking strange, being here with someone like this.

"I'll be right back," I mumble. Bee is so lost in whatever she's drawing that I don't even know if she heard me. Behind me, I close the bathroom door before splashing some water on my face as though that will make a difference.

My cell rings and I almost don't pull it out of my pocket until I remember Laney got hurt and I haven't even checked on her. Phone in hand, Laney's name lights up on the screen.

My thumb lingers over ANSWER before I push it. "Hey."

"Hey. How are you?" Her voice is soft.

Standing in my bathroom freaking out over nothing. "Okay. How are you feeling?"

"Good. Not really in much pain at all. I'm annoyed over this stupid neck brace. I want to take it off."

"When do you go to the doctor?"

"Tomorrow, so I should be able to take it off then. I don't see what a day would change."

"Keep it on till then to be safe," I tell her.

Laney laughs; then it trails off. "I wish you realized how big your heart is, Maddy."

Is it, really? I want to ask her. Wouldn't I have put aside worries about college and money to tell Mom what was happening with Dad? If I had, maybe she'd be better. Maybe Adrian's son would be alive. "I fucked up . . . with Adrian after the accident. I shouldn't have been such an asshole to him."

"You should tell him that sometime." She pauses for a second. "What's going on? You sound different."

I look up at myself in the mirror. "Nope. Still me. Listen, I gotta run. Let me know how things go after you see the doc, yeah?"

"Love you," she whispers.

"You too." I turn my phone all the way off before shoving it in my pocket. Unwilling to let myself hide out in my bathroom, I slide the door open and go out.

"Thought you ran away, Scratch." Bee looks up at me from where she's sitting on the floor.

"Had to get up and move around before I fell asleep waiting for you to finish."

"Asshole." There's a smile on her face and then she lifts the piece of paper so I can see it.

It's me.

A loud laugh shocks me by bursting out of my mouth. "What the fuck is that?" When I get to her, I pull the paper out of her hands.

"It's you."

"Need your eyes checked?" Her body touches mine when I go down beside her. It's crazy how I can tell it's me, but she's obviously trying to be funny too. It's a caricature of me, like the ones people draw at carnivals. My head's huge, my hair floppy, and there's a smile on my face that's so big, I'm not sure I've ever had one like it. "And what the hell's up with the *bike*?"

"You ride one!" She grabs the paper from me.

"Motorcycle. Not a bicycle." Then I'm laughing again and it feels kind of good. There's this rumble in my chest and usually the only vibrations inside me are anger or lust.

"Where's my shirt?" Of course she had my piercing in there, too, but it's oversized as well. "You hinting you want to see me without it again?"

"I'm sure any girl would like that and you know it."

Her words send a sort of jolt through me because they're so honest. She's not shy about anything and she says whatever she feels, whatever she thinks. It's crazy and the urge to ask her questions just to see what she'll say hits me.

"Gimme that." I pull the pencil out of her hand before grabbing a piece of paper. "Now go away." Turning slightly, I bend over the table and wrap my arm around the paper so she can't see.

Bee sits forward and grabs me, trying to pull me away from the table. "Lemme see."

I nudge her back. "Don't be scared, baby. I'll draw you exactly how you look. I promise."

A fist squeezes around my throat because of what

came out of my mouth. I've never called someone
baby in my life. Sure I was only giving her shit but—

"If you *can*. Let's see how good your art skills really
are." The way she rolls right over it like it's nothing
makes me want to do the same thing. It should be
that fucking easy, so I'm going to make it.

"You've never doubted any of my skills before, so
why would you start now?"

She looks at me and rolls her eyes before picking
up another pencil from the table. "We'll see who has
the best kills, Scratch."

When she huddles over her paper to start drawing,
I do the same. My fingers easily sketch her out without
having to look at her. It's as though she's been
embedded into my brain.

This is different. I make the diamond in her nose
bigger, put a big tattoo gun in her hand, and make
it so her tongue is out of her mouth.

"What the hell ever!" She peeks over my shoulder,
but then Bee drops her head back and she laughs. It
slips between the cracks and crevices until it finds its
way inside me. I concentrate on the column of her
throat, which I really fucking want my mouth on
right now, but then she's showing her newest picture
of me and I'm laughing again.

On and on we keep drawing pictures of each other.
Each time I want to make her laugh more because
I love the sound and it makes me feel amazing that

I'm the one making her sound so happy. We draw each other for two hours before she tosses her pencil to the table and says, "I'm done. I won."

For some reason, I don't argue with her.

"It's getting late." Bee stands and stretches, her shirt lifting to show her flat stomach and belly button piercing. My fingers itch to play with it.

Instead, I stand too. "You can take my bed. I'll sleep on the couch."

Before I finish getting all the words out, she's already shaking her head. "No. That's not fair."

"And I don't work that way. You're not sleeping on the couch while I sleep in a bed." I'm used to sleeping on couches anyway. After Dad went to prison, I didn't have my own room anymore. Mom got pissed but I always gave the extra bedroom to Laney.

"I can go home—"

"No. It's late. You're here." My pulse is speeding.

"Then we'll share the bed. I can handle keeping my hands to myself. Can you?"

No. "Yes."

She's right behind me as I turn everything off. I could be a gentleman. Maybe I fucking should but the thought of being next to someone like that, the thought of being next to her, fills me up a little when I've been used to being empty for so long.

My stomach is in knots, but I ignore it. I show Bee the bathroom and give her a pair of my sweats and a T-shirt. She lets me in the bathroom first to clean up and then she goes in. I'm in my room when she steps in. My clothes drown her, but my cock instantly gets hard. There's something sexy as hell about seeing a woman in your clothes. I want to savor it and strip her out of them at the same time.

"It's not much," finds its way out of my mouth even though it has nothing to do with how gorgeous she looks. "My room."

It smells slightly of cigarettes. There's no headboard on the bed, just a queen mattress, dresser, side table, and more art stuff.

"Who said something has to be extravagant to be something?"

There's this strange thump in my chest and this urge to grab her and pull her to me that has nothing to do with how beautiful she is. I want to *hold* her and I've never wanted to fucking hold anyone in my life.

Speak, say something. Like they so often are, my words are lost, so Bee fills the space with hers.

Her eyes dart around, suddenly looking a little insecure. You wouldn't be able to tell by the sound of her voice, which doesn't waiver as she speaks. "On my ninth birthday, Rex and Melody forgot. They were both busy working on a painting. I knew it wasn't because they didn't care. They were just like that sometimes. They got in the zone and everything else left their heads. To make it up to me, Melody made really shitty chocolate chip cookies and we put up a tent in the backyard. The cookies were so bad we built a fire and made s'mores and looked at the stars all night. It was so simple, Maddox, but it was perfect."

Simple. Perfect. That's what I want. Not to stress about shit or have my mom try to kill herself or my sister who's always been so emotional. I love her but it's hard, so fucking hard when I'm the only one to deal with it, especially when I know it's my fault.

Suddenly, I really wish I could see those stars on her side again. Wish I could make s'mores with her and sit outside all night. "Who are Rex and Melody?"

Bee shakes her head. "Not tonight. Maybe . . . I don't know but not tonight. Okay?"

I nod and walk over to my bed. "I get it. I'll never push you to talk." And then I pull the blanket back. Bee crawls into my bed. *My bed.* After pulling off my T-shirt, I toss it to the floor.

"Did you clean your piercing?"

"Yes." The light flickers out with the push of a button and then I am in my bed with a woman. With Bee, in nothing except a pair of sweats, knowing I'll stay in them.

We're both quiet in the dark for what feels like forever.

"It feels good . . . to have someone," she whispers. "Someone who doesn't push or expect me to be anyone I'm not. Just Bee . . ."

Without replying, I reach for her and pull her against me. My arm around her waist as the back of her molds to the front of me. She tenses for a second before it melts away.

Bee lets me hold her all night, and I don't let go.

CHAPTER NINETEEN

BEE

It's been almost a week since I woke up in Maddox's bed. Since I woke up in his arms after talking to him about Rex and Melody and telling him my name.

Even though those things are small in some ways, I still can't believe I told him.

And he hasn't brought it up since. I'm not sure what I would do if he did. Probably be a bitch because that's easy for me. But he hasn't and I wish I could thank him for it—wish I would have the next day when we got up, got dressed, and he drove me to Masquerade like nothing happened.

Nothing did happen, I remind myself. It feels like it did and that has me slightly stressed out.

Glancing toward my computer, I look at the time. My next tattoo will be here in ten minutes, so I pull out a piece of paper and start the sketch. It's nothing big, just a name, so it doesn't take me long to come up with a couple ideas while I'm waiting for the girl to show.

A couple minutes later, a girl with short black hair walks in. "Hi. We spoke last week. I have an appointment for a tattoo." She smiles at me.

"Yep. I have a few ideas here if you want to check them out. I'm not sure exactly what kind of look you're going for." She walks over to my desk and looks down. There are a couple aspects of two designs she likes, so after we chat for a minute, I put together another quick drawing for her.

"You can have a seat." I nod toward the chair. "Maddox will set everything up for us . . ." My feet plant in place on my way to the sink as my words die off. Maddox won't be doing anything for us today because he's not here. Goose bumps pebble across my arms. I wanted nothing more than Masquerade to be only mine, and now my brain is automatically going to Maddox being here to help me like working with him is something I've always done.

The bumps spread up my neck but I fight to ignore them. *It's a slipup, that's all.*

"Scratch that. I'm setting up. I forgot he's not here today." I hand the girl the release and get a copy of her ID. After things are signed and taken care of, I lay the drawing on her ankle so the ink transfers to her skin.

"Right here?" Scooting back, I nod at her leg.

"Perfect."

The rest of the routine happens as easily as

breathing: getting the ink, washing my hands, paper towels, Vaseline, putting together the gun, opening a new needle, gloves. And then I rub Vaseline on her and it's needle to skin. She gives a small jump at first, then relaxes comfortably.

"Is this your first ink?" The needle skates a line. Her skin is easy, like butter. It's perfect for tattooing.

"Yeah. I've always wanted a tattoo, though."

"Whose name is it?" Glancing up at her, I see her cheeks go pink.

"You don't want to know."

Which means it's a boyfriend. I smile as I continue concentrating on what I'm doing. "Don't let anyone give you shit. Some people are like that no matter what your tattoo is of. You might regret it one day, and you might not, but at this point in time it's important to you. Even if that changes, this will be a memory. If he turns out to be an asshole, it will be your reminder about the kind of guy you don't want or if you stay together, then there's the obvious there." After pulling the gun from her skin, I wipe her leg, dip in my ink, and then rub more Vaseline on her before starting again. "And if you want it gone, it's not like we can't come up with something kick-ass to cover it up." I wink at her and she looks relieved.

"Thank you. You're the only person who's not giving me a hard time about it. Elliott . . . he's had cancer before. He's okay now, but you never know, right? I think it's important. I want a piece of him with me all the time and no one understands that."

I think about the ink on my body. The sunflower, the Gemini, my stars. I remember Mom's reaction when I came home with my Gemini sign. How she was upset, then made the comment about how at least it was only one and it was small. Little did she know I'd keep going . . .

Looking up at her again, I tell her, "They don't have to understand." Most people don't.

We're quiet after that as I continue to engrave Elliott's name into her. It's crazy, loving someone like that. I can't imagine ever doing it myself but I'd never give someone else hell for it. And then . . . Rex and Melody loved me enough—or they loved the idea of a child enough—to steal for one and that reminds me how possessive the feeling is supposed to be.

It only takes about fifteen minutes to finish her tattoo. Her eyes get teary when I'm finished and this swell of pride blooms in my stomach. This little flash of Mom fills my head, this foreign wish that she got this. That on some level, she didn't love me because she has to but because she understands me.

It doesn't take me long to get things cleaned up. I look around online for a little while, check the supplies, and then go back to my chair, drumming my fingernails on the desk.

It's not strange without Maddox here. It's not strange

without Maddox here. Only it is and that kind of sucks. It's cool having him to talk to and to come up with tattoo ideas with and, hell, to give him shit. The knife twists in my stomach at the thought. At the strange way I actually miss him.

"I really need to go out and have a good time tonight," I mumble. My phone rings, my hand shooting out to grab it like I'm expecting an important phone call or something. "Hello?"

"Hi . . . Bee? This is Laney. Maddox's sister."

My heart jumps a little. Maddox isn't here. If something is wrong, Maddox isn't here again and that will kill him. "Hey . . . is everything okay?"

"Yeah. I'm fine. God, you sound like my brother." She laughs and I frown. The urge to say, *I do not*, dances on my tongue, but I ignore it.

"I wanted to tell you I'm having a little get-together for my birthday next weekend. Nothing big or anything. Just Adrian, Cheyenne, Colt, and Maddy. I'd love it if you could come."

I fight down the instinct to blurt out a no. She's nice and she's Maddox's sister, so I don't want to be a bitch. *And I want to go. At least, I think I want to go.* But my thoughts start running. It doesn't take a genius to see where she's going with this. That it will be two couples and then Maddox and I. Maddox doesn't see how alike they are. He and Laney are both fixers. I can see her trying to fix him by setting him up. The difference between them is she would do it for anyone and he would only go there for her.

Besides, I'm pretty sure he wouldn't want me at this party. I'm pretty sure I shouldn't want to be there either. Not after the other night at his house, and hell, how everything has been between us since we met each other.

"Saturday or Sunday?" *That's not a no. I should be saying no.*

"Sunday. You guys are closed, right?"

"Usually, but I actually have someone coming in this Sunday, so I'm not sure if I can make it."

"Oh."

There's no doubt in my mind that she knows I'm lying. I can't seem to say yes or no, though. "I'll see what I can do. I'd love to come but it depends on Masquerade, okay? I'll keep you posted."

"Okay. I really hope you can make it." She pauses for a second. "Is my brother there?"

"No. He had to work extra today. Ever since they made him head of security, he's had to pull some extra shifts."

This time her pause is so long I wonder if I said something wrong. "Maddy got a promotion?"

Dropping backward, I lean against the back of the seat. Shit. This isn't my business to be in the middle of. "Yeah, it wasn't that long ago, though. I'm sure he was going to tell you."

At that Laney laughs, though it's not a happy sound. "You don't have to cover for him. That's Maddox. He never talks to me about anything. Maybe one day."

"I'm sorry," I say, not quite sure why.

"Yeah," she whispers. "Me too."

It's 11:00 p.m. and I'm standing in front of Lunar, dressed for a night out. A million times I've told myself it's only because I want to go out and Lunar is the only cool place close by. I haven't decided if it's the truth or not.

Having a good time is definitely high on my list, though, because I didn't even bring my car. I want to be able to drink and have fun, so it's a cab kind of night.

As soon as I step inside, the colored lights flash in my face. The loud music pumps through me, filling me with the urge to dance. My first stop is the bar. Trevor is there like always with two other guys I don't recognize. There's a ton of people up here, so while I wait, I fight the urge to look around for Maddox. It doesn't matter where he is because I'm not here for him.

Trevor glances up and catches my eye. He smiles and I shake my head before he makes it down to me. "Beer?"

"I almost said Cosmo to throw you off, but I can't drink those things."

He opens a Corona, pops a lime in, and hands it to me. I hold it up to him before taking a drink.

He says something, but I can't hear him, so I lean forward. "What?"

"Your man. He's in the back."

A shiver rocks through me. *Get it together, Bee.* "What man? I don't have one of those."

"Hmm. I didn't think you were the type to play games." His mouth is so close to my ear I feel his breath.

Jerking away from him, I flip Trevor off. "You don't know me, so don't pretend you do." He grins, and I take a couple more drinks of the beer. "And I don't play games."

The rest of my beer goes down smoothly and quickly. He's already handing me another one when I set the bottle on the counter.

"So you're available?"

Smirking at him, I say, "I didn't say that either."

Trevor laughs and shakes his head. "That's what I thought."

Before he has the chance to say anything else, I walk away with the beer in hand. I'll pay for it later. I'm not playing his games tonight. My eyes immediately land on Maddox, leaning against the wall in the back. His arms are crossed, his face tight, and his eyes lasered in on me.

Little bitty explosions feel like they start to go off

in my stomach but I ignore them and move through the crowd, straight for him. The whole time I beg the fireworks to slow down but they don't.

Maddox doesn't move an inch when I step up in front of him. "He wants you."

More pops and cracks ignite. "Jealous?" I swallow a drink of the beer.

"Haven't we had this conversation before?" He's still not moving and this quiet whisper floats through my brain: *Touch me . . .*

"You didn't answer the question."

Then he grabs me and pulls me to him. His mouth comes down on mine and that same stupid little whisper says, *Finally . . .*

Maddox's tongue pushes into my mouth and I wrap one of my arms around his neck and bury it in his hair, trying not to spill the beer in my other hand. He turns and my back is suddenly against the wall, my body squeezed between the hard brick and Maddox's heat. His kiss gets deeper, his body moving against mine, and as stupid as it is, I wish we weren't here. Masquerade, my house, his house, anywhere but here.

My thoughts start pushing their way through and I gather enough strength to move my hand to Maddox's chest and shove him far enough away to say, "Don't kiss me because you're jealous."

"You'd rather I did it for other reasons? That's not what we're about, remember?"

The words are harsh, tiny lashes across my skin that I didn't expect. He's right but it hurts and it's not supposed to.

With my hand on his chest, I push him again as I try to move around him. Maddox curses, steps in front of me, and grabs my waist. "I kissed you because I want you. Because you're gorgeous and even though I shouldn't give a shit, I don't like seeing him touch you."

He's breathing hard, so hard I hear it even with the music blaring around us. It's then I realize I'm breathing just as hard. My chest heaving under my tight, long-sleeved shirt.

Maddox brushes his finger over my shoulders, left bare because of the cut of my top.

"I'm not saying . . . It doesn't mean . . ."

With my fingers, I touch his lips. "Shhh." I set my bottle down and then I kiss him this time. My tongue moves with his, *in out, in out*. Maddox holds me between the wall and his body again, his mouth taking over. Moving so expertly against mine. My body thrums with energy . . . need. I want him too. Want him the way I've never wanted anyone.

When his mouth trails down my neck, I say, "I'm not saying it means anything either. Let's not use any words. Let's . . ." *Have fun. Forget everything else. Pretend we're something we're not.* "Dance."

"I told you I don't dance." His mouth is still close to my skin.

"I'm asking you to make an exception."

Maddox pulls away and I expect him to keep going. Instead he hooks his finger in the loop of my pants and starts to back up, pulling me with him.

"Will you get in trouble? I know you're working."

His eyes haven't left mine since he started walking. "I don't give a shit what Trevor thinks and Tyler's not here."

Then I'm pulled tightly against him. His hands are on my waist; then they slide up and down my back as we move together. I rock my hips, sway with him as I wrap my arms around his neck. We're close, so very close our bodies touching and moving as in sync as they do when we've had sex.

It feels good and he feels good but still I grab on to what I said to him about not using words. Not defining anything. It can be like it was at his house the other night. We can laugh and dance and kiss and then walk away like last time and nothing will change. Neither of us want it to change, so it's okay. We're okay.

His hand goes up the back of my shirt, skin to skin, rubbing and caressing. I moan and move with him as one of his legs slides between mine.

"You can dance," I whisper.

"There are a lot of things I'm good at."

I don't doubt that. "Okay, then I'm surprised you *are* dancing." Sure, I asked him to but I don't know if I thought he would really do it.

His mouth drops to my ear. "There are a lot of things your body inspires me to do." Again, I wish we weren't in public.

And then he nips my lobe with his teeth and we keep dancing. When the song's over and it goes into the next, Maddox pulls away. "I need to get back to work."

"Yeah . . . yeah, okay." I step back, trying to catch my breath. Holy crap that was sexy as hell.

"You hanging around or are you out of here?"

"I figured I'd stay for a while."

His finger starts at my neck and slowly trails down the column and across my shoulder. "Good."

Just like that, he steps back, trying to hide who he is again for this crazy masquerade we keep maintaining, and goes back to his perch by the wall.

I'm in a fog, not even sure what happens for the rest of the night. Before I know it, Lunar is closing and Maddox is off work. We don't touch as we walk outside together.

"Your car here?" he asks, not really looking at me.

"No. Took a cab."

He nods toward his bike and I take the first step to walk there. Maddox is right behind me. The helmet slides on easily and then there's a weight on my shoulders and I realize it's his jacket.

Give it back. I don't. After slipping my arms through the holes, I wait for Maddox to put his helmet on and then get on the bike. Behind him, I throw my leg over and pull tight against him, right before it rumbles to life.

Wind makes us fly the whole way to my house. When we pull into my driveway, he kills the engine. We get off the bike and I take off the helmet and set it down.

"Thanks for the ride, Scratch."

"No problem." His voice is raspy and he needs a shave, both things extremely sexy on him.

"Your sister wants me to go to her birthday party. I wasn't sure. I told her—"

"You should go." He shrugs.

"Okay." I don't let myself dwell on how quickly that answer came out.

Maddox raises his hand and cups my cheek before his lips drop to mine softly . . . so very softly. He's never kissed me like this—with such slow deliberate strokes that turn me inside out.

He pulls about an inch away from me. "I want you so fucking bad."

"I want you too."

Maddox presses one more, soft kiss to my lips before he's grabbing his helmet and putting mine away on the bike. Want. We both want each other but we know it's not smart to act on it. I hate it but love it at the same time.

"I'll see you at Masquerade tomorrow, yeah?"

"Yeah . . ." My voice is husky.

Maddox climbs on his bike, puts his helmet on, and nods toward the door. Smiling, I shake my head at him, then go to the door and let myself in. After he pulls away, I realize two things: I still have his jacket, and it felt kind of good to have him want me safe inside before he left.

CHAPTER TWENTY

MADDOX

S itting on my bike in front of Bee's house, waiting to take her to Laney's, I try not to think about the fact that her legs will be wrapped around me in a couple minutes. I've done good all week not acting on the impulses I felt like at Lunar that night. Done well not imagining her hands on me and my mouth on her and remembering how she felt and wanting more of it.

Okay, so I thought about it but that's all. And then . . . there were times we just work at Masquerade or talk like when we started redoing my art portfolios. In those times it's like we *are*. Where I don't fight the attraction or succumb to it either. Times like sitting in my living room drawing pictures of each other where we're two people like any other. In those moments we're not keeping distance neither of us wants. We're not sleeping with each other and then pretending like it didn't happen.

It's easier than I thought. I've never really had those things with someone before and there's a part of me that really likes it. Maybe more than a part. She's cool, and I'm working toward tattooing. I try not to focus on it all because I don't want it to go away.

"Hey. I brought your jacket. Sorry I forgot it all week." Bee steps up to me.

"You can use it. I have another one." I shrug and she slips it on before putting on the helmet and climbing on behind me as though it's something she's done a million times.

The October air feels colder on the bike as we ride toward Laney's. November's right around the corner but we've had some pretty decent days.

It doesn't take long to get there. I wait for Bee to get off the bike before I do. "There's a little courtyard out back. Laney said they'd be out there." I grab my bag and start walking with Bee toward my sister's.

My sister's. With Bee. I reach into my pocket to pull out my cigarettes and light one.

"Haven't seen you do that in a while." I wait for more. Wait for her to tell me how disgusting it is or wonder what's up. She doesn't do any of it.

This little pang of regret hits me. This strange part of me that wishes she would have. What the hell is going on with me? I'm taking this girl to a party with my family. The only real family I have and I keep waiting to freak out or to get pissed at myself for doing it but none of it's coming.

"Do it when I feel like it." I shrug, then stop to put the smoke out. Laney will complain and I don't feel like fighting with my sister today.

We walk around the building to the courtyard. There are two picnic tables there. The graffiti I've seen on them before is covered by tablecloths. Balloons and streamers decorate light posts and trees. Orange and brown leaves are all over the ground, a stereo sits on one of the tables, and the grills are going.

Laney, Adrian, Colt, and Cheyenne are all standing there with their backs to us, and something makes me stop. Makes me take it in. These people love my sister. They did this for her, and maybe it's not much for a lot of people but it's huge for her, which makes it important to me.

Mom didn't do shit for our birthdays after Dad got locked up. We were lucky if she acknowledged us, and even though Laney never said it bothered her, I know it did. She's happy and wants everyone else to be happy.

My stomach sinks as I take it in, wishing I was the kind of brother who would have thought to do something like this for her.

"He loves her . . . Most of the time love doesn't make sense but it kind of does with them," Bee whispers, and I wonder how she knew what I was thinking. Adrian's standing behind Laney with his arms around her as they talk to their friends.

After everything that's happened, he really fucking loves her and that makes the guilt churn inside me more.

"She deserves it." Before I get the chance to walk toward them, Bee grabs my wrist.

"You're a good brother. She loves you."

Half of her sentence is true. "I know she does." We're facing each other. Standing here looking at her, I struggle to remember what I was thinking about. What had me upset because she's gorgeous and she's so fucking different from anyone I've ever known. I can't believe I'm lucky enough to have her. No . . . She's not really mine, though, is she?

Still, I'm glad she's here. I don't remember ever really being glad to be around someone like that.

"Maddy!" Laney yells. "Get your butt over here."

Bee's hand slips off my wrist and I realize I'd forgotten she was holding on to it. "I have a feeling we better go or she'll come drag us there," Bee says.

That makes me laugh. "You know her already."

When we get to the tables, I set my bag by the gifts. "Hey." I hug Laney and then nod at Adrian and Colt. "What's up?" I say to Cheyenne.

"How are things going at the shop?" Cheyenne asks. I've hardly spoken to her but I know she's my sister's best friend and she's trying to be cool to me because of it.

"Pretty good. I'm not tatting yet but—"

"He will be soon," Bee interrupts. "He's doing well. He's a natural. Kind of pisses me off how good he is for a scratch."

Everyone except me laughs. Her words were light and playful, yet for me they feel heavy. No, not heavy—deep, important because I want this. Want to be good at this one fucking thing because all I was ever good at was ball and that's not me anymore.

"Jealous?" I tease her back.

"Of what? I taught you everything you know."

This time I laugh too. Something makes me wrap my arm around her shoulders and pull her to me. "You wish. I'm a natural, remember?"

"You have a naturally big head." She tries to pull away. I hold her tighter.

Bee's pretending to pout, with her arms crossed and I really want to suck her bottom lip into my mouth. I've never seen her act like this before. I don't want it to stop either.

Turning, I put my mouth next to her ear. "My head isn't really a conversation I want to have around my sister." She tenses and then jerks away. Honestly I'm a little freaked out I just pissed her off but she bends and lets out the biggest laugh I've ever heard from her. The sound vibrates through me and I wish I could hit repeat to hear it over and over.

"What did we miss?" Cheyenne asks.

"I'm pretty sure you don't wanna know, Tiny Dancer," Colt tells her.

Bee's still laughing and my skin starts to prick, so I look over and Laney and Adrian are both watching . . . dissecting me. I wish I could put up a shield between us so they can't find whatever they're looking for. With Laney, I know what it is. Know that I'm not being like myself right now and she sees it. *Or am I being me? Who I used to be?*

That can't be it because Adrian's looking for something too. He's seeing something and he doesn't know shit about who I used to be.

"You're such an ass!" Bee's voice breaks through me and I turn away to look at her. Tears are on her face she was laughing so hard and damned if it doesn't feel good. Seeing her that happy and knowing it's because of something I said makes me want to find a way to do it again.

I'm sitting on the top of one of the picnic tables with my feet flat on the seat. We finished eating some barbecue not long ago. Colt and Adrian are standing by the stereo talking while Bee, Laney, and Cheyenne are under one of the trees. Laney says something to Bee and then she laughs before shaking her head.

Laney says something else and then Bee replies

and then Cheyenne adds something too. I don't know why I feel the urge to walk over to them. To find out what they're talking about to make her smile like that. She looks comfortable with them in a way she doesn't often look. Yeah she's strong and confident but she's also closed off. In the beginning I remember noticing how she seemed to turn her emotions off but they're shining bright as hell over there right now.

And they have been lately. At my house and at Lunar and hell even when we sit around Masquerade it's like she's showing me new pieces of her. Only she holds back. She hasn't mentioned the thing with her names again and never talks about her parents, but she's not locked in the invisible box she was in when I first met her. Her eyes and face are more honest.

The wind blows and a brown leaf breaks off the tree and falls on her. Bee picks it off her shoulder and looks at it. Studies it like it's something important.

Laney says something else to her and Bee smiles before replying, still holding that leaf in her hand. Cheyenne says something to Laney as Bee looks toward the ground, bends over, and picks up another leaf, this one orange. As stupid as it sounds, I feel like I'm interrupting a moment for her—seeing something that's important, though I don't get why it would be.

Then she holds them and launches into some other conversation with Cheyenne. It's the perfect way for Laney to escape as she turns around and heads my way.

I'd get up and walk away but I know she'd follow. I feel like an asshole again, because what kind of brother wouldn't want to talk to his own sister on her birthday?

"Hey. What are you doing over here all by yourself?" She sits next to me and drops her head to my shoulder. She does that a lot and has since we were kids.

"Nothing . . ." I feel like I should say more but I don't know what.

"She's great, Maddy. I really like her."

With my eyes, I find Bee talking to Cheyenne and holding those leaves in her hand. *I like her too.* "She's cool."

"She's strong too. It makes sense. You need a strong girl."

I shrug my shoulder and she lifts her head to look at me. "We're friends, little sister. Don't start doing that."

She rolls her eyes. "Fine. I'll stop being honest. Actually, after I say one more thing, I will. Today you've laughed in a way I haven't seen you do since we were younger. You're different and I think you know it too. You like her, Maddy, and she makes you happy. I hope you recognize that and don't blow it. You deserve to be happy."

This is where I'd usually walk away from her. Tell her she's crazy and an optimist and to stop seeing shit that isn't there. I don't do any of it. Instead it's Laney who stands up. She gets a few feet away when I say, "Hey." She stops to look at me. "Happy birthday."

Laney smiles at me. "Thank you. It is a happy birthday."

Shaking my head at her, I get off the table. "I have to piss. I'll be right back."

"Nice, Maddox." She shakes her head. I start toward their apartment and go to the restroom. As soon as I come out, I hear someone. When I step into the living room, Adrian's there with the gifts from the table. He had to have come up right behind me.

"The wind is cold, so we're coming inside." He sets them on the small coffee table without looking at me. Not that I blame him. I'm always a prick to him. Even went as far as to follow him out of the state when he found out our dad's the one who killed his son. Back then we thought Ashton was his nephew. I hit him and called him a pussy for walking away from Laney, not knowing it was his son he'd watched die.

"Thanks."

Adrian looks at me, obviously as surprised at my word as I am.

"And what's that for?"

"For taking care of her. For this party. It means a lot to her."

"I know. It doesn't take much to make her happy."

"But you did it. Doesn't matter if it's not much, you did it." *And I didn't.* Mom probably didn't call her even though I have a missed call from her on my cell right now. If I listen to the message, I know it will be bitching at me because she has to know I'm with Laney today.

There's more to say but I can't find the words. I'm saved anyway when the door opens and Bee, Cheyenne, and Colt come in, everyone carrying some of the stuff from outside.

"Hey, Little Ghost. Let's open your gifts." Adrian kisses Laney and she smiles at him. This big fucking smile that holds so much happiness.

Bee walks over and stands next to me against the wall while Adrian, Laney, Colt, and Cheyenne all sit on the couches and chair around the coffee table. We're leaning against the wall to the hallway behind the couch.

"Wanna go sit by her?" Bee asks, but I shake my head.

"Nah. I'm good here."

Laney opens her first present—gift certificates for a dance class from Cheyenne.

"I need someone to dance with me!" she tells my

sister, and I can see from the look in Laney's eyes that she wants to do it too.

"I got you something else because I felt all fucked up giving you dance lessons." Colt nods toward one of the gifts, which Laney opens next. It's an iTunes gift card to get more music for when she runs, he tells her.

"I'm giving her my present later." Adrian nudges her and everyone laughs. I suddenly want to kick his ass again. That's not the stuff a guy wants to hear about his little sister, even though I know he's giving us shit. He probably got her something that is perfect for her because that's how he is with her. It's fucking crazy to see but I'm glad she has it.

"In my bag." I nod toward it and immediately wish I had decided to give her my gift later too. It's not something I want all these people to see but I can't be a dick and say anything now.

Bee scoots closer to me and I glance down at her, wondering how she knew to do that, even though she's not looking at me.

Laney grabs my bag and opens it. My body is begging me to walk out of the room as my pulse kicks up. With one of my hands, I dig my nails into my arm as she pulls out the square gift.

Slowly, like it's a fucking treasure or something, Laney starts pulling the wrapping paper off. The second it's open, she freezes, her eyes not leaving what's in front of her.

My muscles tighten and I feel eyes on me that aren't there. Adrian's looking over her shoulder at the picture in the frame.

Laney still doesn't look up, so Adrian says, "It's a drawing. It's a beach with a sand castle and two kids next to it. Fuck, this is really good. Did you do this?" He looks at me. Turing from him, I nod.

"It was my favorite day with all of us together," Laney's soft voice breaks through the room. "We were on vacation. Dad had been gone off and on for a while and we finally got to spent time together. Maddy was upset. He didn't want to go and I didn't know why."

Because it was a lie. I knew it was a fucking lie and Dad was a cheat and a gambler.

"I was bugging him like I always did. I wanted to have fun and I didn't get why he was so angry. When we got to the beach, he tried to go off by himself. I wouldn't let him. I begged him to teach me how to make a sand castle. He said no at first, but then I cried and so he did it."

Finally she looks up at me and her eyes are wet with tears. "You always tried to make me happy."

Because I was lying to the family. Because I was selfish and kept my mouth shut so I could have money for college to play ball.

When I don't reply, Adrian asks, "What happened next?"

He's like that, I've noticed. He wants words, talking in a way I've never fucking seen.

"We built three of them. The first one fell when we were half done and the second got messed up with the water. I told Maddox it was okay and he said no, that we'd make another one. And so we did and it was incredible. Perfect and then we lay next to it like we could somehow protect it. Later, Dad came over and talked to me about it. Maddy left and I told my dad how we made three of them because Maddox wanted me to have the perfect sand castle and Dad said he'd make another perfect one with me too. A few minutes later, Mom tripped on it and it got wrecked."

Laney shakes her head. "Which obviously she screwed up on purpose because she was angry that Dad and Maddox were paying attention to me. I cried again and then Mom and Dad walked away and got into an argument. Maddox came back over and said we'd make another one but then we had to leave. We never went back to the beach after that."

It wasn't long after that everything went to shit. Dad got drunk and killed Adrian's son.

I shrug. "Thought I'd keep my promise. No one can fuck this one up." At that I turn for the door, really needing some space for a minute. "I need a smoke. I'll be right back."

Behind me, I slam the door, wanting nothing more than to get the hell out of here.

CHAPTER TWENTY-ONE

BEE

Laney stands as though she's going to go after Maddox. Adrian grabs her hand, while at the same time I ask, "Can I go?" I'm not sure what makes me think I will be any good talking with him, but there's this pull coming from deep within me, drawing me his way.

"Yeah . . . of course." She sits back down and I'm already halfway to the door, not quite sure when I even started moving.

Behind me, I close it softly and walk down the stairs in search of Maddox. There's a strange tingle in my belly. It's not quite nerves, though definitely not excitement either. Whatever it is, I concentrate on the fact that I called off Maddox's sister—the only person he really cares about—so I could go and talk to him myself.

The first place I can think to look is by his bike. Maddox is sitting on the curb, cigarette in hand. Even from behind, I can see how rigid and tense his body is. What he did back there was huge for him and honestly I'm surprised he did it.

"You know I'd have to kick your ass if you tried to leave without me, right?" Stepping next to him, I hope light is the best way to play this.

He doesn't reply.

I walk past Maddox to his bike and throw my leg over it, grip the handles that feel welcome in my hands. "Did you decide I can drive it yet?"

He takes another drag of his cigarette but doesn't reply.

"It's been a while since I've had a good ride—I mean drive."

At that he looks up at me through his dark lashes and half his mouth rises in a smile.

"Hasn't been *that* long."

"Of course you speak when I start in with the sexual innuendoes."

Maddox puts his cigarette out on the concrete, reaches into his pocket, pulls out a mint, and pops it into his mouth. "What are you doing out here, Bee?"

Still sitting on the bike, I let go of the handles so I'm straight. "I would have thought that was pretty obvious." I pause for a few seconds, then add, "The drawing was incredible, Scratch."

He rubs a hand across the dark brown stubble on his face, then smiles cockily. "I know."

An unwelcome warmth spreads through me. Damn he's gorgeous. "Then why are we out here?"

"You know why."

Yeah, yeah, I do. Because he's like me. It's hard to open yourself up for people. I wonder if he also fears that people who are important to him won't like what they see. "You knew it would be hard going into it. Before you gave it to her—hell, when you drew it— but you did it anyway. That's something." Something I wouldn't do. All Maddox has is Laney and he tries to be there for her. I have a whole family of people who love me and I run away from them. Guilt ignites a wildfire that scorches through me.

"Yeah?" he asks.

"Yeah." He's staring at me with those deep gray eyes of his. My skin savors the feel of them on me but my brain makes me turn away. It's too much, especially knowing I like his gaze there.

"You looked like you were getting along well with them—Laney and Cheyenne."

His change of subject is surprising and welcoming at the same time. "She's cool. I like her. I didn't go to school when I was younger, so I didn't really hang out with a lot of girls in high school. I lived in a wealthy area and most of the girls weren't too into hanging out with the chick who had her nose pierced and didn't date guys but had sex."

Two things spar for my attention at once. First, I told him something about myself. The words had come out without a thought. The second is that for the first time, I feel a little embarrassed about my past. It's not that I've slept with a ton of guys. But I've never been an angel either. It's not something that has ever bothered me but I don't want Maddox to think I sleep around. *Why does it matter? There's nothing wrong with safely enjoying my sexuality.*

It's not like we didn't meet trying to have a one-night stand anyway. Whatever he thinks about me is probably already engraved into his mind.

"Not that there were a lot of men—"

"Holy shit." Maddox pushes to his feet.

"What?"

Within a couple strides, he's reached me. His right hand comes toward me and cups my face, his thumb brushing over my cheek.

"You're blushing. I thought you were too bad-ass to blush."

I smile. "I know lots of good tricks."

"Don't do that."

Maddox hasn't lowered his hand, so I pull back. "Do what?"

"Feel like you have to make excuses. It's like you said the first night, there's nothing wrong with a woman knowing what she wants. And I can tell you're not the type of person to sleep with everyone you meet."

Person. I love that he said person and not woman.

"I worry about you, Leila, I mean, Bee. I don't

*want you to get hurt or wake up one day and regret
where you are. You're such a beautiful, smart young
woman. You could have anything. Your sister has
someone she'd like to introduce you to. We could go
shopping and get your hair done. I think you'd be so
happy if you met a nice boy . . ."*

If I could do anything, what was wrong with picking
to be a tattoo artist? Did my happiness revolve around
meeting a nice guy? Being like everyone else in my
family? Not that there's anything wrong with that,
except that it's not me.

But then Mom had hugged me. Hugged me and
told me she loved me. And it only made me question
love more. How can you love someone you want to
change? I know she wishes I was that girl who wants
nothing more than to meet a nice guy. The girl she
probably thinks I would be if she'd raised me.

"Where'd you go?" Maddox's voice breaks through
my thoughts. He has his finger tilting my chin up so
I'm looking at him.

He's so close that I can see every little detail about
him, like the small dimple below his lip that doesn't
show often. I want to rub my cheek against the stubble
on his face and feel his lips as they possess mine.
"Nowhere . . ." whispers past my lips.

"My bike's too big for you to handle but you look
sexy as hell on it." Maddox leans closer. "Mmm, I
wish I could see your ink."

He might not be a nice boy and I am definitely not the perfect, nice girl but I've never wanted him with the burning passion engulfing me right now. Before I have the chance to kiss him, Maddox's lips come down on mine. Both his hands are cupping my face as I straddle his bike and he kisses the hell out of me. His tongue pushes past my lips, deep inside my mouth like he's starving for me the same way I'm suddenly starving for him. I've never wanted—needed—anyone the way need surges through me right now but he feels too good and tastes too good for me to worry about it.

I'm wishing he was on this bike with me. That we were somewhere else so we could do so much more and he could cure the ache inside me.

Suddenly, he's pulling away and I'm fighting not to pull him back to me. He doesn't go far, pushing a piece of hair behind my ear, his mouth only inches from mine.

"We keep ending up this way." His hand slides away and I wish he'd put it on me again.

"I know."

"I've never . . ." He shakes his head. "I don't know what the fuck to think about it."

At that I laugh. *Me either*. "Your sister's probably wondering where we are."

Maddox closes his eyes for a second as though he's trying to gather himself before he steps back. "Let's go. I don't trust you alone with my bike." When he smiles, I see the dimple again. Then he holds out his hand to help me off the motorcycle, and I let him.

When we go back inside, Laney gives Maddox a hug and then we all move into the kitchen where I assume we're about to do the cake. I'm surprised when Adrian pulls out one cupcake with a candle in it. After lighting it, we all sing "Happy Birthday" and then Adrian opens the fridge and pulls out caramel apples for everyone.

Laney looks at him like he had just handed her the world, and then he leans forward and whispers to her, "Such a sweet Little Ghost."

Maddox and I stand back from the rest of the group as they talk and laugh with each other. He should be there with them, laughing and talking, but I know he never would be. If I wasn't here right now, he'd stand back from the group alone.

The urge to reach for him teases me. I don't let myself follow through. "What's with the apples?"

Maddox shrugs. "Hell if I know. It's not the first time he's given her one."

My eyes are drawn to them as they stand close. Laney right next to Adrian and Cheyenne the same way with Colt. It's like they complete each other. They give each other something that no one else in the world can. I've seen that in Mom and Dad, even in Rex and Melody, but with them . . . it almost feels like seeing it with someone like me.

A strange sort of longing comes out of hiding inside me and I wish it would go away. That's not me. I don't want things like this. Hell, Maddox and I can hardly talk to each other about anything important. He doesn't know much about me at all.

But he knows me . . . somehow he knows me.

And I like that he does.

"Are you ready to go?" Maddox has leaned over, his mouth next to my ear.

After looking at the group one more time, I tell him, "Yeah . . . I think so."

"Laney, we're going to head out." Maddox nods toward the door.

"Good seein' ya again, man." Colt nods at Maddox as Cheyenne comes toward me.

My body tenses when she pulls me into a hug. "I think I want another tattoo!"

At that I laugh and then pull back. "Name the time."

I'm not sure if Adrian and Maddox say anything to each other because when I look, Laney is hugging Scratch. Her face is angled toward the other side of him and I can tell she's saying something in his ear. She's so relaxed but he looks slightly uncomfortable. Laney pulls back and he ruffles her hair and says, "I know."

It's so not my business; still, I want to know what she said. Or maybe it's that I want to know what he heard. Everything about Maddox makes me curious.

"I'm so glad you could come." Laney turns to me next and pulls me into a hug as well. It's so crazy being around these girls. I'm not used to being around women I feel comfortable with—women I feel like I can be myself around—and it gives me this strange sort of happiness I didn't know I missed.

The whole way home I can't stop thinking about it. I hardly register my arms and legs around Maddox as he drives his motorcycle through town. Today was a good day. I had fun and felt okay being me . . . like I had when I lived with Melody and Rex? They loved me for me. Mom and Dad love me even though they wish I were someone else. I can't keep putting my parents down and not Rex and Melody, though. It's not like they are perfect either. They stole me.

Little flashes of fear flicker through me again. The feeling of being grabbed . . . of being confused. They stole me and told me my parents were dead. And it hurt. I never let myself remember that I'd been sad at first. How could they hurt me if they loved me? Or did that mean they loved me more? Because they risked it all for me and wanted me so badly.

The world would be easier without so many questions of what love is and how to do it properly. I see it when Laney and Maddox look at each other or between Adrian and Laney and Colt and Cheyenne. I've seen it with my parents looking at me or Rex and Melody looking at me and I've felt it too. And still I don't understand it. Don't get how people can love someone and want them to be someone different or love them and hurt them.

Before I know it, we're pulling into my driveway and Maddox is turning off his motorcycle. With a kick, I pull my leg over the bike and pull the helmet from my head. "Tell me about your sister and Adrian." I don't know why I need to know but there's suddenly this thirst that I can't quench. There has to be a story there. Maybe if I know it, it'll help me understand.

One, two, three, four, five. Maddox sits on the bike, not looking at me. Then he pulls the helmet from his head and I know I struck a chord—that the way his sister and Adrian got together somehow ties to him too. I see the ache in him that he tries so hard to bury. "Shit. I'm sorry. It's not my business. You don't have to tell me anything."

Slowly, he turns his head, looks at me. He does that thing again where he closes his eyes for a second before taking a deep breath and opening them.

"I shouldn't have asked," I say, trying to make up for inadvertently pushing him.

"My dad killed Adrian's son." He turns, his jaw tight, eyes trained in front of him instead of on me.

Words escape me. Fighting, I try to find them in

the maze of my mind but I can't. His father killed Adrian's son. And he's with her. He loves her. And Maddox told me.

"Maddox . . . shit. I'm sorry."

"Why?" He looks at me. "You didn't do it. You didn't get fucked up and get your girlfriend to go down on you while you were taking a corner too fast." His hands tighten into fists. "He was two years old and my father ran him down in front of Adrian. That's what started the shit with my mom."

"How?" I'm shaking my head. We shouldn't be doing this in the middle of my driveway. We maybe shouldn't be doing it at all. Holy crap. His father killed Adrian's little boy.

"Laney thought she could make it better. She wanted to find Adrian, tell him and apologize, like that would somehow fix all our lives. She thought Ash was Adrian's nephew. But instead of telling him the truth, she fell for him. When she told him, she found out it was his son."

Finally . . . *finally* he looks at me. "As you can imagine, he lost it. He found his way back to her, though. He loves her enough that he would do anything for her regardless of what we took from him."

How do you love like that?

"What do you mean, 'we'? You didn't take anything from him. Just like you said, I wasn't in that car, you weren't either."

"I should go." Maddox's hand comes up to put the helmet back on his head, but I grab it. I don't know what's come over me but I need him here. Can't let him leave.

Not after the truth he gave me.

"Don't."

I look at him. Really look at him. Yes, I've always thought he was gorgeous but that's not all that's there. I know that only now I'm seeing it. Seeing the pain inside him as though he's wearing it for me. I don't know where it all comes from or why he feels any responsibility for his father, but it's there.

And my heart breaks for him.

"Why? Why should I stay, Bee? So we can keep fucking around? So we can draw pictures again or sleep in the same bed? Why do we keep playing these games?"

He's right. We are playing games but I don't know how to stop them. I also don't know how to let him go and I don't think I want to. I want to give him something. Want him close to me in a way I've never wanted anyone close to me before. If I could, I'd cure that ache inside him. I don't know how to tell him that. Don't know how to show him or even what the hell it all means.

"I don't know," I admit, at a loss for words.

His eyes bore into me. "Tell me about your parents, Bee. You wanna talk all of a sudden, tell me that. Is that why you want me to come inside?" His words are angry lashes across my skin.

I think about his sister and her friends. How much they care about each other and how they made me feel like I fit. How I feel like that with him, too, and Maddox has given me both those things.

How he came to me and let me pierce him because he knew that was all he had to offer. It was his way to say he kind of trusted me and I want him to know the same thing about me. That I trust him. *I'm falling for him* . . . Or maybe I'm already there.

When I open my mouth, those aren't the words that come out. "No, those aren't the reasons I want you to come in. I want you to mark me."

His eyes fill with fire and I know he understands exactly what I mean.

CHAPTER TWENTY-TWO

MADDOX

I want you to mark me.

I'm cemented in place. My feet nailed to the ground and my eyes glued to her. There is no doubt in my mind what she's saying. She wants me to give her ink—to put something into her skin and it's the biggest fucking honor to even have her say it but also scares the hell out of me. This is huge. This is *Bee* and the last thing I want is to screw something up that's this big.

She straight up told me she hasn't let anyone except the Professor give her ink but she's asking for it from me—someone who's never put needle to flesh before.

There's no fucking way I will walk away from this either. I want my mark on her. Want her to have a piece of me with her for the rest of her life.

"Here?" Cocking my head, I nod toward her house.

"I have everything we need."

As if my body has a mind of its own, I reach for her. Wrap an arm around her shoulder and pull her close. I like having her near, like the way she feels and how she makes me feel. My body molds to hers as though we're supposed to fit together.

We walk to her house and she unlocks the door. Bee steps in first and hits a light. Words are trapped in my throat as I look around her house. It's . . . perfect. Her furniture is white and there are dried flowers on the entertainment center and paintings on the walls that you can tell cost more than all the secondhand shit in my house put together. It's not her.

"Mom did it for me as a surprise." She looks at me. "Surprise! It's a very grown-up house, I'm told. My sister helped."

There's so much history behind her words that I hear it coating them—dripping off but still leaving residue behind.

Bee doesn't give me time to ask, though. Honestly, I'm not sure if I would. My hands itch too much to tattoo her to think of anything else.

"Drink?" she asks.

"Water. Where can I leave my jacket? I don't want to fuck anything up."

Her back is to me as she walks into the kitchen. "Put it anywhere, Maddox."

A couple seconds later she comes out with two bottles of water. Instead of moving toward the living room, she heads to a hallway and I go right behind her. Four closed doors line the hall, two on each side. Bee picks the last one on the right. When she turns on the light, I see the room is full of tattoo supplies but it looks like an art room too. There's a desk with a lamp and a light board for drawing. Pencils are in a cup.

In the corner there's a chair. Not a tattoo chair but one that will definitely serve the purpose. A cabinet is in the other corner, with no doors on the front and stocked full of brand-new supplies.

Bee grabs something from against the wall and I see it's a foldout table. After I help her set it up, she nods toward the table. "You going to start drawing?"

Her words send electricity shooting through me. She could easily draw whatever she wants, exactly how she wants it. Instead she's asking me.

Trust. She fucking trusts me.

"What do you want?" My mouth feels dry, so I open the bottle and take a drink. Fuck, this girl does something to me. She ties me in knots and makes me feel free at the same time.

"Leaves, on my shoulder blade." Her eyes dart to the desk and back at me. "Everything you need to get started is right there. I'll be right back. I'm going to change."

And then she's gone and I'm at the desk. After taking off my jacket, I toss it in the corner. Leaves. What the hell? A little flash of memory hits me. Seeing the leaf fall on her shoulder. Watching her pick it up, then another one.

I think of the stars going down her side and the story she told me about camping. Her Gemini, the mask like someone would wear at a masquerade on the back of her neck and I know. I fucking know what she does. Those things are important to her and the leaves from today are too.

This burst of pride like I haven't felt in so long fills me. I brought her today and it was important to her. She trusts me to put this piece of her life into her skin forever.

I'm not sure anything has ever been so special to me.

My hands actually shake a little as I sit at the desk. As soon as I put the pencil to paper, it's like something takes me over. This need and desire to create something incredible for her possesses me and it starts to flow: one leaf on top, another floating below it, and a third under that. The second two are both bent whichever way the wind chooses to fold them. With the side of the pencil I shade some curving lines for the wind. I draw little spidery lines in each leaf, smearing some of the lines. What happens next is automatic. In each of the leaves is a letter, spelling her name.

Not Leila. Not Coral. Even if she goes back to either of those names, she needs to know she gets to decide who she is. And she chose Bee.

By the time I finish, I know it's been at least

forty-five minutes. Bee isn't back yet but then I didn't expect her to be. She's waiting for me. I don't let myself overthink how I know that.

Sticking my head out the door, I call, "We're good."

It's not five seconds later she's coming out of the room across the hall wearing short-shorts and a tank top with a thin strap. Her hair is up and all I can think about is how much I want to taste her neck. To put my hands through her hair and kiss the skin I'm about to mark to show it some sweetness before the pain.

"What'cha got for me, Scratch?" She walks in the room and I follow. Bee heads straight over to the desk, her back to me as she studies the drawing. My heart kicks up as I crack my knuckles.

"If you want something else—"

"It's perfect." She turns. "It's beautiful."

I think about that sunflower on the back of her calf, I know her stars, her Gemini, the mask, and her leaves but I don't know that.

"Are you sure you want me to do this?" It fucking kills me to ask but I have to. I can do it. I'll make it fucking beautiful but I need her to be sure.

"I wouldn't let anyone else."

Christ I want to kiss her so bad. I know if I do, we won't stop. And I want to do this tattoo for her. "This is going to get in the way." I run my finger down the strap on her tank top.

She looks up at me, all strength and honesty. "Then take it off."

I slide my hands down—down her shoulders and her arms to her waist. Bee shivers when I reach my destination but I start going back up, this time with the bottom of her shirt in my grasp. She raises her arms and I pull the fabric off her before tossing it to the floor.

I swear it's like my fucking insides are shaking. My tongue traces my lips and I wish I was licking hers instead. Or a tattoo, or each peak of her perfect breasts as she stands in front of me naked from the waist up.

"You're fucking killing me here."

She grins. "Then we better get started. I'd hate for something to get in the way of getting my ink."

My hand slides around her side. "Just worrying about yourself, huh?"

"It's a great tattoo."

Her compliment only reignites the wildfire burning me up. "You'll be the perfect canvas."

She gasps, my words shocking her the same way they do me. She recovers quickly. "There's antibacterial soap in the bathroom down the hall. Wash up. I'll get everything set up."

Before I lose the strength to do it, I head out of the room. It doesn't take me long to wash my hands and she's almost finished with the setup when I get back into the room. The supplies, towels, gun, and ink are all laid out on the table. After grabbing the saran wrap, I put some Vaseline on it.

"Sit down." My voice comes out scratchy.

Bee does as I say, leaning forward so her back is to me, her breasts up against the back of the chair. Laying the paper against the smooth skin of her shoulder blade, I watch as the hairs on the back of her neck move with my breath.

"Do you have a mirror so I can make sure you like the placement?"

"It's perfect." She doesn't even turn around.

"Bee—"

"I know what I'm doing, Maddox. I can feel where it is. I saw the drawing. We're good, okay?"

Without a reply, I slip the gloves on and find the right speed on the machine. Goose bumps travel down her arms when I rub a light layer of Vaseline on her shoulder. All inked up and ready, with no hesitation, I touch the needle to her skin. Bee doesn't flinch— doesn't move at all as I move down the first line.

Neither of us talk for the longest time. No words are needed right now as I make something that's important to her, a piece of her forever.

I do the first leaf and then move to the second. Time passes but I don't know how much. It doesn't matter. All that does is the art. The whole time I don't let myself wonder if I'm ready for this. She thinks I am, and I trust her. Christ, I fucking do.

I've never felt as connected to another person as I do in this moment with her.

And I know it wouldn't be the same with anyone else.

"You good?" I ask her before I start the third leaf. Each of the lines is clean and how they're supposed to be. The skin of her shoulder is red and puffy but it doesn't take away from the beauty of the ink.

"You have a steady hand. I can tell."

"Thanks, but I asked how you are." I lift the needle from her shoulder and she turns to look at me.

"Rock steady up here."

Fuck she gets to me. I wonder if there's anyone like her in the world but know there's not.

Once I'm working on the third leaf, I say, "You have stars because of that night on your birthday. The Gemini because you feel like two people. Your mask because you hide . . . I saw you." After wiping more Vaseline on her skin, I continue, knowing this is the one place where she can't pull away. It's fucking crazy. I want to talk to her, want her to talk to me, push her to open up. "I saw you with the leaves at the party, Bee, and now you want them in your skin. Your tattoos are about what's important to you, aren't they?"

She's silent for what feels like forever. Anger at myself sneaks in, singeing my edges when I'm not sure they have a right to. We said from the beginning what this was about and telling each other about our past wasn't included.

Neither was this . . .

But fuck . . . I want to know, need to know more about her. "If you don't want to tell me, you can say it."

"I always want to be able to take the good things with me. I want a reminder because you never know when everything will change. When you won't be able to tell what's good and bad or right and wrong, so I make sure the good is with me."

It's a struggle not to pull the tattoo gun from her but I keep going, don't break the contact so she can't pull away and so I can't either. She wants to keep the good with her. I fight through my angry memories and try to think of the good. I blocked it out, not wanting to hold on to it because I didn't know which parts of it were real or not.

"That's good. There's strength in making sure you remember, Bee."

She lets out a deep breath. "You think?"

It takes me a minute to reply. I'm working on the hidden *e* in her last leaf, wishing I could wipe away the angry red skin so it will be perfect the first time she sees it. "Yeah . . . you're kind of incredible. Has anyone told you that?" Closing down my thoughts, I focus on the muscle in my chest for the first time in forever.

"No." Her voice is soft . . . sweet in a way I've never heard it. "It scares me that you did, only not as much as it should. That freaks me out even more."

"It's not like you're the only one who's nervous here." Because I'm falling for her. Really fucking falling for her. I think I've known it for a while but it hasn't been as real as it is right now.

"This is different, isn't it?" She drops her head and I really wish I could see her face. She's voicing what I've been feeling.

"You know the answer to that." It's all I can think of to say and I know she'll appreciate me for it. Because that's how we work. We don't need words.

So we don't use them. She stays bent forward as I continue to tattoo her. Soon I'm changing the tip so I can do the shading of the wind. Bee hardly moves, just trusts me with her body.

When I finally finish, I have no idea how late it is. After turning the gun off, I set it to the table. "Done." Obviously, but she doesn't call me on it. It feels wrong to completely study it before she gets the chance, so I pull my eyes away and stand. "Let's go."

Grabbing her wrist, I help her stand. When she turns, I remember she's half naked, and for the second time in the past few seconds, I have to rip my eyes away from her.

Bee lets me lead her to the bathroom. I stand against the wall as she leans forward, her back toward the mirror, neck turned so she can peek over her shoulder.

It's the most incredible fucking sight I've ever seen. Her breasts, her flat stomach with the piercing. Those stars that go up her side, and then my mark in the middle of the puffy skin on her shoulder.

Knots form in my stomach as I watch her, as I wait for her. This is her memory, this is the way she wants to take this day with her wherever she goes and it'd kill me if I fucked that up.

Our eyes meet in the mirror and then she turns her head to face me. "It's even more amazing than I thought it would be . . . Maddox . . . you're incredible. Do you know that?"

It's so close to what I said to her not long before. Words are trapped in my throat, clogged in my brain as I try to figure out how to reply to her. Instead, I do the only thing I can think of—try to take care of her.

She doesn't say a word as I slip out of the bathroom. I grab the saran wrap and find some medical tape in the cabinet. Bee is right where she was when I left her, only again she's looking at the tattoo.

"Let me wrap it for you."

She nods. The plastic wrap sticks to her tattoo because of the Vaseline. I tape it down to be safe. It's a short distance to bend forward and press my lips to the back of her neck, where it meets her shoulder.

This time, it's Bee who turns to face me, looking up at me with a look in her eyes I've never seen from her.

This frenzied need explodes inside me. Nothing can keep me from tasting her. My lips cover hers, soft, pleading for her to let me have her. To give herself to me the way I want to give myself to her.

Her mouth opens and I slip my tongue inside. My hands squeeze each side of her waist. It fucking kills me not to press her against the wall but I don't want to hurt her tattoo.

Her hand goes between us and I'm scared she's going to push me away but instead her hand goes down . . . down until she cups my erection. "Fuck," I hiss, pulling away from her. "I want you, baby. Fuck the rules. Let me have you."

Bee steps back and it's like a fist slamming into my gut. I need her beneath me. Need her bare skin under my hands and mouth. I don't think I can take it if she says no.

"Bee—"

Her voice cuts off my plea. "If you want me, take me."

CHAPTER TWENTY-THREE

BEE

Maddox doesn't give me time to contemplate my words when his mouth swiftly comes down on mine. It's stronger, fiercer, and more intense than any kiss we've ever shared when his tongue passes between my lips and into my mouth. Even though I know it's only been seconds, it feels like years that I've been waiting for him, and I immediately melt into the kiss.

My hands touch his face, feel the rough stubble. It might be one of the best feelings in the world. I keep going, continuing to touch him before tangling my hands in his hair. He palms my ass and then lifts as I wrap my legs around his waist.

"Christ I've wanted to do this again for so long." His lips are moving across my neck and . . . down, as he starts to head out of the bathroom.

"Me too." I lean back, hating the honesty that flows out of me so easily. Confused as to why I *do* want him so much. Or maybe not confused but scared. I don't want to fall in love. It makes people do stupid things.

"Which door?" Maddox's gravelly voice sounds almost like a growl.

"What if I don't tell you?"

His grip on me tightens. "Then I'll use the wall."

He backs me up until my back is only an inch from the hallway but stops. Without him saying a word, I know exactly why. My heart turns to putty. I want to harden it, put in cement, but somehow he won't let me. Even something as simple as him worrying about my tattoo makes me feel soft in a way I'm not sure I ever have.

In a way that I should?

No. I shove those thoughts out of my head. I want to enjoy this too much without thoughts of trying to be someone I'm not.

"The door across from where you tatted me."

Maddox carries me inside, his mouth back on mine again. I dig my heels into him, trying . . . needing . . . to pull him as close to me as I can. He's busting down those walls inside of me, getting closer and closer whether I want him to or not.

Maddox turns before sitting on my bed. I'm straddling his lap, the hard length of his erection nuzzled right where I want him to be.

"Are we doing this?" he asks. The question surprises me. Makes me wonder if I should want to run.

"Don't ask. Just do it."

"No." He shakes his head. "Not this time. I want you to tell me, no rules. Just us."

Desire and . . . love? Need? I don't know what it is but they lure the words from my mouth. "No rules. Just us. We're totally doing this."

His fingers slide across my belly as I stand up. My hands tremble as I push my shorts down.

His eyes skate up and down my body like a gentle caress. I've never been embarrassed of my body before. I'm not now. Still a small urge to cover myself sneaks up on me. It's more personal being naked around Maddox than it's ever been with anyone else. Like he sees more of me than I show. Before I have the chance to think about it, his voice breaks through my nerves. "Jesus Christ, you are so fucking beautiful."

Maddox leans forward, his tongue slipping out of his mouth, flicking the piercing in my belly button. I have the urge to do the same thing to the one in his nipple but know it has to be tender still.

"Your turn." I run my hand through his hair and he looks up at me through his dark eyelashes. Those gray eyes seeking . . . searching. I'm not sure what for.

And then he grabs the bottom of his T-shirt and pulls it over his head. It falls to the floor before he's pushing off my pale yellow bed and going for the buttons on his pants. I can't stop myself from leaning forward. From letting my mouth taste and tease his bare chest, as close to the piercing as I can.

Maddox hisses. I somehow know it's not in pain. When his pants are gone, I look down to enjoy the view, but then he's falling to the bed and pulling me on top of him. This strange happiness bubbles up from my stomach as a laugh tumbles out of my mouth. It's so foreign-sounding that it makes me want to laugh harder.

"What are you laughing at, baby?"

There's a playfulness in his voice that I'm not used to hearing from him.

"Just realizing that since you gave me a tat on my back, I get to be on top." The words weren't planned but they make his gaze turn dark as his grip on my ass tightens.

"You can be on top of me any time you want to."

Maddox pulls my hair tie out, and my blond waves fall over my shoulder before he lies down. I go with him, kissing him, because I need him on my tongue.

He palms one of my breasts, playing with my nipple, and even though we just started, I feel the beginning of my orgasm already burning through me.

"I want you," I tell him.

"Fuck, I love that about you. Love that you're not afraid to say what you want."

My body freezes at the word. I know Maddox isn't

saying he loves me. It still makes a cold shiver run
through me.

"Don't. Don't fucking do that, Bee. You said you
want me, so take me."

That's what I need to hear. Leaning forward, I reach
for the drawer beside my bed to grab a condom. When
I do, Maddox's warm, wet mouth covers one of my
nipples. I can't help but cry out, the need in me
starting to blaze again.

I open the wrapper before scooting far enough off
of him that I can roll the condom down. He doesn't
stop touching me the whole time, and then I'm
straddling him again. I lean forward and can't help
but look down at him. At the stubble on his jaw and
the intense stare in his eyes. He's lying there, waiting,
looking up at me as though it's the first time he's
seen me.

My hair down, brushing his chest, Maddox reaches
up and cups my cheek. "If you don't do this, I'm
going to."

My smile comes out of nowhere.

And then I move, slowly, so, so slowly, as I make
us one. He's inside me and we're moving together
and that satisfied burn starts building higher and
higher again.

His hands are on my hips as I move. He feels so
good and I feel so good that I wish I could hold on
to this feeling forever. When his grip on me tightens,

I know he's getting close. Maddox's hands slide up my body, cup my breasts, and then he rolls each of my nipples between his fingers. That's all I need to push me over the edge. I'm careening down, but it's such a wonderful fall that I want it to keep going. It takes me over as my whole body shudders and then he's pushing deeper and my tremble is transferring to him as he finds the bliss I just held.

Look at him. Look at him, Bee. Yet I can't make my eyes find his. This didn't feel like just sex and I'm not sure how to deal with that.

"I'll be right back." Maddox kisses me, one quick, tender peck to the lips and my eyes start to mist. It's the kiss of a lover. Of people familiar and comfortable with each other in a way I've never let myself be with anyone.

He doesn't seem to notice as he disappears from the room. Fear starts seeping through all the hiding places inside me. I've fallen for him. He means something to me, more than I want to admit. What if I hurt him? What if he hurts me? What if I can't be what he needs?

"Hey." Maddox stands in my doorway, naked and so, so beautiful. "Don't. Wherever you're going in that beautiful mind of yours . . . don't."

Without another word he turns off the light. I hear his footsteps on the carpet and then he's grabbing my comforter and pulling it. When I scoot over, he lies down next to me before lifting the blanket on top of us.

"You shouldn't be on your back." Maddox pulls me over, so I'm half on him, my shoulder facing up and away from the mattress.

My body is stiff as we lie silently in the darkness. After what feels like a million years, he whispers, "It's not easy for me either. Let's not overthink it, yeah?" Like he's known for doing, he goes silent after that.

Some of my tension evaporates with his words. Thinking of the leaves on my back and the fact that they're his mark, I somehow relax. Wrapping my leg over the top of him, I nuzzle into his chest and go to sleep.

I'm not sure what wakes me later. It's as though my eyes open and I'm awake. Maddox is holding on to me, his breath in my hair and his chest rising and falling against my cheek.

The ghost of a memory starts flittering its way through my head and I realize what woke me up. I'd been dreaming about Rex and Melody.

"Where's my mommy?"

"She's gone. We're going to take care of you now. She wanted you to be with us."

Waves and waves of tears had fallen from my eyes. I cried. Cried all night. Cried for days. How could I not have remembered that? How could I not have known I missed my parents? I'd suppressed all that terror.

Not wanting to wake Maddox, I push out of bed as quietly as I can. After grabbing my shirt, I slip it on and go to the room we were in earlier and sit on the chair. With my knees bent, I wrap my arms around my legs and close my eyes.

They hurt me. Of course they hurt me. They stole me.

It's this fog in my brain that I somehow contained all these years. I don't know if I wanted to block out the fact that Rex and Melody had really *hurt* me—that they'd let me cry for the parents I believed were dead. What did I think? That they'd told me and I shrugged that it was okay and that was the end of it?

In the name of love, they'd broken my parents and my sister and . . . *me*, the one they claimed to care about. And now I have my parents back and I know they love me but they wish I was someone different too. All in the name of love. I don't get why in the hell anyone would want to feel it. *Why am I considering letting it get its claws into me?*

As if I don't control it, my hand reaches for the phone. I have no idea what time it is. I know it's late. Still I dial my mom's number, not sure why I'm doing it.

She answers on the second ring. "Hello?" Mom sounds as perfect as ever, not as though I woke her up when I know I probably have.

"Hey . . ."

"Leila? Is everything okay?" The pitch in her tone rises a notch.

Bee . . . my name is Bee . . . Though I guess it's really not, is it? "It's cool. Everything's . . . cool. I don't know why I called. I'll let you go—"

"No! I'm glad you called. I want to talk to you."

She does. I know she does but her love and Rex and Melody's love are still this murky fog that I don't understand.

"Couldn't sleep?" Mom asks after a minute of my silence.

"No . . . not really." *There's a guy in my bed. A guy that I might have feelings for when I've never let myself really love anyone after I lost you and then Rex and Melody were ripped from me.* "I have a headache."

"Did you try a bath? That works for me. I keep the lights low, maybe light a candle and lay a wet washcloth over my forehead. It's really relaxing." There's a rustle in the background and I imagine her sneaking out of bed so she doesn't wake my dad. They're courteous to each other like that.

"How's Dad?" I'm not sure why I ask.

"He's great. He misses you. We all do. We were thinking maybe you could come home one weekend soon. Your sister would love for you to meet her fiancé."

"Yeah . . . yeah, we'll plan something."

"And you know if there's anyone special in your life, you can bring them, right? We'd love it if you did. You've never brought anyone home, Leila—Bee. I know there has to have been someone. You're such a pretty, smart young woman. Any man would be lucky to have you."

"There's never been anyone, Mom." And that's true. There never has been before . . . *but maybe there could be Maddox now?*

"What about . . . if there's a woman, that's okay too. You know we'd love you regardless."

A humorless laugh falls from my lips. "There's not a woman. I like men."

"Honey, we want you to be happy. You're so alone out there. All you have is that tattoo place. What about—"

"I didn't call to do this with you. That tattoo place makes me happy. I'm not like Larissa." *Maybe I could have been. Then we'd all be happy.*

When she speaks again, there's a slight tremble in her voice. "That's not fair. That's not what I meant."

Time to go. "I know. Listen, I better go. I just called to . . ." Nothing comes to me because there isn't a reason.

Mom sighs and she's quiet for a few minutes. There's never been a time she doesn't know what to say. "I love you, Leila. You know that, right? We all do. I want you to trust me."

Love. There's that word again. It finds its way into every conversation. Someone is always declaring their love to someone else but it doesn't stop them from hurting other people. *It doesn't stop me from hurting other people.* "I know. I gotta go. I'll talk to you soon."

When I hang up the phone, I let it slip through my fingers and fall to the couch, wishing I could be more like her. Wishing I could find the Leila inside me I used to be. Or even Coral. Both of those girls knew how to let people in.

CHAPTER TWENTY-FOUR

MADDOX

She's been out of bed about an hour. I can't stop thinking about her. Not only her but also me. Her and I. Whatever the fuck we are, if we're anything. I've never let myself overthink shit because nothing has ever really mattered except for the stuff with my dad and my sister. But here I am thinking about her and wondering about the way she'd suddenly tensed against me, the little moans that snuck past her lips, and wanting to fucking erase her ache.

Instead, I let her go . . . That's me, though, isn't it? I didn't do anything about Dad and I haven't done anything to be there for Bee either.

The crazy part is . . . I want to. Want to learn how for her because she ties me in knots in the best way. I actually want to be with her and even though it's scary as hell, I think she's worth it.

Still, I haven't left her bed. Haven't walked to find her or tried to be a man and take care of her. I've been trying with Laney ever since I let them all down. Things with Bee are on a whole other playing field because I want to wipe her tears and make love to her until she forgets about all those secrets she keeps locked away from me.

The same fucking way I do with her.

Still, I want to try.

My eyes are drawn to the door, seconds before she walks through it. Her shadow, dark in an even darker room as she makes her way back to the bed and climbs in.

I can tell she's on her side, facing me, but her skin hasn't come in contact with mine. I want to wrap her inside me where we can both pretend we're not fucked up and lost. The urge to ask her where she was for so long begs to fucking break through my lips. I don't let it.

"You're awake." Her voice breaks through the night.

"Have been ever since you left."

Ask her what's wrong. Ask her where she went.

"Sorry."

"Why? You want to get up, then you get up."

"Ooookaay." The bed dips as though she's rolling away from me to get up. Need surges through me and I reach for her. Touch her soft fucking skin and pull her to me.

Tell her you want her. That you want to try. "You were making noises."

"Strange dream."

On instinct, I run a hand through her hair, lean

forward, and press my lips to her forehead. "What was it?"

Before she has the chance to reply, my cell rings. A fist lodges itself in my stomach. They called at night when Mom tried to kill herself the last time. We didn't find out about Dad until night too. All I can think of is my sister—of something having happened to her.

"Get it." Bee gives me a light shove as I move away from her. A light comes on from her side of the room, right before I reach my pants and pull my cell out.

My skin tightens when I see my sister's name light up the screen.

"What's wrong?" I ask immediately.

Crying is my reply. Laney's trying to speak but I can't understand anything that's coming out of her mouth.

"What the hell is wrong, Laney?"

"I got it, baby. Give me the phone," Adrian says in the background before he's on the phone. "It's your mom, man . . . She's gone."

My hold on the phone tightens. I don't know if I'm breathing. If my heart is fucking beating. She's gone. Even without being told, I know she finally got her wish and her parting shot at Laney at the same time. "Tell Laney I'll be right there. Don't you fucking leave her alone and you tell her I'm coming, okay? I'll be right there."

Without another word, I hit END on the phone. I'm already shoving my legs into my pants.

"What is it? What happened?" Bee steps up to me.

"My mom's dead."

She gasps and I wonder if it's because I lost my mom or because of the cold way I said it—detached with no feeling because I don't know how in the hell to feel.

"Maddox, I'm so sorry. What happened?"

I shrug. "She did it somehow. What kind of mom would she be if she didn't kill herself on my little sister's birthday?"

Bee gives another gasp at that before she reaches out for me. I'm too angry at my mom and the situation to let myself be touched. My skin is tight with tension. I dodge her as I go for my shirt.

"I gotta go. I need to check on Laney." My voice muffles slightly as I pull the shirt over my head and go for my shoes.

"Hey." This time, I don't move when she grabs my arm. "What about you?"

"Doesn't matter."

She lets me pull away but then steps in front of me. "Let me go with you."

And fuck if I don't want that too. If I don't need it. Someone there for me. *Her* there for me. "You don't want to do that. It's not going to be pretty."

"Don't fuck with me, Maddox. You know I wouldn't

say it if I didn't mean it. Let me go with you."

There are all sorts of reasons I should tell her no. I know Laney is going to want to go back home. There has to be shit to take care of and it's not like I'll let her do it alone. Bee shouldn't have to close Masquerade. This isn't her business and she doesn't want ties, but fuck if none of that matters right now, because I need her. I want her, and minutes ago I tried to tell her that I wanted to be with her and didn't know how. This time, my mouth won't stay closed.

"Yes," is all I say and then I pull her to me. She wraps her arms around me and for a minute, I pretend that we're normal. That we're like everyone else and we're not playing this game where we pretend there's nothing between us when there obviously is. When I want there to be.

"Let me get dressed real quick, okay?" She steps away before getting her clothes. I watch her and wish we could go back to the part where she was taking the clothes off instead of putting them on. I wish this night—no, our fucking lives—wasn't so screwed up.

Bee grabs a bag out of her closet and puts some other clothes inside. She leaves for the bathroom, probably to grab whatever else she needs, and all I can think is she knows—she *knows* that we're probably going to leave town and be gone for days, but she's still coming.

When she's all packed, we head for the door. I stop when I get there and look at her. *My mom is dead . . .* Thoughts fight to push their way to the surface but I shove them down. I can't think about this. I just need to push through. That's what I do. Close the fucking doors inside me and push through. It's worked for years.

"Thank you." I push her hair behind her ear because even though I can't deal with the rest of it right now, I need her to know how much this means to me. "Thank you for coming."

She blinks, biting her lip when she looks up at me—unsure in a way she isn't usually. "It's nothing."

But both of us know it's everything.

I'm so fucking nervous as I walk toward Laney's apartment. Christ, I don't know how to do this. Don't know how to really be there for her. I've done a shitty job of it for years. I can't stand seeing her upset. It makes me feel helpless.

"Are you okay?" Bee asks as we stand in the hallway.

Honesty finds its way out of my mouth. "I don't know how to do this. I'm not like her. She's wide open with everything she feels and this is going to kill her. I don't know how to be there for her."

Bee takes my hand, then goes to let go as if she's not sure she should do it. Before she can, I tighten my grip on her.

"Don't try to be there for her. Grieve *with* her."

How screwed up will it be if the truth comes out there. That I don't feel anything other than anger. That I don't need to grieve after how my mom had treated us. "I'm fine."

Bee looks toward the ground. "I'm always fine too . . . I've been *fine* for years. But we never really are, are we?"

It's like I feel the walls inside me break down. Feel her break them down and find her way inside, into this place that I didn't think was there. "I don't know."

She looks up at me, really looks at me, and I feel her eyes like she can see deep inside, and wonder if anyone has ever seen me the way she is right now. "Bee . . ." I take a step forward, reach my hand out to cup her cheek, but the door opens behind us.

"Maddy. She's gone. She's really gone."

I turn to catch my sister as she wraps her arms around me. She cries enough for the both of us, her tears wetting my shirt. None fall from my eyes, though. I only hold her, be there for her, and wonder what it would be like to ever let go like this. Wonder what it would be like to free myself from the past and help Bee through hers too.

CHAPTER TWENTY-FIVE

BEE

Maddox is quiet the whole way to Stanley. It's a few hours away, and the entire time I keep telling myself I should speak. That I should tell him it's okay or ask him if he needs to talk but fear lodges the words in my windpipe. Even though I hate it, I can't stop myself from wondering if I should be here right now. If it's my place to tell him these things when he didn't even want to hear it from his sister.

So instead I sit back and let him drive my car. Laney's in the car in front of us with Adrian, Colt, and Cheyenne. They're all so close in a way that's so foreign to me—when one bleeds, they all seem to. When one of them needs something, they're all there, and I can't help but think about the fact that if I wasn't sitting in this car with Maddox right now, he'd be on his motorcycle alone. They would have each other and he would have no one, and being that person to him fills this void inside me that I never realized was there. As hard as it is and as frightened as it makes me, I see his shattered soul through his eyes and I want to do this for him because even though he may not know it, Maddox has made me feel when I haven't wanted to for so long. I owe him this.

His mom is dead and I know it hurts him. It has to, no matter what his family situation has been.

When we pull off the freeway, I watch as the other car goes left, and then Maddox turns right.

"We're not going to the hotel?" They'd decided to meet there, no one wanting to go to his mom's apartment.

"No. I called when we made a stop. I need to go to the morgue to ID her. I don't want Laney to have to see that shit."

I never thought I would be the type of girl who would say a guy made her melt. Maybe this isn't the right time and the circumstances are all screwed up, but the way he loves his sister makes me do just that. My hand reaches for the door handle because I need something to do with it. He loves her with the kind of strength that makes people do crazy things.

"Maddox."

His cell rings before I can say anything else. I'm surprised when he answers it but not shocked when he says, "I need a few minutes to process this. I'll meet you at the hotel. Don't leave without me." Maddox tosses the cell down.

"You shouldn't do this alone," I tell him.

"And she shouldn't have to."

"What about you?"

At that Maddox glances at me. "It was her fucking birthday yesterday, Bee. My mom hung herself on Laney's birthday after making her life shitty for years. Laney never deserved any of it. She never could have stopped all of the stuff that happened."

Crossing my arms, I turn in the seat, fighting the urge to reach for him, to touch him, to soothe him. "You don't deserve it either and you also couldn't have stopped it."

His jaw tightens and he doesn't turn to look at me, doesn't even reply.

My heart hurts because he's shutting me out when he usually lets me in. Looking at him, I realize that's what I want. He's trusted me, and he let me come here with him. It's scary—that part of me that wants him to continue to let me in. For it to go farther so I know even more about him. The fact that we're here together speaks volumes for what we have become.

When we pull into a parking spot at the morgue, I push the door open and step out. I don't make it more than a couple steps when Maddox's hand grabs on to me. There's not a bone in my body that even slightly tries to pull away from him. In fact, I squeeze him tighter.

"I'm not trying to be a dick. I . . ."

Maddox's jaw is still tight—that angry look that makes people want to back up—but his eyes are telling a different story. It's those that make me pull out of his grasp and wrap my arms around his neck. "You're not being a jerk and if you were, you'd have the right. You're taking care of your family. You're doing something I never could."

His hands fist in my sweatshirt, gripping me tightly to him. It feels as though he'd climb inside me if he could and I let myself revel in that.

"Thank you." Maddox's voice is low in my ear.

"No problem. Whatever you need. I'm . . . I'm here. If you want to talk or anything."

At that he pulls away. "I'm fine. I . . ." He slides his hand around to the back of my neck. "I'm glad you're here."

My heart free-falls over the edge of a cliff. When I open my mouth to reply, no words come out. Maddox leans forward and kisses my forehead again. It's the second time he's done it and I feel it all the way to my toes. Instead of finding words, I grab his hand. It's the best way I can think of to tell him I'm here for him. I can't help but wonder if I'll be enough.

CHAPTER TWENTY-SIX

MADDOX

*P*eaceful. That's the first word that comes to mind as I look at Mom's cold, empty body. For the first time in years, she looks peaceful. As fucked up as it sounds, I almost envy her for that. I hate what she did, hate it so fucking much that there's this crippling ache in my chest. I hate how she treated Laney. Hate that she still loved my bastard dad. That she loved me, but there's a part of me that is glad she found peace.

When my hand twitches with the urge to reach out and touch her, I squeeze Bee's hand tighter, so fucking glad that she's here. I need her at my side.

"Yeah . . . yeah, it's her."

The gray-haired man standing across from us nods. "I'll give you a few minutes alone with her."

Fuck that. I don't want it, plays through my head, but the words don't come out. He walks away, followed by the quiet click of a door closing behind him. There's a sting in my eyes that I ignore. I haven't cried since I was a kid and I don't plan to start now.

I hate myself for wanting to cry over her after the way she treated Laney. Still . . . when I look at her, I see my mom. The woman who used to play with us and laugh with us until my father betrayed her. Until I helped him do it.

I tense when Bee's arm goes around me and she leans into my side. "I'm sorry, Scratch. So damn sorry."

My lips don't move but the urge to smile slips through me. Hearing her call me Scratch somehow helps. It feels normal when everything else is so fucked up.

"Me too." That sting starts again, making me back up. Bee is right beside me as I turn to go from the room.

"You can stay. I can go out if you want to say good-bye."

Good-bye . . . How do I say it to someone I both hate and love? To someone who hurt me and hurt people I care about but only because I'm the one who let her get hurt?

"I'm good."

This is where my sister would try to get me to talk. Where she'd tell me it's wrong and I should grieve and talk to her or whatever the hell else she thinks is important. Bee doesn't say any of that, even though the words play in her eyes. She knows me and in this moment, that's more important to me than anything ever has been.

We step out of the room and turn the corner, down the hall and then outside. The second we step out, I can't stop myself from kissing her. From trying to tell her thanks in a way that is comfortable for both of us. She opens right up for me, letting my tongue stroke hers. It's comforting and I don't remember anyone ever making me feel like this. Fuck, I don't remember wanting anyone to but then I think about the fact that my mom is dead inside that building. That she wrapped a rope around her neck and hung herself in her apartment and I'm standing out here being as selfish as I was when I kept Dad's secret.

Pulling away from Bee, I say, "We should go." The sun peeks through the clouds and sparkles off the piercing in her nose, reminding me of the ink I put in her back. I'm a part of her and fuck if I don't like that.

It doesn't take us long to get to the hotel where my sister got a room. Bee and I get our own before I text Laney to find out where she is. She sends a room number back to me, and even though I wish like hell I could turn around and walk right out of here, I head toward my sister. She needs me and I'll be damned if I let her down again.

Adrian opens the room when we get there. There are two beds, Laney sitting on one and Colt and Cheyenne on the other.

"What's up, man?" Colt nods at me. Adrian doesn't

say anything, just moves back to sit by my sister.

"I went to the morgue. Everything down there's done. You don't have to worry about it." *Except for paying for the services.* He'd made sure to talk to me about that first thing.

"What?" Laney pushes to her feet and walks toward me. "You went there without me?" Her eyes are red and I wonder if she's stopped crying since she found out.

"You shouldn't have to do it."

The look in her eyes changes to an anger she's directed at me only one other time. "Fuck you, Maddox! Fuck what you think I should have to do!" she yells.

Adrian's to his feet and by her side as Bee steps toward her. "He did something really fucking hard so you didn't have to."

Laney's eyes dart to Bee as though she's shocked she stood up for me, but I'm not. She would do it for anyone. That's just her.

"Don't." My eyes don't leave Laney as I talk to Bee. "If she has something to say, let her."

Her voice is softer but still hurt when she says, "You should have told me you were going, Maddy! We should have done it together! I need the closure as much as you do! No matter what, I loved her and I'm tired of you treating me like I'm so breakable. I should have had the *choice.*"

Adrian's grabbing for her, but Laney pulls free.

"You didn't fucking need to be there! Look at you. You haven't stopped crying and you want to go in there and see her dead?" The second the words are out, guilt slams into me.

"Don't give her shit for feeling something because you don't." Adrian pulls Laney closer to him as though I'm going to hurt her. It's a stab through my chest.

"Dude," Bee says to him. "You need to stop—"

"Nah." I step closer to Adrian, cutting Bee off. "Keep going, man. Say what you want to say." Adrian moves closer, too.

Colt gets off the bed and then Cheyenne, probably expecting to have to break up a fight that would feel really fucking good to start. I open and close my hands, my eyes right on Adrian.

Don't give her shit for feeling something because you don't . . .

My anger at him, at fucking everything, tries to block out those words but it doesn't work. That's me, right? The cold bastard who doesn't feel anything. Just like our dad.

"It's not the fucking time for this shit. Your mom fucking died," Colt says to me, then looks at Adrian. "Your girl's mom is fucking dead. All of you need to grow the hell up." There's a depth to his voice that I don't understand. Pain laces his words.

Laney doesn't stop, though. She grabs my arm with

both gentleness and anger, not letting go when I jerk away. "You need to stop doing this. Adrian is wrong—I know you feel something, but you need to *stop* trying to protect me. I love you and I know you love me but I can't deal with being babied. We've been through this, Maddy. She was my *mom*; you're my brother. I should have been there with you! When are you going to see that? We're all each other has left now, but all you do is push me away."

Her voice cracks, splintering me apart. Because she's right. And because I know that I'm not a good brother. I'm not as fucking *good* as she is. "You heard your man, it's because I don't feel anything. You want to see her, go fucking see her. I'm done."

Bee moves out of the way when I jerk the door open.

And then she slams it behind us, never farther than a foot away from me.

She doesn't say anything as we head to our room. Part of me wonders if she thought I would leave but I can tell she doesn't. That she knows me better than that because no matter what I said, I won't walk out if Laney needs me. I might not be the best kind of brother, but this is the only kind I know how to be.

"I'm texting her that we're in our room."

I don't have it in me to argue. It takes me three times to make the stupid keycard work before the green light flashes and I open the door. My hands are actually shaking as I pace the room, trying to breathe, trying not to think about beating Adrian's ass or how much I disappoint my sister.

"Don't feel guilty about what you did. It might not have ended up being the right thing but your heart was in the right place. Don't let them make you feel like it wasn't."

"Was it? Was it in the right fucking place?" My feet won't stop moving. "I did it because of guilt. Because I let them both down and that's not being in a right place. It's being selfish. It's trying to make up for all the shit that I screwed up. *That's* what I did, Bee. Don't try to make a hero out of me."

Once the words leave my mouth, there's not even a second I want them back. I'm so tired of staying fucking quiet. I want this shit out of me. "Everything I do isn't because I'm some great guy with a big fucking heart. It's because I *owe* people. Because I let them down and this is the only way to make amends for it."

Bee crosses her arms. "Bullshit. I don't believe that for a second." She leans against the table looking almost relaxed.

"Why? Do you see the good in everyone like my sister? Do you think you can save me? Honestly, I'm not that fucked up. My kid didn't die. My mom didn't hate me. I'm an asshole who kept his mouth shut for selfish reasons when I should have spoken up."

"You've lost stuff too. Don't try and pretend you haven't."

At that, I laugh. "What? Football? A dad who I don't give a shit about anyway?"

"A dad who was still your dad. Football, which was something you loved. And what about your mom? Your sister? Your childhood? You can pretend all you want that you've never been hurt before and that you've never lost anything, but I will continue to call bullshit, Scratch. Loss is loss. It's not a contest about who's been hurt more. We all have our own battles to fight."

I'm suddenly begging my mouth to stay shut. I'm going into territory I've never traveled before. I wish like hell I had a cigarette on me, but since I don't, I walk over to the window and push the curtain open. It's something to keep me busy because as much as I've never wanted to talk, I know I'm about to do just that. I have to tell someone and she's the only person I can imagine seeing inside me.

"Did you miss the part where I said it's my fault? That I could have stopped it?"

"Well I'm about to get to the part where I say it doesn't matter."

Her reply almost makes me laugh but it's stuck inside me. She doesn't get it. How much everyone has lost. Turning around, I look at her—at her blond hair and the determined look on her face. At her gorgeous fucking body and know that I want her to know me in a way no one else has. That even though I never thought I would fall for anyone that I've somehow fallen for this woman.

That I love her . . . because everything almost feels okay with her standing with me. Going to the morgue was easier and seeing Laney too. There's always this anger inside me that she somehow soothes.

She deserves to know who I am.

"I knew, Bee. I knew Dad gambled and I went with him—races, illegal games, whatever he could find. I found out later about the cheating and I never told. I let myself believe he wasn't going to hurt Mom anymore and let him continue to lie about his trips out of town so he could make money for me. Because I wanted football so fucking bad and scholarships weren't a guarantee."

She takes another step closer to me, so close I feel the heat of her and wish I could lose myself in it.

"You were a kid. It wasn't your job to fix it. He put you in a bad position with all his secrets."

Nausea turns in my gut at what I'm going to say next. At the thought of how much my silence has hurt other people. "I knew he wasn't where he said he would be the weekend he killed Adrian's son. I knew and we fought and he told me to keep my fucking mouth closed and I did. I sat back and pretended he was working when I knew he wasn't. I let him go and lied to my mom. He got in that car with another woman and killed Adrian's kid!"

The words are almost choking me now but I can't stop them from coming out. My heart is beating so hard my chest hurts and I see Adrian's son's eyes, which are engraved into my brain after as many times as I've looked him up online over the years.

The same man who loves my little sister more than anything. Who takes care of her better than I ever could despite the fact that she's connected to the worst fucking moment of his life—not knowing that one word from me could have stopped it all. I hate it that I let myself be a silent bystander.

"He was two years old when he died. *Two*. And even though I hated my father and stopped playing ball with him, I still let my stupid fucking dream get in the way of doing what was right. I let him go and he killed Ashton and broke Adrian and I've *still* kept my mouth shut this whole time. I don't have the balls to step forward even now.

"I've hated Mom for being so broken all these years when it was partially my fault. When she died, I almost felt . . . Christ it was almost a relief because she won't be hurting anymore and she can't hurt my sister. What kind of guy feels relief when his mom kills herself?"

We're standing only a few inches from her. I'm breathing heavy, my chest heaving in and out, my fists tight as I wait for her to tell me I'm as weak as I know I am. For her to be disgusted because I've let so many people get hurt and I treat them all like shit, even though I could have stood for something important for once in my life.

When everything went down with Adrian and Laney, I accused him of being a pussy, when I'm even worse. I'm weak and I'm a liar.

"He was a kid, Bee. And Mom . . . fuck, she loved my dad. I hate her for how she treated Laney but she really fucking loved him. My sister lost both her parents and lives with the knowledge of what our dad did every time she looks at Adrian. One word from me could have changed everything."

We could have been happy. People didn't have to die.

My eyes find Bee again, afraid of what I'll see there. I wait as she crosses her arms, looks up at me before she finally speaks, her words completely unexpected. "Are you done now, Scratch?"

CHAPTER TWENTY-SEVEN

BEE

Maddox is speechless. He's standing in front of me with his mouth open and I'm praying like hell I'm doing the right thing. There's a part of me that wants to reach for him — to pull him to me and hold him because he's living with so much misplaced guilt. He's taking the blame for Adrian's kid, his sister, his mom, and everyone else his dad hurt when none of it was his fault.

Because he loves them?

When Maddox still doesn't reply, I continue. "You're too smart to think all that is your fault. I can imagine how everything you've been through hurts. None of it was your doing, though."

When he steps to the side as though he's going to go around me, I follow, keeping in front of him. Maddox could easily push me out of the way but he won't. I know it.

"If I would have told —"

"Then maybe, *maybe* things would have turned out differently, but there's a good chance they wouldn't have. Your mom still would have been hurt by him. He probably wouldn't have quit gambling or left the other woman for her, which means he still could have been on that road."

"But he might not have too!" he yells, his eyes slightly wet. No tears fall because that's not Maddox. I wonder if he's ever opened himself up enough to cry, even when he's alone.

"I need to get out of here." He moves to step around me again. Before he can, I grab his arm.

"You said you don't want to be a pussy, so don't. I'm telling you something here. Don't run."

"Pfft." He pulls away but makes no attempt to leave. "Look who's talking. I know shit about you, Bee. I've told you things about me I've never told anyone else, and I don't know why you run from a mom who obviously loves you or why you needed a new name. I know shit about you, so you have no right talking to me about running."

His words stab me, a truth that I wish I could change—wish I could be like him because I actually want him to know me in the way he's let me know him.

"I never claimed to be anything other than who I am. You're right and I know it."

"Then what room do you have to talk?"

"I don't! You think I don't know that?" The urge to cry burns behind my eyes, in my chest, and *God* do I want to reach for him. To stop dancing around in this masquerade and figure out who I am, to be proud of it and to learn to love the way he does.

After taking a few deep breaths, I reach inside me and find words. "I've never let anyone in as much as I've let you. It's scary as hell and my instinct is to run like crazy but I'm here. I might not be as strong as I'm telling you to be but I'm here . . . for you." The words make my chest ache; I'm embarrassed because I know how crazy they sound.

"It scares the hell out of me. I've seen people ruin lives in the name of love, feel like lesser of a person when they can't be what others want them to be and I've seen it given unconditionally too . . ." That's how Mom loves Dad. How my whole family loves each other and how I know they want to love me, but how can they? I was gone for so long and I came back a shell of the person they knew. Maybe they loved Leila, but Leila isn't Bee.

I turn my head, unable to look at him anymore, scared to see what reflects in his gray eyes because I think I told him I want to love him. Or that I do. Hell, I don't even know what I said. Maddox doesn't let me off easily. Gentle hands touch my chin and push until I'm looking at him again.

He's breathing so hard I feel his breath. Wonder if he hears the wild beat of my heart.

"And?" His voice comes out raspy.

And I don't get love. Don't want to feel it even though I worry I already do. I was stolen and shown love only to be told it was wrong. To remember how they hurt me and then returned to find out I couldn't be the same girl my real family loved.

"I've seen the way you love your sister. You would do anything for her. You lied to my mom for me and you've been there for me when I haven't been able to give you anything in return. Nothing that happened with your family is your fault. You couldn't have known what your dad would do and telling your mom probably wouldn't have stopped him. I guess"—I shrug—"that's what I can do for you. What I want for you, Maddox. For you to know that you're probably the best person I know. None of what happened was your fault. Your dad is responsible for his actions, and your mom is responsible for her reactions. It's not a child's job to police their parents."

And even though everything I said is true, I still avoid telling him about me and it feels wrong. Maddox drops his hand from my face and I know he knows it too. He thinks he's a coward, but it's me. I've let him down the way I let my real family down as well.

He steps away. "If that's all you have for me, it's not enough."

My legs go weak but I manage to keep myself standing. That's what I do. I'm strong. I push through.

I lived through losing my parents the first time and then losing Rex and Melody. This is something else I will make it through. It's not like we didn't know it would end anyway. It's gone on too long as is.

My hand longs to reach up and grab my chest like that will somehow ease the pain there.

Oh, God. I love him. I really think I love him.

"Okay . . . We'll finish with things you have going on here. I'm sure you and Laney will need help with arrangements for your mom and I want to be here for you. I—"

"What's the point, Bee? It's not going to change anything. You didn't want ties anyway, so I'm not going to force them on you. You might as well leave now."

Breath catches in my throat. I might not have wanted ties but they're there now . . . only he wants to cut them.

"That's what you want?" *Say no. I'm sorry. I'll be what you need me to be—no!* I am who I am, and I won't change that for anyone.

"It's what's going to happen." Without another word, Maddox turns and walks from the room. After letting myself take three deep breaths, I grab my things before I leave.

It feels like it takes years to get to my car. I turn it on, letting the engine run as though sitting here will make a difference. It doesn't.

I can do this. I've done it before. I've lost before.

The whole time I've planned to lose Maddox, and that's exactly what's happening.

Car in reverse. Back up.

In drive. Go forward.

For a good fifteen minutes I drive. Keep going until I feel like I'm going to burst out of my skin. Until a scream climbs up my throat and I'm scared I won't be able to hold it in. I jerk the car to the right and pull over. The second it stops, aching cries rip from my mouth. My face is wet and my shoulders shake as I cry. When was the last time I cried? When I was taken and thought I lost my family? When I had to understand why I had new parents and couldn't tell anyone that I used to have different ones? When Rex and Melody made me cry because they wanted me too much—because they wanted a child to love?

Or was it when I went home? When I laid in bed at night trying to figure out how to be Leila for these perfect parents who loved me so much. For a sister who missed me? When I had to force myself how to forget about Coral, when both Coral and Leila were suddenly strangers?

Who am I?

Because Bee isn't enough. Not for Maddox at least and even though I want to feel okay with that, I can't. *Because I love him.* That strange fucking word that people put so much stock into that causes nothing but pain.

All I know is I'm tired of hurting, tired of losing. Tired of running and avoiding.

My eyes hurt from crying so much but it's nothing compared to the emptiness in my chest. That space I never wanted to fill and then Maddox snuck inside, took it over, and now he's gone.

Because I couldn't say good-bye to my past. I couldn't for my parents, and now I can't for him either.

No matter what, my past continues to haunt me.

Shaking my head, I hope to evict the thoughts there. After wiping my face on the sweatshirt in the passenger seat of my car, I start it again and drive away.

CHAPTER TWENTY-EIGHT

MADDOX

I'm up before the sun, which would piss me off if my head weren't full of so much other shit. Mom, Laney, Bee. They're all pulling me in different directions, three voices yelling for attention in my brain, making me get why people like Adrian turned to shit like weed when things go bad. Not that I would because that's not me. I hate that shit but right about now, I would give almost anything to forget.

Forget she died.

Forget I hated her.

That I hurt my sister.

Took something from her.

And Bee. Jesus Christ I wanted her to stay. Wanted her to tell me she could give me more because I want that with her. Wish she could open up to me the way I did with her. Only with her. She didn't want me enough to try, though.

My fists tighten, wishing like hell I could hit something, but instead I shove out of the bed I've been lying awake in for hours and head to the bathroom.

The shower doesn't help, so after I get dressed, I grab my phone and the keycard so I can walk down and get a pack of cigarettes before going to see Laney. As I'm heading down the outside walkway, I don't know what makes me do it but I pull my cell out of my pocket. I let my finger ghost over the missed call button.

I know exactly what I'll see. I still do it anyway. My finger presses down.

One, two, three, four, five . . . they keep going—one missed call after another, all of them with the same name.

Mom.

Fire burns through me and for the first time in my life, I wish it would burn me alive. Wish for something, anything, to swallow the guilt that's inside me.

Just like Dad did, I pushed her aside. Yeah, she was horrible to Laney and that shit was so fucking wrong, but I never even tried to do anything to change it. Never tried to help. I pushed her away and drowned in all my fucking anger, casting her aside like Dad did.

I had no idea how to help her. And now she's gone.

Stopping, I drop against the wall and close my eyes. Try and calm the breaths rushing from my lungs. I want to lose it, really fucking lose it. Shaking starts in my insides and burns outward. Heat engulfs me—anger, rage, pain, whatever the fuck else I can find in there, and it's crazy because I actually want to let it out. I never lose it. I just become an asshole and walk away. I want to be free of it. And I sent away the only person I can do that with.

And she left easily.

"Last time we met in a hotel walkway like this, there was a lot of fucking blood. Think we can skip that part this time so we don't hurt your sister anymore?" Adrian stops beside me.

"Fuck you."

"Heard that from you before. It's getting old as hell. Called your room and you weren't there, so I told Laney I'd come check on you. I'll tell her you're being your typical asshole self."

It's on the tip of my tongue to tell him *fuck you* again. It doesn't matter right now. He doesn't or I don't. "How is she?"

Adrian shakes his head like it's a stupid question, which I guess it is. "She's hurting, man. How do you think she is? She loves her mom and now she's gone. She got into it with you last night and that always fucking kills her. But like you told me the last time we stood together at a hotel like this, she's strong—stronger than all of us—so she'll be okay. Even if she didn't have me, which she always will, she'll be okay." He crosses his arms and I know he's not done yet. I don't know why I don't walk away from the bastard.

"Which is exactly why you shouldn't have gone without her, man. Is it a shitty thing to see your mom like that? Yeah, and I wish like hell she didn't have to but she can handle it and it was her right to be there—with you. She doesn't need you to save her—never has."

I hate him more for telling the truth. Hate myself because he's still manning up in a way I won't.

"I didn't think she'd want to go and see her like that. I want to do right by her."

Adrian studies me. His eyes narrow but not like he's pissed—like he's trying to put together some kind of puzzle. He crosses his arms, and again I want to tell him to fuck off. Whatever shit he wants to give me, I'm not in the mood for it right now.

"I know you do. You've loved her better than I did my own sister but you need to let her live too."

His words are needles sticking into me, prick after prick. Because they're almost . . . cool. I didn't expect them and wish they weren't both truth and lie.

"I know she can handle it and I haven't been a good brother to her."

Adrian shakes his head. "Christ, I can't believe I'm going to do this. I should have brought a bottle of whisky like you did. Would be easier."

I almost laugh at that.

Adrian leans against the wall, looking forward. I turn

from him, too, knowing whatever he's going to say, I'm not going to want to see him while he does it.

"I don't know how much Laney told you about me, but my dad used to beat us. I watched as he beat my mom and I let my sister Angel take beatings for me too. I was young, so fucking young, but that doesn't matter. What does is I let them down. Then Angel took me to live with her and the first thing I do is get some girl pregnant at sixteen. Then I had a son—Ash—and . . ."

It's as though Adrian's hand is fisted around my throat. He's cutting my air off and cutting my heart out and I know I deserve it. Still, I don't know if I can listen to him talk about his son.

"He was fucking incredible, ya know? Only two but it was like he knew the world better than I did. Angel helped me with him too. She took care of both of us and when he died, I bailed on her. When have you walked away from Laney?"

"I wasn't there . . . when Mom slit her wrists."

"That's a fucking bullshit answer and you know it. You didn't leave. You were working. You've never fucking left her. You came with her to Brenton even though you didn't believe in what she was doing. You sacrificed loving your own mom for her."

My eyes snap to him at that and he's looking at me. Looking like he knows shit about me that I don't. "I'm not playing let's open up and talk with you.

That's not me." Pushing off the wall, this strange thought filters into my head. *I want to take those words back . . .*

Because he's being fucking real. In a lot of ways, that's who I am. I'm real and honest and don't sugar-coat anything. Maybe that's really a lie. That's what I want people to think. I've been a prick to him. Our father killed his son and he's standing here talking to me about him.

"Fucking pussy." Adrian's hand comes down on my shoulder. His accusation is another truth because I am exactly what he said. "You play that game real well. You accused me of being weak when you're just as bad. You hide behind being a prick, the whole fucking time pretending all you want to do is take care of your sister, but that's not all, is it? There's more to it than that but you aren't man enough to face it."

At that I whip toward him, words doing what my fists have done the other times we've fought. "You want to know the truth? Is that going to change so fucking much? Fine, I used to go with my dad when he gambled. I kept it from Mom and Laney, pretending it was for their own good and that I thought he would stop. Really it was to be selfish. I never said a word — just gave up playing football with him, telling myself I was sacrificing something so it wasn't wrong.

"And then I confronted him one day when he was

leaving. Threatened to tell but as soon as he brought up money, I let it go. I let him walk out the door and I didn't tell Mom or Laney and then he killed a little boy."

Adrian's face pales at that. His jaw tightens, fire burning in his eyes.

"Every fucking day I hate myself for that. Not for me but because a kid died because of my selfishness. And then my sister fell in love with the boy's father and I look at him and pretend to fucking hate him when I know he's more of a man than I am. I watch him love my sister better than anyone in her life has and all I see are my own failures. I would do anything—*any*-fucking-thing—to get that day back! I will never . . ."

I let out a deep breath. Adrian still isn't moving. His hand has fallen from my shoulder, and he looks sick. Looks like he could pass out and I know I'm screwing with him more by finally opening my mouth and telling him the truth.

"I will never regret anything like I do that day. All these years I've been trying to make it up to Laney, trying to be what she needs so she doesn't feel her loss, but it's nothing compared to what I owe you. Every day of my life, I will hate myself for that. I'm sorry. I'm so fucking sorry."

One, two, three, seconds I close my eyes. Brace myself for the hit that I know has to be coming. He deserves to do more than punch me. When it doesn't come, I open my eyes to see Adrian still staring at me.

"I'm sorry," I tell him again before I turn and start walking away.

The end of the walkway gets closer and closer. I don't know where I'm going. I only know I can't fucking stay here.

My foot hits the top stair when I hear, "Wait."

And as much as I want to keep going, I owe him this. Owe him to at least hear him out. Slowly, I turn and walk back to him. And he's shaking, fucking trembling. I wish like hell he would hit me. It would be easier to deal with than this.

"You weren't driving the car." A pause. "You couldn't have stopped him." Adrian's words are slow . . . measured, pain traveling from them to me. I see how much he's struggling, how much he wants to believe the words he's saying. "It's not your fault, like it isn't my fault. I let him play in the yard when I knew I shouldn't. I wasn't standing next to him to protect him like a father should . . . but I also wasn't behind that wheel." He runs a hand over his face. "And . . . and neither were you."

When I was younger, before I really got what Dad was doing, I looked up to him. Once the truth came out, I stopped. I've respected people since then—Laney, Bee, and even Adrian for still loving my sister—but I've never *looked up* to someone until this second. "How can you say that?"

"Because it's true."

For the first time since I found out what Dad did, a tear slips out of my eye. Christ, we have all lost so fucking much. Parents, kids, dreams—way more than our fair share. We've hurt people we've loved and we've hurt ourselves and we've been lost. Through it all, we're still fucking standing. Adrian's doing more than that now; he's learning to live.

I want to live too . . .

"I was wrong about you. I've known it but I want you to know it. I was wrong. You're more of a man than I've ever been, and I can only hope like hell I'll be this strong one day. My sister is lucky to have you. I'm lucky to have you take care of her. I've hurt Laney and my mom and treated you like shit. And Bee . . . Christ, even her. I told her to go. I let her walk away from me instead of trying to be what she needed. Instead of showing her I love her so she felt safe enough to let me inside."

I've made such a fucking mess of everything. I've acted like my dad and I will never let myself do that again.

"Then fix it. Start with her."

Shaking my head, I say, "I can't. She left. I don't know where she went and Laney . . . I need to do this with her."

"When will you ever fucking learn, man? If you really love Bee, Laney would rather you fix shit with her. She can take care of things here, and I'll be here with her every step of the way. And . . . and she'll be there for me too." His eyes are hard on me, making sure I know what he's saying. That he has to talk to my sister about what I told him because he needs her. That's what they do for each other.

That's what I want to do for Bee.

"You managed to Sherlock your way into finding me when I left Laney. Do that for yourself." Adrian reaches into his pocket, pulls out a set of keys, and tosses them at me.

Looking at him, I know what he's going to do. He's going to Laney to face what I told him and deal with it head-on. They'll face taking care of Mom's arrangements together too. I'm so tired of fucking running. I've never faced anything. I kept quiet about Dad. I walked away from football. There isn't one thing in my life I've had the balls to fight for—until now.

Just then my sister walks up the stairs and stops when she sees us. "I was worried about you guys. Is everything okay? Maddy, I'm sorry for—"

"I'm in love with Bee." Shock colors her face at my admission. "I love her and she left. I want to fight for her, Laney. Adrian . . ." My eyes dart to him and then back to my sister. "He taught me I need to fight for those I love—no, to fight with them."

Her chin trembles and tears drip from her eyes. "Adrian?"

"Yes." For the first time in possibly my whole life, I'm the one to pull her into a hug. I don't stiffen, only hold her as tight as I can. "I'm sorry for everything I've done to you. I'm sorry for how Mom treated you and sorry I hurt her too. And . . . he loves you. I've known that and I should have told you. I'm glad you have him."

Her hand fists in my sweatshirt as she hugs me tightly, crying on my shoulder. "I love you, Maddy."

"I know, little sister. I love you too." When I pull away, Adrian has walked partway down the hall, waiting, without looking at us. "He needs you. Go to him. I . . . I told him some things I should have told you a long time ago and I'm sorry for that."

Laney nods. "Go, find Bee."

"Mom . . ."

"Is gone. You're still here. I can handle this. For once you need to let me take care of something. I want you to go."

Once more I hug her. "Thank you." And then I do exactly what she said. I go to find Bee.

As soon as I get back to Brenton, I go straight to Bee's house. Her car isn't there but somehow I knew it wouldn't be. Still I ring the doorbell a few times before going to Masquerade.

It feels fucked up using my key to get in without her being here but I do it anyway. Wherever she is and whatever she's dealing with, I want her to know she doesn't have to do it alone anymore. Finding her—going to her—is the only way to do that.

I look through the stockroom, the back room, any and everywhere I can think of that might tell me something about where she might have gone. I don't even know her last name or where her parents live. I love this girl and I want to know everything about her—to fight for her and with her until we know every part of each other.

Each place I look and each time I come up empty I feel more like a failure. I told her to leave for being exactly how she told me to be, how I've always been, and now I can't get to her either.

Dropping into the chair at her desk, my leg hits the bottom left drawer. The one she always keeps locked. It would be locked right now if it wasn't for the corner of a folder, sticking out, holding it open. That little voice in my head tells me it's wrong to open it. Part of her secrets are in there but damn it, is it wrong if it's done out of love? I don't really know. I've never felt it before and damned if I don't want to try and keep on feeling it, so I rip the drawer open.

Without hesitating, I pull one of the folders out and open it. Newspaper articles are stuffed inside. One after another, I pull them out, each of the headlines making ice slither through my veins.

LOCAL GIRL KIDNAPPED

GONE WITHOUT A TRACE

AFTER YEARS PARENTS STILL FIGHTING THE ODDS TO FIND MISSING GIRL

MIRACLE! NINE YEARS LATER, MISSING GIRL BACK HOME

It keeps going on and fucking on. Trials and sentences and interviews with her family. Leila, mixed with Coral, but all really about Bee. The girl with the tattoo of the twins because she doesn't know who she is. Who the fuck would?

The more I read, the more my stomach constricts. There aren't a lot of details about it. Still, she was *kidnapped*. She was taken from her family only to discover the truth nine years later.

Tossing them on the desk, I bury my face in my hands, my eyes still drawn to the papers in front of me. It doesn't make sense—why she thought she couldn't share this with me. Then, whose ghosts really make sense to someone else? You have to live it to understand it no matter how much people might think otherwise.

Scanning the top newspaper article again, my eyes stop on the word *Kansas*. I power up her laptop, hoping I can find more information online. I don't know how in the hell I expect that to help me find her but it's the only thing I can think of to do.

Kidnappings with the word *Kansas*, her name and *Kansas*. I keep looking, my eyes burning from lack of sleep, but I'm determined to do this one thing right. To do it for her.

Scrolling down through the links, my eyes stop when they come to a picture of a sunflower. The same flower she has tattooed on her right calf.

One click tells me why she has it—the Kansas state flower.

Pushing to my feet, I grab the keys off the desk and I'm gone.

CHAPTER TWENTY-NINE

BEE

I sit on one side of the clear glass, waiting. My leg's bouncing and my heart's jumping and I've gagged three times, so close to vomiting I'm still not sure I can hold it back.

But I'm here.

I'm not leaving.

My body goes numb when the door opens and they walk her in.

Melody.

That simply, my heart rate slows, happy memories I don't know if I have a right to feel creating pictures in my mind. Baking cookies, looking at stars, burned dinners, and laughs. They morph into pictures of Mom. Of her trying to do the same kinds of things with me, but my heart fighting the happiness just out of reach.

It doesn't make sense—my feelings for either of them. It's not that I don't love my parents; it's that I don't know how.

Melody's green eyes are teary when she sits down.

Her red hair shorter and tied into a little ponytail in the back.

She picks up the phone, so I do the same. "Coral. I can't believe you're here. It's so good to see you."

"My name is not Coral." She flinches as though my words are a slap to the face. The anger in them surprises even me.

"You're right. Leila. I'm sorry."

That makes me laugh. Melody's eyes crease in confusion as she looks at me, making more of the past flicker in, turning my feelings into a tornado of sadness and anger. "Funny you should call me that because I'm not Leila anymore either. You took that away from me. Did you know that?" My eyes dart down because it's hard to look at her, but then I focus on what I came to do and tilt my head up again.

The phone in 'her hand shakes but she doesn't hang it up. She sits there, listening, waiting. That's one thing she has in common with my real mom. They're both strong.

"I never thought I would come here. Honestly, I wasn't sure if it was because I was scared of hating you more or not hating you enough."

Melody nods, her face wet with tears.

"My mom and dad, did you know they tried to call me Coral at first because they thought it would be easier on me? Because I didn't know how to be Leila and all they wanted was to find a way for me to be

happy. Then . . . then I felt guilty, guilty because
they kept my room the same and had pictures of me
all over their house. They missed Leila and they
thought she came home but I was Coral instead."

Wetness rolls down my face. I'm crying. God, I'm
crying and I didn't even know it.

"So I told them to call me Leila. I tried, *tried* so
damn hard to be the girl they lost but I never could.
They did game nights instead of movie nights like we
did. We went together somewhere as a family once a
month. Mom never, *ever* got so busy she forgot to cook
dinner and at first I hated her for it. Hated her for not
being like you, for not being who I was used to."

Now that the words are flowing, I can't stop them.
My brain and mouth are working together without
me having the ability to stop them. I hate that my
words hurt Melody but I need to evict them from me
if I ever want to be free. And as much as it pains me,
she hurt me too. She needs to know that.

"For years it went that way. Hell, it still is. I'm
fucking trapped in between two lives, neither of which
are mine and both adding this weight to my chest
because in some ways they both feel wrong and they
both feel right."

"Cor—Leila. I'm sorry. I can never tell you how
sorry I am but I wanted . . . the moment I saw you
I fell in love. We loved you so much."

"Love?" There's that word again. The one that

makes people hurt and still it threatens to take over my heart. "I used to believe you. I wanted to but now I don't know. You didn't know me when you *stole* me. How could you have loved me?"

She wipes her eyes. "We wanted a daughter. Wanted someone to love so much. I couldn't have babies and with both mine and Rex's past, we couldn't adopt."

"I get that and I'm sorry, but I wasn't yours. That didn't give you the right to *take* me. To hurt my family and ruin my life . . . in the name of what? Wanting a baby? If that's what love is, screw that. I don't want anything to do with it."

Her voice rises. "Don't you think I know it was wrong? That there isn't a day that goes by that I don't wish we'd made a different decision? I will never forgive myself for what we did to you and your family but I also don't go a day without hurting because we lost you too. No matter what you believe, we loved you."

My grip on the phone loosens, and it almost falls free. My eyes flitter, trying to rid themselves of the tears. "I loved you too . . ."

This time it's me who wipes my eyes. Fear lodges in my throat, trying to keep me from talking. I force the words around it. I'm here and I'm doing this no matter what.

"I remember . . . I don't know how I forgot, how

I could have thought you guys explained to me that my parents had died and I didn't realize that hurt but I hadn't. I remember now. I remember the pain of losing them. The memories of being grabbed keep resurfacing. I cried for them, for my family, and you guys let me believe they were dead . . . in the name of love.

"And eventually I moved on. I had you and Rex and I loved you guys and you loved me but then they found me and I lost you too. My family was back, only now I cried tears for you. My parents didn't have a choice in their loss and neither did I. I'm still fucking losing because I'm scared—scared to love them because I don't want to lose someone again. Scared I'm not worthy of them because I'm not Leila anymore. Because I don't know how to love them like I don't know how to love . . . What is it to love?" *Maddox.*

"Sweetie—"

"Don't. Don't you dare call me that. It's not fair." I push to my feet, ready to leave.

"They love you. It doesn't matter if you're Coral or Leila. They love you." Her words make me pause, still holding the phone to my ear. "They always loved you. We . . . we watched them. They brought you to the park almost every day. They loved you so much, and that makes what we did even worse. Don't be afraid to let them love you. Don't be afraid to return their feelings. What we did . . . God, I loved you, too, but what we did, that isn't what love is. Don't ever think that. Love is support. It's doing your best to take care of people instead of hurting them. It doesn't mean you're perfect. It means doing everything you can to be there for the ones you love. Wanting what's best for them and loving them for who they are too. That's how your parents feel about you, Leila. And I know that you feel that way about them too."

My hand is shaking so bad I have to squeeze the phone tighter. Her words unlock my heart. No, I wasn't Leila anymore but that never stopped them from loving me. They don't understand my tattoos yet they still helped me start Masquerade. We don't always see things the same way, but I have no doubts in my mind that they want me happy. *Still, is being Bee enough?*

"You fell in love, didn't you?" Melody's voice is soft in my ear.

"Yes." The word comes out automatically. A part of me wants her to know it before I say good-bye.

And he accepts who I am and tries to be there for me too. I know to the marrow of my bones he would be there for me with this. He's tried. All I do is push him away. "I don't know if I can love him the way he deserves." One more time, I look at her. "I can't forgive you for taking me but . . . I don't hate you either."

She gives me a sad smile.

"Good-bye." After hanging up the phone, I walk out of the room.

The house I lived in with Melody and Rex is empty. I don't know anything other than that, which means at any moment, someone could find me here. It doesn't matter.

I'm wrapped up tight in a sweatshirt and jacket as I sit in the backyard, waiting for the stars. Actually, I don't even think it's for them I'm waiting on, but for answers.

Somehow I thought telling Melody how I feel—by getting a good-bye—I would magically change. That didn't happen.

It's late afternoon, probably an hour or so before dusk. Mom's called but I ignore it like I do pretty much anything important in my life.

My eyes dart to the side of the house when I hear the gate open. I don't try to move. What's the point? Whoever comes through will see me and know I'm not supposed to be here, and I'll deal with it.

"Bee?" A cocktail of excitement and fear shoots through me at the sound of Maddox's voice, right before he steps around the side of the small house. "Hey . . ."

"How . . .?" It doesn't even occur to me to be mad. He had to have talked to my parents or something to find out enough about me to think to look here.

Instead of that anger, the tenseness in me releases and my heart slows.

"You're going to be pissed." He smirks but it's obviously an effort.

"Tell me anyway."

"I looked in your desk . . . I found the articles, did some more detective work that led me here, and people in town are quick to answer questions. Finding the house was the easy part."

I feel a moment of panic and shame at the thought of him reading about my past, but I'm so numb that it fizzles away.

He kneels in front of me and I wish like hell he would touch me.

"Why didn't you tell me, baby?"

My chest swells at the endearment. It's not something I ever would have thought I'd like—to be called *baby*. "It's not usually my conversation starter, Scratch."

He frowns. "And that's still where we are? We haven't moved forward at all since we met?"

There's a pain in Maddox's voice I've never heard directed toward me before. "You know that's not true. You're . . ." *Everything.* "You know I suck at this." He still hasn't shaved and I wish I could rub the dark stubble on his face.

"You know that's a bullshit excuse. I don't know how to do this either."

This time I can't stop myself from touching him. I haven't been able to since we first met and I don't think I want to. "You do, Maddox . . . You might not know it but you're good at it."

Maddox sits next to me in the middle of the lawn. "If I was good at it, I wouldn't have told you to leave. I would have told you I loved you and if you weren't ready to say it back, I would have supported you and been there for you. Probably would have fucked up a few times but I would have been there until you were able to trust me."

This is how you love. Right here, what he's doing.

It's probably the wrong thing to do, most girls probably wouldn't, but I need to be close to him, so I crawl forward and climb into Maddox's lap. Facing him, I straddle his lap and touch his hair to make sure he's really here.

The things he said I never would have imagined hearing coming out of his mouth and they were scary, but somehow that fear is eclipsed by their beauty. "I trust you probably more than I have anyone in my life. I . . . That's why I came here. I thought maybe if I understood how they felt or why they took me, I could . . ."

When my words trail off, Maddox speaks. "I talked to Adrian. I told him about Ash. He's telling Laney. I would have. I needed to go, though. I had to be here—"

"Oh my God." I try to push off him. He holds me

instead. "You shouldn't be here. I'm so sorry. How could I have forgotten? Your mom. You need to be with your sister. You shouldn't have followed me all the way to Kansas."

Maddox shakes his head, holding me tight. "I needed to do something for me."

A tear slips out of my eye. "You came here."

"Because I need you."

I have never wanted to swoon over a guy before. I never thought that was me. There have been hot guys and I've screwed around with them or admired them but that's all. Maddox is so much more than that. His words burn me alive and make me melt at the same time. They fill me when I've made myself empty for so long.

"I'm scared."

He pushes my hair behind my ear. "I am too."

"I've lost so much. I lost my parents, my sister, and then Rex and Melody." In this moment, I'm glad he read the articles . . . glad he knows everything. Still, there's a part of me that wants to be the one to tell him.

"I was so scared to love them when I went back home. I didn't know how to be who they expected me to be and felt guilty for it at the same time. They love me and I hurt them. Rex and Melody claimed to love me but they hurt me. What if . . . I don't want to lose you too."

"My dad hurt all of us. I hurt Mom and Mom hurt us. I think . . . that's life, baby. It doesn't come with a guarantee. Just know I'm not walking away from you. I've never wanted anything in my life enough to actually fight for it. I've folded and given up but I'll be damned if I give up my fight for you."

Wrapping my arms around him, I cry into Maddox's neck. I hold him so tightly that I fear I'm hurting him before I realize nothing can hurt him. Not really. He's strong and he'll keep going and he makes me want to do the same. Like him, I realize I've never really fought for much. I've spent my life like I'm living some kind of masquerade. I became Bee instead of fighting to be Leila. I didn't accept my parents' love so I wouldn't lose it and I clung to Rex and Melody because I knew I could never really have it. They were in prison so it wasn't like I could really have their love; therefore, I wouldn't have the pain of losing it.

Melody and Rex love me. I don't doubt that and . . . I know my parents do too. I'm tired of holding back, so I don't show them the same.

"We'll fight together. We'll learn how to do this together. I love you, too, Maddox. You made your mark on me that first night I met you and it hasn't gone away."

"You mean it wasn't my mad tattooing skills?" This time when he smiles, it's real.

"No."

A serious look crosses his face again. "You don't need to be anyone other than who you are. Not for me."

I drop my forehead to his. He's never wanted me to be anyone else. He never pushed even when he should have. "I know . . . Thank you. I love who you are. I love who we are together." And I want more. I want it all. I want my life back. "I want you to go home with me. I have to fix things with my family. I'd like you to meet them. If it's too much—"

"It's not."

At that, I smile. "I need to start over. I think . . ." When I look at him, I know. "The only way to find myself is doing it with the people I love."

"You're you. The name you go by doesn't matter."

And I know he's right. I also know he needs to fight some of his demons and I want nothing more than to be by his side. "You need to go home, too, Maddox. You have things to work out with your sister and—"

"I need to say good-bye to my mom."

The look in his eyes tells me there's more he needs to say to her than that. He needs to make amends, even if it's with a ghost.

"Do you want me to go with you?"

"I need you to go with me. Just like I need to go with you to see your family." With that, Maddox's lips come down on mine. It's an urgent, needy kiss. My hands go into his hair and his go under my sweatshirt to rest on my waist. The kiss is wild and passionate, and a mixture of so many emotions just like love is. It's raw, all of us open for hurt when we choose to let love in. But open for beauty too. A tattoo on your heart with the colors and images of who each of us really is. Emotional art.

We're not perfect, though none of us are. We're works in progress and what matters is we're moving forward and we're doing it together. In love.

EPILOGUE

MADDOX

July, eight months later

"We're putting all the food and shit on that table on the right." I point the caterer to the corner, as Laney smacks my arm.

"Food and shit?" Laney asks as I shake my head before looking over at Leila, who smiles and winks at me.

It was about two months after Mom died that she told me she wanted to start going by her real name. I'd seen it coming before that. The more time we spent with her family, the more comfortable she became with them. The more she wanted to fight for her life back.

"Remember how I told you it felt good to be Bee because I chose it? She was who I wanted to be?"

"Yeah." I kissed her neck as we'd lain in bed, then kept traveling down. I'd gotten to her stomach before she continued.

"It feels even better to tell you I'm choosing to be Leila again."

I'd stopped, kept my lips to her skin before I looked up at her. "It's a sexy fucking name."

That had been the end of the conversation and she'd been Leila ever since. Leila who is still a tattoo artist and is learning to ride a motorcycle and is the same person I've always known. It's not that none of us ever slips up and calls her Bee, but it's like a nickname now.

I wrap my hand around the back of her neck and pull her to me. She comes easily, her arms going around my waist as she looks up at me.

"Is it bad to say *shit* in front of a caterer?" In the background, I hear my sister chuckle before walking away.

"Fuck if I know." Leila pushes up on her toes to kiss me.

For a second I let myself forget we're in a room full of people. That Laney, Adrian, Colt, and Cheyenne are lurking around somewhere. That Leila's parents and sister are all huddled around Leila's portfolio on the desk. Cheyenne's family, an aunt and an uncle, are here somewhere and Adrian's sister too. Hell, even Trevor, Tyler, and a few other people from Lunar are here, though I had my last day a couple weeks ago. Definitely won't have time to run security for them while I'm working full-time at our new shop.

Mine and Leila's. Masquerade hadn't been big enough for us to both have our own workstation plus . . . that's not really our lives anymore, living like we're in some masquerade, hiding behind our hardened exteriors. We both wanted a clean slate.

"That's why I love you so much. You don't care about my mouth."

"Oh, I care about your mouth very much, just what you do with it, not how dirty it is."

I laugh as Colt and Cheyenne step up. "Let's not talk about mouths because Colt has the dirtiest." Chey twists the engagement ring on her finger and grins at him.

Colt shrugs. "It was good enough to make you mine."

He'd proposed on his mom's birthday. They're taking their time, though, finishing school first from what Leila said. Hanging out with him and Adrian more, I heard about how he lost his mom and how important she was to him. It's crazy because it helped me make peace with my own mom's memory. Colt would have done anything for his mom and it made me wish I would have fought harder to help save mine . . . or maybe not save her, only make sure she knew she wasn't alone. Who knows, maybe it would have helped. Maybe not. I try not to dwell on it.

Everyone laughs, making me notice that my sister and Adrian stepped back up.

"When you open the doors, I was thinking you could do a piece for me," Adrian says. Today we're having a pre-celebration or some shit. Leila's mom planned it. She likes doing stuff like that and Leila actually had fun helping her.

"Hell yeah. What do you want?"

Adrian pauses for a second, his eyes hitting mine. Laney wraps her arm through his and I notice he relaxes into her a little, letting her support him. "Ash."

The five of us all stare at him.

My body stiffens. "You're not talking a name here, are you?" Faces are hard as hell, but I know that's what he wants.

He shakes his head.

"It would be an honor, man. I'd love to do it for you, but it should be Leila. She has more experience and I can't fuck something like that up."

"You won't. We'll talk later."

Christ he's a good fucking guy. I'm so lucky my sister has him. Honored to call him my brother even though there's no ring on Laney's finger yet. I know one day there will be and even without it, he would be a brother to me. "We'll talk."

There's a chiming sound and without looking, I know it's Leila's mom. Everyone quiets and we look over at her as she stands by the desk. "I know everyone isn't here yet and we're not officially starting but I wanted to take a minute to . . ." She pauses before her eyes land on my girlfriend. "Leila, come over here for a second."

She doesn't hesitate to go and then her mom looks at me. "You, too, Maddox." Since the first day I've met them, they've treated me like family. They've showed us both love.

Leila and I stand on each side of her before she continues talking. "I wanted to thank you guys for coming to Leila and Maddox's pre-opening. This shop isn't only important to my kids."

My stomach bottoms out as I look at her, and she smiles. "Both of my kids."

A breath leaves my lungs. I've lost both my parents — one to death and one I can't find it in myself to forgive. I've gained so much, though. It's fucked up but it's at this moment I realize everything is good. We're all going to be good. I have regrets with my mom and I wish things had been different. But I'll be okay. Leila has her family, who she loves. Things aren't perfect with them, but they work hard to understand each other and they love each other regardless.

She has me too. Always, like I have her. Laney and Adrian have each other and Colt and Cheyenne . . . and I wonder. I've never in my life thought of shit like this but I can't help but wonder if Colt's mom, Cheyenne's mom, and mine aren't sitting up there somewhere, taking care of a little boy with Adrian's eyes and looking down at us.

Leila looks at me and smiles before she grabs her mom's hand, and I take the other.

"Reality Tattoo is important to all of us. It's brought so many of us together. My daughter is so talented and I love that she can share her art with the world and with Maddox."

Everyone claps and I smile, feeling like I never thought I would.

"I think it's time to crack a bottle of wine!" Leila's mom says.

"Or beer!" Leila adds, because I'm pretty sure most of us will be drinking that.

Everyone starts moving, grabbing what they want and going for the food but instead I go for Leila. She's what I want. Her arms wrap around my neck; her hands thread through my hair as I tighten my fingers around her hips.

"Reality Tattoo. I like the sound of that . . . and the fact that it's ours."

"I love you. Even without this place, I'd have everything I want, because I have you."

She grins. "Mmm. You make me want you when you talk sweet like that." Her face goes serious now. "I love you too. You taught me love is worth it. I can't wait to keep showing you how much of it I have for you."

For the first time in so long I have a future to look forward to. One that I will fight like hell for, no matter what because that's what you have to do in life.

Reality. It's not living a lie like so many of the people we know have done. It's not treating life like a game of charades or living behind any type of façade. Life is fucked up, it hurts, and it's not always pretty, but damned if it can't be beautiful too.

Read on for exclusive deleted scenes from

MASQUERADE

Deleted Scene from Chapter 7: Bee's phone call with her mom. This scene takes place when Maddox comes to Masquerade and finds Bee upset. It's the phone call that happened while he was gone which leads to them making love again.

Looking down at my sketch, I can't help but smile. It's good. Damn good. I'm confident in my abilities but it's not often I think something like that. I don't even know what it's for—if I'll ever use it for anything, but I love it.

I'm still smiling when my phone rings. After tucking the drawing away, I answer with a "Hello."

"Leila. Hi. I didn't expect you to answer."

Without even meaning to, she just dealt me two blows in one shot. Bee . . . My name is Bee. Which of course I can't say because technically it's not. After all this time, I should be able to be Leila by now. The fact that I can't feels like a spoon, digging out the happiness I felt while drawing.

And the second blow is knowing I'm such a crappy daughter, she didn't expect me to answer. Yet, she's such a good mom that she still calls.

"Sorry." This is always how it goes with us. I don't know if she knows it or if I'm crazy for feeling it. When I talk to her I automatically feel like I'm doing something wrong. "I've been busy."

"How are things going at Masquerade?" she asks.

"Okay, I guess. Could be better but it takes a while to get off the ground."

Mom sighs. "I know you don't want to hear this but it would be irresponsible not to talk about it. I know you want this, just remember Masquerade might not work out. Odds are it won't. It's important to have something to fall back on."

Would it be too much for her to have some faith in me? If it was my sister, she would.

"Why did you help me if you don't believe in me?"

"That's not what I meant. I'm sorry if it came off like that." Mom sighs. "Let's not do this. I called with good news! Your sister's boyfriend proposed! I wasn't surprised when she told me. He's such a sweet boy. They'll finish school first, of course. They both know it's the most important thing."

It's not fair but all I hear is that that's why Masquerade will fail. I didn't do the right thing—the important thing. I never do. You'd think by now I would be used to it but damn, there's part of me who wishes for once, I wasn't different. That I could have still been the perfect Coral for Rex and Melody and then been the perfect Malone for my real parents too.

Mom keeps going after that. She tells me my sister is on her way to making top of the class and how proud they are of her.

She wants to be a lawyer and I'm a tattoo artist. Only a slight difference there.

The longer she talks the emptier I feel inside. Then the angrier I get because this is me and I want to be—no, I am proud of who I am.

The more she talks the harder it becomes until I can't stop myself from saying I have to go.

Mom sighs. "Okay, sweetie. It was good talking to you. I hope . . . I hope you'll answer the next time I call. The wedding isn't for a while but there are so many plans to make! I know it's not your thing but it would mean a lot to have you involved."

I never said it wasn't my thing. She's my sister, of course I'll help.

Even though I don't know if she means it like that, it hits me as another way I've failed.

I hate the tears that pool in my eyes.

"I will."

"It's important."

"I said I will."

"I know . . . I'm sorry. You're right."

But I'm not. She's much better than me for being the type to apologize to smooth things over.

When we get off the phone, Masquerade isn't the place where I just felt happy. It's something to hold me over until I discover my real career. It's not important.

It makes me nauseous to think like that. The place is empty. No clients.

Odds are it will fail.

Hitting the lights, I disappear into my office.

Deleted Scene from Chapter 29: Maddox and Bee reconnect after he finds Bee at the home where she lived with her kidnappers, and they talk. They head to a motel before going to Virginia.

Bee's arms and legs wrap around the back of me as though she physically can't let go. It's not tight enough and I have a feeling it isn't for her either. I need her close, need to be inside her in every way I can be.

Still, I wait, motorcycle revving beneath us as she looks at the house she'd lived in with people she thought were her parents—people who she loved.

I'll stay as long as it takes for her to say goodbye.

When her hand wanders down and squeezes my leg, I know she's telling me she's ready. We take off down the street and even though the ride is freeing, it's not all we need. Right now I really fucking need her.

The first hotel I come to, I pull my motorcycle in. She doesn't question anything, just lets go of me and gets off the bike. We need to get back to Virginia, we both know that. It doesn't make us need tonight any less.

We pull our helmets off and Bee reached for my hand. I thread my fingers through hers as we head into the office. Less than five minutes later we're in our room. It's nicer than the one we had our first night in together. I'm grateful for that. She's not the type of girl to care about shit like that but I still want nice things for her.

Tossing my helmet to the chair, I say, "Come here, baby. I want you and don't think I can wait."

She grins and gives me a wink. Holy shit I love this woman.

She gets rid of her helmet too before wrapping her arms around my neck. My mouth comes down on her, starving for her taste. Matching my intensity, she kisses me back. I cup her thigh and she lifts her leg, so I pull her up as she wraps herself around me.

"Don't think I can go slow," I tell her.

Bee drops her head back so I can kiss her neck. "Don't think I asked you to."

That's all I need and then I'm leaning her down on the bed. Her legs are still around me as I lie on top of her. "I need these clothes gone." I slide her shirt up and she lifts enough for me to pull it off. As I work the clasp on her bra, she's already unbuttoning her jeans.

I move away just far enough to take my shirt off and then it's my hands tugging at her pants, pulling them down her legs. They fall out of my hands and I look at her. Let my eyes wander over this girl who is mine. The only woman I've ever really wanted.

"You are so beautiful."

I swear a slight pink colors her cheeks. I like that I can make this tough girl blush.

"I can't believe you're making me shy, Scratch."

"You don't ever have to be shy with me." Then I'm taking a condom out of my wallet and getting rid of my pants. Bee moves up in the bed so she's lying with her head on the pillows.

Her eyes study me as I climb onto the bed. "You're not so bad yourself." She pauses and then adds, "You're beautiful too."

"Sexy," I say before I cover her mouth with mine. Our tongues tangle, work together to pleasure each other and then I'm letting my mouth trail down her neck. I like that hollow spot at the base of her throat, before I keep going down. Her nipple is right there and I can't help but taste it.

Bee cries out, arches forward as my mouth teases one breast, and then the other. Her nails dig into my back. As much as I want this to last forever, my body burns to be inside her.

"Want you. Now," I mumble against her.

"Then take me."

I moan because, Christ, how fucking hot is she?

With my teeth, I rip open the condom wrapper before sliding it down my length. I tease her swollen flesh with my finger, feeling how ready she is for me.

Slowly, I push inside and it's everything it always was to be inside her and even more. It's where I belong.

My thrusts are fast and hard. Her nails bite deeper into me, making me need to be deeper inside her.

"Oh, God," she gasps. It's sexy as hell, the breathlessness in her voice.

"You feel so good."

Leaning forward, I kiss her again. Take her mouth the same way I'm taking her body. I'm already close, so fucking close to losing it, that I know I need to hurry up and get her there too.

Again, I let my tongue tease her nipples as I pump inside her.

"Maddox . . . Holy shit . . . I'm . . ."

And then she does. Her body spasms around me and it's all I need to fall over the ledge with her.

Rolling to the side, I toss the condom in the trashcan before I pull her into my arms. She comes easily. There will be no walking away anymore. No pretending this isn't what it is. No walls up when we really want to hold each other.

"That was incredible." Bee buries her face in my neck.

"You're incredible."

She turns a hand through my hair, tightening her grip there. "I love you."

Pride swells inside me—that she feels that way about me. That I'm worth it.

"I love you too, baby."

Deleted Scene from Chapter 29: Maddox and Laney talk. This scene takes place after Maddox and Bee leave Kansas to go back to Virginia.

"Hey." I close the hotel door behind me. Bee and I just got back from Kansas today. Laney planned a small memorial service this afternoon for me, her, Bee and Adrian.

"Hi." She's sitting on the edge of the bed but scoots over, which is my sign to sit next to her, which I do.

"Listen, I'm sorry you had to do this on your own. I know it sucks that I wasn't here but I had to go." I shrug my shoulder. "I need her."

"You know I wanted you to go. It's the first thing you've done for yourself since I can remember. I'm glad it worked out. I'm glad you have her and I'm trying really hard not to say I told you so right now."

Her response makes me chuckle. "You'd deserve to say it. I've known for a long time she meant a lot to me. It was a lot easier to be an asshole than admit it, though."

"Eh, you were good at being an asshole. Gotta go with what works, right?"

I nudge her. "Smart-ass." We're both stalling and we both know it. The truth is, I know there are things I need to say but that doesn't make saying the words any easier. People can't change over night no matter how much we might want to.

Finally it's Laney who opens the discussion. "Why didn't you tell me, Maddy? All that time you were dealing with that misplaced guilt. You should have told me you blamed yourself for that day."

I sigh. "There are a lot of things I should have done over the years. There's no excuse for why I didn't and . . . fuck, I don't even want to try to come up with one. Nothing's going to change it. I think we've all spent too much time living in the past. It's time to move forward."

"I agree. That's what I'm trying to do."

"Me too." Glancing over, I see her hand sitting on her leg. Reaching over, I grab it. Laney's hold is loose at first, as though she can't believe my hand is really there, and then she tightens her grip.

How fucked up is it that my own sister is shocked that I'm not tensing away from her? That I reached for her first? We've always been best friends and I would have always done anything for her but hell, I never even hugged her first. Those are the kinds of things she needs—to know someone is there for her, and I was too big a prick to support her.

"I'm sorry for everything, Laney. You were always the best of all of us and all I did was give you shit about it. I know there's nothing I can do to make up for it. All I can do is promise to try a whole hell of a lot harder now."

With her other hand, she wipes a tear from her face. "There's nothing to make up for. We were all hurt and none of us knew how to deal with it . . . but we're better now. And no matter what, you've always been there for me. I always knew I could count on you."

Giving her hand a squeeze, I say, "You couldn't always count on me. You'll be able to now though. No more trying to protect you. Hell, little sister, I might be coming to you for help now. I have no idea how to do this relationship thing."

Laney laughs. "You'll be great. You love her. That's what matters."

"I do." I pause for a minute before continuing. "How's Adrian? I dropped a fucking bomb in his lap. He has every right to hate me."

"But you know he doesn't."

Nope. Not him. He's too good a guy for that. "I know. He's dealing okay though?"

She sighs. "It didn't change anything, Maddy. There's no way you could have known what would happen anymore than Adrian could. And you couldn't have stopped it either. He still misses Ash just like he always has but . . . He wants to move forward too. Like we said, we've all spent too much time living in the past."

"Good." I nod. "Bee too. She's had a hard time. After we say goodbye to Mom, I'm going home with her. I don't know how long it'll take—"

"What about your job?"

"She's more important. She needs to see her family, to talk about stuff she held in too long just like I did. As long as she wants me there, that's where I'll be."

Laney gets this huge-ass smile on her face. "You will have no problems being a good boyfriend to her, Maddy."

I roll my eyes even though I think it's honorable the way she looks at the world. The way she's positive and looks for the good. Everyone would be a lot better off if more of us were like my sister.

"It's getting close. We should probably go."

I stand and then she does the same thing. On reflex, I grab her and pull her into my arms—hugging her in a way I should have done a long time ago. "I love you, little sister."

"I love you too, Maddy."

I take her hand and we go out to meet Bee and Adrian—go to say goodbye to our mom, with the two people we love by our sides.

Don't miss Book Two in
The Games Trilogy . . .

FAÇADE

Read on for an electrifying extract

CHAPTER ONE

ADRIAN

I didn't sleep for shit last night. Not that I ever really sleep that well, but last night was particularly bad. About 1:00 a.m., I was sick to death of all the drunk, high, loud-ass people in my house. Jesus, I wanted them gone. Wanted quiet, normal, but instead I'd smoked another bowl, lied, and said I was going to bed before locking myself in my room.

The party went on without me because that's what people do. It's not that they really need me to have fun. I just have the house, shitty as it is, and everyone thinks I'm always down to have a good time. Scratch that. I *am* always down to have a good time. One look at me shows I'm stoned half the time. Weed? It clouds out the past. Parties drown out the stuff in my head I don't want to hear. But last night of all nights? I deserved to hear that shit, since I'm the one who caused it. So that's what I did. All night. Got blazed out of my head but kept myself awake so I could think about today.

Around six this morning, I jumped in my car like

I have every January 12 for the past four years and drove my ass here. Rockville, Virginia. Home sweet fucking home, except I hate this place with a burning passion. When you spend your childhood getting beat by your dad, all you want to do is escape where you came from. I wouldn't have come if I didn't have to, but after everything, I figure it's the least I can do.

Not that my sister, Angel, will ever know I came.

After all this time, I wonder if she'd want me here. If I were her, I wouldn't.

Shaking my thermos, I realize I don't have any more coffee. I toss it onto the passenger side floor and lean back in the seat. Four hours is a long-ass time to sit in my car, but I don't want to risk getting out and her seeing me. Probably a good thing I ran out of coffee; otherwise I'd have to piss again.

Looking across the street, I see all the headstones. Most of them are laid flat, so I can't see them from a distance, but I still know exactly which one belongs to Ashton. It's under the big tree. He would have liked that. I bet he would have wanted me to lift him up and put him in that tree if he'd ever had the chance to see it. He thought it was cool to ride on my shoulders. I'd carry him all around the house and he'd laugh like it was fucking Disneyland or something.

Pain grabs hold of me, threatens to pull me under, and for the millionth time I wonder why I don't let it. It would be so much easier than walking around in the masks I do now.

"Fuck." I drop my head back. Run a hand through my dark hair. Feel my pocket for the pipe there and wish like hell I could light up. Seems kind of wrong to smoke weed at a cemetery, especially under the circumstances.

I hate the drugs anyway. You wouldn't know it, though. No one does. *Adrian's always down to smoke. Adrian's always good for it.* That's what everyone thinks, but really I just want to be swept away. To ride a tide or the wind or whatever the fuck will take me far from here. Weed is the only thing I can find. Sometimes it works; most of the time it doesn't.

I'm itching to shove the key into the ignition, to push down on the gas pedal and get the hell out of here. Not that I ever went real far. I only live four hours away in Brenton because I couldn't make myself leave the state. But I can't live in Rockville anymore. I don't want to see this. Don't want to be here. I wish I could wake up and find out this has all been some fucked-up nightmare. Even if it meant going back in time before Ash and having to deal with shit from my parents.

Leaning forward, I push the useless thermos out of the way and reach for *The Count of Monte Cristo*, which is shoved under the seat. The cover's all old and ripped. The spine's cracked so much from how many times I've read it. It'll probably fall apart any day now.

The thing is, I've always respected Edmond. He went through hell and back but fought despite it. He didn't fold. He pushed through and worked his ass off to become so much more than he was. He was strong. Not me. I just can't seem to make myself overcome the past.

There's nothing to do but deal with it. And maybe lose myself behind a cloud of smoke or a girl.

I need to turn off my thoughts.

Even though I can't stand hats, I grab the one from beside me, push it low on my head, open my book, and read. Maybe Edmond can help me clear my head.

Hours later, when I see my sister, Angel, walk over to Ash's grave, I don't get out of the car. When some guy walks up and grabs her hand, I don't know who he is and yet, I don't bother finding out. They hug and I don't walk over and do the same thing to her. It's not our thing to stand around having some group mourning session over the two-year-old boy who died too soon.

Nope. This is real life. Not like all the stupid fucking books I read or the movies people watch or the reality shows that couldn't be farther away from reality.

Without moving an inch, I watch her. Watch as she sets flowers on Ashton's grave. As the guy pulls her into a hug. As they kneel on the ground, probably talking to him in a way I'll never have the balls to do.

The guy says something to her and then gets up and walks away. I duck lower in my seat, but no one is paying attention to me. He heads back to a little car and waits.

Angel's hands go to her face and I know she's crying in them. Know she's mourning the loss of Ash, the boy she loved so much. The boy she took care of better than any mom could. I know she sent the guy away because she's like me and needs to handle shit on her own. Only unlike me, she'll never run.

She cries out there for probably thirty minutes. The whole time my chest is tight. Aching. It's hard to breathe and I want to turn away, but I don't. I deserve to feel this way and deserve to see this.

A fist squeezes tighter and tighter around my heart. My face is wet, but I don't bother to wipe away the tears, either. Real men don't fucking cry. That's what Dad always said before he hit me in a series of body shots, until I couldn't stop myself from doing just what he said I shouldn't do.

Then he'd beat me harder for being weak.

Angel's shoulders are shaking. I can tell from this far away.

I'm not an idiot. Never have been. I know it wouldn't

make me weak to walk over there and hug her. To hold her and tell her it'll be okay, but I still won't do it. What right do I have to try and console her when I'm the one who destroyed everything?

When I'm the one who let Ash die?

So I sit here and watch her, just so I'll never forget the pain I caused.

CHAPTER TWO

DELANEY

I'm yanked out of a deep sleep by the sound of my cell. My room is still pitch-black, which means it's the middle of the night. My heart immediately starts setting off rounds to the speed of a machine gun.

"Hello?" my voice squeaks out.

"Is this Delaney Cross?"

The official-sounding female does nothing to slow the rapid-fire beating in my chest. If anything, it makes it worse. "Yes. This is she."

"I'm Doctor Marsh over at Three Valley's Hospital. Your mother was brought in a little while ago. She's okay, but—"

"What happened?" Now I pray for my heart to pick up again. It's silent, almost as if it's gone, and I miss the pounding in my ears. Miss it because as ridiculous as it sounds, it takes the loneliness away.

"We'd really like you to come down. It's not—"

"It's not something I haven't dealt with before," I cut her off again. I don't need her to try and make this easier on me. The fact is nothing would make me deal with it better. Saying it on the phone won't make it any less real than in person.

"We're assuming it was a suicide attempt. She took pills. We don't know if she changed her mind or if she wasn't lucid enough to make decisions, but sometime after, she must have tried to leave her apartment. A neighbor found her collapsed in her doorway and called nine-one-one."

The tears that I didn't realize had formed in my eyes are brimming over and starting their slow descent down my face. This is her third suicide attempt in the last four years.

"I'm sorry," the doctor tells me.

"Me too," I whisper. I'm sorry about all of it.

I push out of bed and race to my closet. "We'll be there soon," I tell the doctor before dropping my cell to the dresser. Yanking a sweatshirt over my head, I'm already shoving my feet into my tennis shoes. My heart seems to have found its beat now and as I finish shoving my other foot into my shoe, I try and concentrate on it. It's a crazy thing to do, but it keeps me from cracking apart.

"Maddox!" I yell as I run into our small hallway. "Get up!" My fists come down hard on my brother's door. "Come on! We have to go." I try for the doorknob, but like I knew he would, he locked his room. Before I can knock again, he's jerking the door open, his eyes wide and frantic with worry.

"What the fuck happened? Are you okay?"

"It's Mom. She . . ."

Anger washes away the worry on Maddox's face. His jaw tenses. Veins pulse in his hand; he's gripping the doorknob so tightly I think it could break. Quite the pair, aren't we? While I worry, he gets pissed.

"What did she do?" It's almost as though he blanks out in times like this. Goes numb. All I have to do is bring up either of our parents and I can see the emotion drain from him and I hate it. He and Dad used to be so close . . . and then something switched and I was the one who got his attention, yet Mom was all about Maddox. Now he can't stand to talk about either of them.

"Pills. We need to go, Maddy."

"Don't call me that. I hate it when you call me that."

I reach for my older brother's hand, but he jerks it away. "Yeah, because that's what's important right now. We need to go see her."

He's shaking his head and I know what he's going to say before he does. That he doesn't want to go. That he doesn't care if she needs us. Before he can, I say the one thing that I know he can't say no to. "I can't do this without you. I need you."

"Fuck," he mumbles under his breath. "Gimme two minutes." The door slams, guilt tingeing the edges of my pain. I shouldn't manipulate him like that, but he's my brother. Her son. Mom and I both need him. She can't help that she fell apart after what Dad did.

Realizing I forgot my phone, I grab it and the car keys, and I'm pacing the living room when Maddox comes out, his dark hair all disheveled. He doesn't look me in the eyes. He's pissed and I know he knows what I did.

We head out to the car and I drive us to the hospital because I don't trust him to do it when he's mad. He likes to go too fast and the last thing we need is to get into an accident on the way.

I'm shivering by the time we walk through the hospital doors and only part of it is from the cold. Maddox isn't wearing a jacket, even though it's a frigid cold January in Virginia.

"We're here to see Beatrice Cross," I tell the desk clerk. Maddox doesn't step up beside me. He has his arms crossed about five feet away from me.

"Are you family?" the clerk asks.

"Yes. We're her children."

She puts bands on each of our wrists and directs us where to go, as if we don't know where the ER is. We could find anywhere in this place.

I'm not surprised when my eyes pool over again. No matter how many times this happens or how many times she slips back into her depression, it doesn't get easier.

Right before we leave the sterile white hallway and

head for the emergency room, Maddox grabs my wrist.

"Don't cry for her, Laney. Don't cry for either of them."

Maddox is so much older than his twenty-one years. He's always been the strong one and both of us know it. It's not that simple for me. My mom just tried to take her own life. My dad is in prison and my brother—my best friend—hates the world.

"Why did this happen to us?" I ask. He grabs me and pulls me into his arms, letting me cry into his chest.

I can feel his awkwardness as he holds me. He's not real big on affection and it makes me feel like crap that he has to console me again. But that's what he does. He hates it, but he tries to make everything better. Mom couldn't take care of stuff, so Maddox did. He's still doing it.

"I don't know," is all he says. Honestly, I'm a little surprised I got that much out of him.

"We need to go see her." I wipe my eyes with my sweatshirt.

Maddox nods at me, but before we can go in, a nurse stops us. As soon as I tell her who we are, she gets that small smile on her face that says she feels bad for us, but she's trying not to let it show.

"Let me get the doctor first, okay? She wants to speak to you." She disappears behind the sliding doors, the sound echoing through the halls. The emergency room is quiet tonight and I almost wish for more people around to distract us.

Right away, the door slides open again. A woman with graying hair, wearing the same smile as the nurse, comes out. "You're Ms. Cross's children?"

"Yes." Of course it's only me who answers.

She leads us over to a small room with a couch. Goose bumps blanket my skin the second we walk in. It reminds me of the place they take family members to let them know when someone has passed away.

She's okay . . . she's okay. They would have told me if she wasn't.

"As I told you on the phone, your mom overdosed on pills. Some of them seem to be medications that have been prescribed to her, but we're not sure if that's all she took."

Oh God. Has she been buying pills illegally? How did this happen? How did we go from a normal family—with a mom and dad who used to laugh together, a mom who used to love cooking dinner for her family, a brother who could have gotten a football scholarship, and me, who was just happy to have the people I loved close—to this? "Okay . . ."

"She's sleeping right now, but she's been in and out of it. You need to know that she's still a threat to herself. She . . ." The doctor pauses for a second before sighing. "She's continued to say she wants to die and she attacked one of the nurses. I just want you to be prepared when you go in. We had to strap her down for everyone's safety."

A cry climbs up my throat and I clamp my mouth closed, hoping it won't be able to escape. Why aren't we good enough to make her want to stay? I don't understand her not wanting to be with me. With Maddox.

My brother's hand comes down on my shoulder and he gives it a comforting squeeze. No matter how angry he is, he's always here for me. I hate how all of this has scarred his soul.

"Where do we go from here?" Maddox asks her, but I want to be the one who's angry now. I want to yell that we've been through enough. That I'm eighteen fucking years old and Maddox only twenty-one. We're not supposed to be dealing with this. We're supposed to be in college and going home for long weekends instead of being alone.

"We did a psych consult and we think it's best that she be admitted to our inpatient ward. It's a thirty-day stay. They'll be able to help her better there. I would hate for her to be in a situation where she's able to hurt herself further or, God forbid, someone else."

It feels like a fist squeezing my chest so tight it shatters my ribs, shatters everything inside me, but I just want to be whole. Why can't we all be whole again?

I look at Maddox and he's emotionally gone again. His hand is still on me, but the rest of him looks as though he's checked out, leaving me alone.

"Okay . . . I agree. Can we see her now?" Is it bad that part of me doesn't want to? That I'm scared to death to walk in there and see her? To risk that her anger will come out at me like it always does?

"Of course. Follow me."

I know before he stops me that Maddox isn't going. His eyes that look so much like mine soften as though he's trying to tell me he's sorry—words he'll never say out loud.

"It's okay," I tell him, but really it's not. I need him and he knows it. Mom needs him. We both know she'd rather it be Maddox with her than me.

My legs tremble slightly as I walk into the room. She looks so small in the bed. Her blond hair, so different from my dark brown, is stringy and matted. I just saw her two days ago. Two days and she didn't look like this.

"Hey, Mom," I say. The doctor is gone, leaving me alone in the room with her. Gray cloth shackles keep her hands tied to the metal on her bed, almost covering the scars on her wrists from the first time. The time I held her while she bled.

Of course she doesn't answer.

I stand next to her bed and touch her hair, but then pull back, afraid to wake her. Instead, I stand there wishing I would wake up and we'd be the family we were four years ago before everything changed. Before my dad got drunk and, while his girlfriend went down on him, drove into a yard and killed a little boy. Before we found out about his gambling and the other women. I guess we were never the typical family I thought we were. That isn't true either. I knew that even then, when Mom would get pissed at me for spending time with Dad and Maddox stopped playing ball with him.

Tears roll down my cheeks in synchronized wave after wave, like a crowd at a football game. Maybe one of Maddox's old games.

I think of the woman, Angel, who I visited a few weeks ago.

The pain in her eyes when I told her who I was. But also the forgiveness she showed even though my father took away her little boy.

Maddox hates the idea bogging down my brain, but I don't know what else to do. Maybe the only way to end our family's suffering is to continue to make amends, the same way I did with Angel.